VIRAGO
MODERN CLASSICS
573

Rumer Godden

Rumer Godden (1907–98) was the acclaimed author of over sixty works of fiction and non-fiction for adults and children. Born in England, she and her siblings grew up in Narayanganj, India, and she later spent many years living in Calcutta and Kashmir. In 1949 she returned permanently to Britain, and spent the last twenty years of her life in Scotland. Several of her novels were made into films, including *Black Narcissus* in an Academy Award-winning adaptation by Powell and Pressburger, *The Greengage Summer*, *The Battle of the Villa Fiorita* and *The River*, which was filmed by Jean Renoir. She was appointed OBE in 1993.

BREAKFAST WITH THE NIKOLIDES

Rumer Godden

Introduced by Rosie Thomas

virago

VIRAGO

This paperback edition published in 2013 by Virago Press
First published in 1942 by Peter Davies, London

Copyright © The Rumer Godden Literary Trust 1942
Introduction copyright © Rosie Thomas 2013

The moral right of the author has been asserted.

A CIP catalogue record for this book
is available from the British Library.

ISBN 978-1-84408-845-4

Typeset in Goudy by M Rules
Printed and bound in Great Britain by
Clays Ltd, St Ives plc

Papers used by Virago are from well-managed forests
and other responsible sources.

MIX
Paper from
responsible sources
FSC® C104740

Virago Press
An imprint of
Little, Brown Book Group
100 Victoria Embankment
London EC4Y 0DY

An Hachette UK Company
www.hachette.co.uk

www.virago.co.uk

*I should like to thank Kumar Krishna Das
for his courtesy and help.*

INTRODUCTION

In the decades since they were written, Rumer Godden's India novels have floated in and out of fashion, yet whatever tidal shifts have affected current tastes in fiction these distinctive, delicately poised and entirely unsentimental books have never lost a shred of their almost hypnotic appeal.

The three early novels *Black Narcissus* (1939), *Breakfast with the Nikolides* (1942), and *Kingfishers Catch Fire* (1953), along with *The River* (1946), reflect the themes and settings that are central to her works. Godden was a writer who continually drew on her own life experiences, frugally mixing and recasting the elements to give them fresh significance, but always relating her work back to the people, places, human passions and frailties that she knew and understood best. Here, the place is northern India, the people are the pre-Partition British and the Indians they governed, and the themes are sexual desire, treachery, the conflict of cultures and the loss of innocence.

Margaret Rumer Godden was born in England in 1907, but while still a baby she was taken by her mother to rejoin her father in Assam. The Godden parents soon sent Rumer and her elder sister Jon 'home' again to boarding school, as did most of their contemporaries, but the First World War intervened and the girls happily returned to live with their parents and two younger sisters at Narayanganj, a small town on a tributary of the Brahmaputra River in East Bengal where their father was the manager of a steamship company. Their eventful childhood in the big house on the river bank, with its large garden, complex hierarchy of family servants, and with the town's hectic bazaar on their doorstep, was close to idyllic for all the Godden children and they looked back on it with yearning. But even so, Rumer sensed that she did not quite belong – that necessary credential for a writer in the making. All her life she believed Jon to be the more talented writer, and she knew that she was the plainest of the four sisters. At Narayanganj she was an outsider to the life of India and Indians that she observed with such clear-eyed fascination, and when in her adult years she chose to live elsewhere in India she did so mostly outside the narrow boundaries observed by British residents. At 'home' in England she was set apart too, as much by her exotic upbringing and her struggle to bring up her two daughters after a difficult divorce from her 'boxwallah' husband, as by her beady cleverness and intense involvement in her work. The expression of exile from physical place and from the ease of conventional society is ever present in her books.

Black Narcissus is the story of a small group of idealistic English nuns who travel to set up a convent school community at Mopu, in the mountains to the north of Darjeeling. As in her other novels, the setting is described with sensuous but precise exactitude – a neglected palace with a scandalous history in a landscape of butterflies, blossom, forests and snowy peaks. The sisters' intentions are of the best, but as the local agent of

Empire, the whisky-swilling Mr Dean predicts, their mission is a failure. The nuns' blithe confidence in their power to do good is undermined by the complexity of local conditions; they fail to understand or even investigate the rules that govern the people and they are correspondingly unbending in their own beliefs and traditions. Everyone they try to draw into their Christian sphere is more knowing, more corrupt, and better at calculating the odds than they are, from Mr Dean and the young Indian princeling General Dilip Rai to the ripe young student Kanchi. Sister Clodagh, the leader of the mission, is on the exterior authoritative and temperamentally cool, but within she is troubled and questioning of her own capabilities. Clodagh's antithesis is the outwardly dissolute Mr Dean, a man who is nevertheless able to summon compassion and strength when these are required. For all its convent setting, the novel thrums with sex, portrayed with a subtlety that seems only to intensify its power. The story is simple but the narrative takes an unshakeable hold, building to a climax involving sexual obsession, insanity and tragic death, which despite the gothic elements is handled with masterful restraint. The final image of a lonely grave which the villagers will not pass by for fear of the *bhut*, or spirit, that haunts it, is one that Godden took from a real burial place.

Breakfast with the Nikolides and *Kingfishers Catch Fire* both feature a young girl who is obliged by events to recognise and absorb into herself the consequences of adult shortcomings. Such children are recurrent figures in Godden's work; they are vulnerable, observant individuals who are deficient in charm but gifted with perception beyond their years. As the child Emily declares to Louise in *Breakfast with the Nikolides*, 'I see you, Mother. I cannot help it.' Both Emily and the child Teresa in *Kingfishers Catch Fire*, with the premature pucker of apprehension between her brows that her mother so dislikes, contain aspects of their creator as well as of her two daughters, but the writer and her experiences are most clearly discernible in their vivid, disconcerting mothers. Sophie and Louise, in their respective narratives, draw and hold the reader's attention like flames dangerously leaping in the dark.

The setting of *Breakfast with the Nikolides* is closely based on Narayanganj, with the bazaar lying 'like a patch of plague' against its walls. The atmosphere is heavy with the unspoken; Emily's queasy stomach is an emblem of the invisibly churning entrails beneath the sunny surfaces of the family house and gardens. The girl is caught in the sticky threads of her parents' passionately unhappy marriage; there is further sexual tension close at hand between a young student, an Indian vet, and the vet's uneducated wife. The edifices of social and marital relationships are fragile, but they hold up until an incident with Emily's pet dog triggers the cataclysm. Louise, Emily's mother, is imprisoned by her circumstances. She hates India – as symbolised by the squalor and brutality of the bazaar – but she is trapped in the country as she is trapped in her marriage. Her treatment of the dog is an act of blazing revenge and repudiation of both. Rumer Godden adored her pet Pekinese, and family dogs recur through the books – as does the perpetual threat in India of rabies.

Kingfishers Catch Fire is the most autobiographical of this trio of autobiographically inflected books. The setting is Srinagar in Kashmir, where Godden lived with her daughters on far too little money after separating from her husband. Sophie

Barrington-Ward is a widow, left in poverty after the death of her handsome but inept husband. Full of headstrong enthusiasm and naive idealism, she takes a house in a remote village on the lake. Here she and her daughter and infant son will live on next to nothing, exactly like their peasant neighbours. "'We shall be poor and simple too," she said with shining eyes [...]"Peasants are simple and honest and kindly and quiet."' Teresa bears witness to these declarations with the telling pucker of apprehension showing between her brows. She is a priggish child but, like Emily, she cannot help seeing her mother.

As with the nuns at Mopu, Sophie at Dilkhush never stops to consider what she represents to the people who live at her gate. She believes she is poor, but to these villagers she is rich and profligate, and ripe to be cheated. Sophie is maddening but she is also brave, ingenious and determined. She does everything in her power to make the venture a success, but, between the harsh weather of the mountains and the cruel poverty of the village, her peasant idyll never takes on more substance than a dream. Everyone cheats her except the noble Nabir Dar, the caretaker of the house, and she does not appreciate his worth until it is too late. Discord erupts between the two tribes of the village, on Sophie's account. The little family suffers but Sophie clings on, wilfully blind to the truth, until she is no longer able to discern the danger she and her children are in. From a languorous start steeped in the luscious beauty of the Kashmiri scenery, the narrative gathers pace and pitches towards its climax: all of Sophie's illusions collapse in a miasma of threat, sickness and confusion, while through her benign neglect Teresa is swept into jeopardy.

The novel is perfectly poised. Each strand of the taut narrative is woven with precision, each character is given his due, with restrained sympathy but with an absence of sentimentality that is almost forensic. Sophie and her children survive Dilkhush; the shocking events are explained and the ending provides a necessary fictional full stop – though even that has its tensions. It is significant of their era that both Sophie and Louise make an eventual pact of submission to their men in exchange for economic and social stability. Only the nuns walk away, and even they are returning to the mother house and the Mother Superior of their order. Rumer Godden underwent the same ordeal as Sophie Barrington-Ward, but the reality of the matter was less clear-cut. The truth behind the events at Dove House, the original of Dilkhush, was never properly resolved.

The books are remarkable for the way that powerful adult themes underlie their glimmering surface. I devoured them as a teenager, racing through the stories and revelling in the lush landscapes and exotic peoples in the (then) certainty that I would never see them for myself. It's hard to think that I appreciated any of their true qualities. They have repaid rereading from an adult perspective, and they will continue to reward both returning readers and new ones: such is their narrative grip, clothed in its silken dress of delicacy, subtlety and understanding of the human state.

Rosie Thomas

2013

BREAKFAST WITH THE NIKOLIDES

I

It was in the little agricultural town of Amorra, East Bengal, India.

In the night Emily Pool's small black spaniel, Don, slipped down the stairs. He ran into the garden and out through the gate into the College grounds where the lawns lay smoothly between the buildings and the trees and ended in grass beside the tank. He ran with curious intentness, his head down, his wide ears brushing either side of his hot serious face, and very soon his ears were soaked with dew and stuck with twigs and ends of grass. The featherings of his legs were filthy too.

He was hot. He lay down and panted; but in a moment, pricked with some intense discomfort, he was up to run again, round and round without any point or reason. There was nothing he wanted, but he could not be still, he could not feel or behave like himself at all. He had been a serene and normal dog, quietly engaged in completing himself from a puppy to an adult, but now, and all day, he was like the mirage of a spaniel, lifted out of himself and thrown distorted and heightened on the air. He was forced to run, and run, and run – foolishly to run.

At times he was invisible, quite lost in the shadows and the leaves, and presently he was invisible altogether because he had lain down behind a small balustraded platform that led down to the water tank; it was here the old professors of the staff liked to bring their chairs and their shawls and sit out in the evening. Now it was deserted. Don lay on the grass and pressed his side against the stone. He needed to press himself down where it was cool. The stone was warm from the day's sun but underneath that veneer of warmth there was real old coldness, a damp and chill, and it eased him to feel it beyond the warmth. He needed to be cool, to be still, to be dark, but he was mysteriously compelled to stand up and run in circles round and back to his place below the platform; he did it again and again and each time he circled back to lie invisibly there.

II

In the night the Government Farm at Amorra seemed to grow smaller. By day it was impressive with its colonnaded buildings, its straight well-sanded roads with railings that led through model fields; through the seasons the fields had model crops of jute and paddy-rice, grasses and pulses and fruits, sugarcane and cotton and wheat; they stretched field by field towards the horizon sweeping in a wide half-wheel with the bank of the river, acre after acre. Only Charles Pool knew how big it really was; he knew exactly, because he had made it. He had pushed it out and across the plain, patch after patch, crop after crop; and it had not been easy, for with every field he pushed out into the waste, he was pushing the whole of India before him.

The Indian cultivator is rooted in deep slow prejudice and he is convinced that he is without hope. He knows too well that he is born to live and die in monotony and poverty with nothing but toil, and debts and perhaps hunger and still more toil. Charles's talk of manures and water-conservation and crop-rotation only made the villagers lift their eyes for a moment and sink back into the ways of their great-grandfathers' great-grandfathers' grandfathers again.

Charles talked of peculiar things – of pits for instance; and at first thought, what had pits to do with farming? Charles still talked of pits, pits for rubbish, compost pits, pit-latrines. He talked of dreams, of 85 per cent germinating seed, of bigger crops and better crops and different crops and crop-rotation. 'It does not matter how we farm,' they said. 'If we farm well in a bad year, still we get bad crops; if we farm badly in a good year, still we get good crops. What is to be will be. What does it matter how we farm?' 'There shall be no bad years,' said Charles and talked of wells, and Persian wheels, and levelling and terracing the rainfed land to hold the water and conserve the topsoil.

'Do it now. Combine,' said Charles.

'We'll do it tomorrow.'

'No, now. Now. Today.' He was like a gnat in their ears. Grudgingly, in one or two villages, they began to follow him.

Charles's young men went with white banners like preachers or warriors into the villages. They took with them a bull, and an English cock and hen, and the people's eyes stayed open with astonishment when they saw the size of these creatures. The young men showed them eggs from the hen, they talked of stall-fed milkers for the bull. They had a model village, a model house, a haybox, mosquito nets and quinine, and they had a magic lantern with slides: *Cowdung for Manure, Not for Fuel. Use the Haybox. Light and Air. The Poor Man's Pestilence – Litigation. Good Seed Costs Four Annas More, Bad Seed Loses Twenty Rupees.* They had posters to match the slides – *Fever is Cheap, Quinine is Cheaper; Motherly Love* (the mother who drives away the vaccinator – 'Go away, you cruel man!' – while her baby's ears and nose are pierced for ornaments); *Send Your*

Girls to School, the Mother Makes the Home; Who Profits? (when the crocodile of litigation holds its clients in its jaws) – all with lurid highly coloured pictures. They had gramophones and records. Later they had wireless.

There were not enough young men, not one for a hundred villages. The Indian lives to and for himself and his family, his sense of social service and citizenship is small, and voluntary workers were almost nil. The Legislative Government was slow and very cautious in providing paid ones. Already Charles was the fellow who always wanted money and when money was given to him it went like drops of water on dry sand. 'But you only give me drops,' said Charles. 'I want bucketfuls and gallons.'

'That is impossible,' they said.

'It may be impossible but it must be possible,' said Charles. 'It may be useless but it shall be of use. I don't know how you can do it, but you must do it, all the same.'

Charles won. Results are quick in India, once work is started and sustained, and in eight years the Farm had become an Industrial and Research Centre, with an annual exhibition; it had a Stud Farm and a Veterinary Research Annex, and recently the College had been added to it with a roll of nearly three hundred students who came from all parts of the province to study livestock, crop-husbandry, bacteriology, agricultural botany, mycology and entomology.

Now, the mail steamers came up to Amorra; it had a light railway; it was visited and conferred upon; its grant had been raised and doubled, and raised and doubled again. It had equally outstripped its boundaries in land, the gates led one into the other along its roads and new houses were springing up for its staff all along the river in surprising shapes and colours,

'Primrose Villa,' 'Lucknow,' 'Jolly Garden,' 'Riviera View.' One with pink concrete with wrought-iron balconies in silver, one had strips of looking-glass let into its walls, one was completely in the shape of a ship with a railed bridge, a ventilator and a concrete life-belt on the roof. Charles looked at it through his monocle. 'It seems I started more than I knew,' said Charles.

He was held to be a connoisseur of houses though no one quite knew why; rumours also said that his own house was very beautiful and very peculiar, but not many people had been in it to see.

Everyone knew Charles but no one knew him very well, except perhaps the Principal of the College, Sir Monmatha Ghose. Charles was the old as well as the new Amorra, and he never left it. He lived alone in a fixed ray of limelight as the only European in Amorra except for an Anglo-Grecian combine managed by a Greek, Yorgo Nikolides, on the river two miles away. The whole town knew everything Charles did, but that told them very little about him. Naturally a network of rumour and gossip and small coloured lies had woven themselves round his name; his appearance encouraged them.

He looked a little like a pirate; he was burnt so brown that he hardly looked European – though he was too big, his bones too heavy, for an Indian; his walk was commanding; though it was commanding it had a slight roll. He was tattooed on the inside of his arms, and his eyes were a peculiarly brilliant blue, and he had a small cast in one of them that gave him a blind, wilfully obstinate look, a suggestion of a patch, particularly as in it he wore a monocle without a string. His hair was as black as his eyes were blue, and he had hair on his chest and arms and legs. The students to whom he lectured occasionally called him 'One-eyed Carlos' or 'Charlie Chang' – but unlike a pirate he had sober tastes, and unlike a monkey he would never chatter and never hurry. Sometimes he was terse and explosive and the students were in awe of him, but usually he was genial, venial and serene; and on the whole he was popular.

Among the rumours there was one that persisted; it said he had been degraded to Amorra from a very senior post. The curious tried delicately, or bluntly, to find out from Sir Monmatha Ghose if it were true. Sir Monmatha Ghose did not know, but he had been in Charles's house and knew that many of the rumours told of it were not far wrong.

The house was old and deep-walled and cool and spacious, but Charles had insisted on having the whole of it altered. That was odd in Charles, who liked and valued true old Indian things. It was washed yellow, and turreted at one side, with long verandahs and a columned porch, where creepers grew. It stood like a fort with a moat of old bazaar on three sides of it, trenched in upon by the new houses and new streets that were spreading out across the plain. On its fourth side it was joined to the College, and its garden led into the College grounds.

Inside the rooms were still immense, the doors and windows nearly as high as the rooms, the verandahs nearly as deep; it was floored with Mexican red stone except the drawing-rooms, which now had marble in faint grey and white squares; the floors were carefully kept and oiled so that they shone like mirrors, the walls were leeped in delicate lime washes, the panelling and the furniture polished and waxed, and the gardener spent an hour every morning arranging bowls and vases of flowers that were beautiful in the empty rooms.

'Where did you get your *mali*?' said Sir Monmatha Ghose. 'He has one heavenly arrangement of flowers after another.' There was a square glass jar that held marguerites and lupins in blue and

pink and orchid colours, with forget-me-nots and deep red car-
nations, and a vase flat against the wall, with roses, and the small
cream double jasmine that has flat, pale green glossy leaves; and
a ring on the table in the next room, where they were to dine,
that picked up every colour on the tablecloth: nasturtiums and
white candytuft, marigolds, and tips of stock. 'But I suppose,' said
Sir Monmatha, 'you imported him with the others.'

Charles's servants were hill-men, of high order and meticu-
lous, who did not gossip in the bazaar.

Sir Monmatha noticed them, and he noticed the flowers, the
faint exquisite colourings of the rooms and furniture; and he
noticed – what many people would not have seen – that, under
the polish and orderliness, nearly all of it had been broken or
defaced and put together again.

'This poor table,' said Sir Monmatha Ghose, running his
finger down an ugly joining, 'why do you live with it like this?
It is so badly broken that it is a pity it has ever been mended.
Why do you keep it like that?' As Charles did not answer he
took it that he might go on. 'This house,' he said, 'is like a shrine
that has been defaced,' and he turned his small deep-seeing eyes
on Charles and said, 'It isn't good for you, Pool.'

'On the contrary,' said Charles, 'it's very good for me.'

'You should try to forget.'

'No, I should try to remember,' answered Charles, and after
a moment he added, defensively, 'I'm perfectly happy.'

He was perfectly happy. He lived chiefly in two small rooms
beside the office; he woke up at dawn and worked into the night –
and that was what he liked to do, get up at dawn and work all day
into the night. That was how he had made Amorra; but in spite
of all his years of work, in the night it looked curiously small in
the plain. Its edges seemed to shrink back on themselves as if the

plain might swallow them, and the night picked out the great belt of the river that changed its course and its bed through the years, that could perhaps defy the engineers and change its course again and sweep the farm and Amorra out of sight with one twist of its flank. The farm in the night was small between two enemies, the snake river and the tiger plain, but Charles did not see them in the night; in the night he went to sleep.

'You are not afraid of the river?' asked Louise, his wife. 'It might turn again.'

'It might. If the dams won't prevent it, I can't.'

'Why didn't you build more inland?'

'We are growing inland, but we have to irrigate.'

'But there are the rains . . .'

'The rains might fail and the crops would dry.'

'So – famine and flood – even here!' Her eyes were dark with melodramatic lashes. 'Even here.'

'Everywhere,' said Charles.

Suddenly after eight years Charles had produced a wife. That had disconcerted, most horribly, his Indian friends. Granted that it was quite possible and usual for anyone in a foreign country to have a hidden past, in spite of the rumours they had not really believed it of Charles. Europeans in India are like cut flowers; that is why most of them wither and grow sterile: they cannot live without their roots, and so few of them take root; but Charles had taken root. They had almost forgotten that India was not his native soil, and they were deeply hurt. They were deeply curious too.

One morning Charles went down to the jetty to meet the steamer; and on the steamer was his wife, and not only his wife – there were two children of perhaps eleven and eight. What were they like? The wife was elegant, handsome but fragile, with a very white skin that made her more than ever noticeable in an Indian community. Her hair was a deep dark gold; 'The colour,' said the sentimental students, 'of the wheat of the fields when it is ripe'; 'The colour of curry powder,' said the not-so-sentimental, 'very hot indeed.'

Her dark eyes under the small veil tied over her hat looked this way and that, quickly as if she were afraid or searching for something, and she lifted her hand to shield her face to ward off the stares, or the sun, as she walked down the jetty to the car. Her hand was small and gloved; gloves had not been seen in Amorra before, nor had the Pekingese, the two dogs feathered like birds that walked down after her. The little girls came behind, one larger, one smaller, like the pictures of the British Princesses; they were dressed alike, one had long hair and one had not, one was pretty and one was not, and they carried attaché cases with foreign hotel labels. Except for the beauty of the mother, they looked very neat and urban, not at all the sort of family anyone would have imagined for Charles. His friends were disconcerted and an immediate unbridgeable gulf opened between them.

Where had this family come from? It appeared that they had been driven out of Paris by the war, and escaped by Lisbon to the Canaries, where they had taken a ship round the Cape to Colombo, and another from Colombo to Calcutta.

Why had they come? Why had they not come before? Why had no one ever heard of them? On all these questions Charles shut his door and gave no word of explanation. Soon, Louise and the little girls might have been living in the house in the bazaar always.

They came in on the paddle-wheeled mail steamer, Louise and Emily and Binnie, on the last stage of the journey from Paris, by Spain and Portugal, by the Canaries and the Cape, by hot little ports on the eastern edge of Africa, by Madagascar and Ceylon to Calcutta; from Calcutta they caught the steamer that took them down the mighty tributaries of the Brahmaputra through East Bengal; and, as they went, a line like a taut string unwound from a tightness under the child Emily's heart, between her heart and her stomach; it slackened as if the thread were casting her off. As the water of the river closed over the track of the steamer, smoothing it back again into calm, these hours began to close over the track in Emily's mind, smoothing it away.

The steamer rode high above the plain, and the hot empty landscape suited Emily. It was the end of the rains; though it was hot there was a promise of freshness; there was a small wind and the river was full to the brim, and on the plain were flat expanses of water, like shallow lakes, rippled by the wind and touched with brilliant green of floating water weeds. There was nothing else but the steamer going slowly and quietly along, coming in now and then to touch the bank near a village of huts in the trees; a plank was put out from the lower deck, a few people with bundles or a wicker crate of hens walked off, a few more people walked on, and the plank was drawn in, the steamer backed off and turned upstream again. It was gentle, unhurried and completely quiet.

Emily rested her arms on the wooden rail that was hot from the sun; she rested her chin on her arms and shut her eyes and the sun began to warm her eyelids and her face. She sighed, and the sigh ran through her like a ripple from the same warm wind that blew across the lakes, and she settled down more comfortably to lean on the rail. Then she opened her eyes and saw her mother's face.

Louise was standing at the rail too, looking down into the water, but what did she see in it to make her look like that?

Louise did not see the water; she was looking at a ghost and the ghost was herself. She was on another steamer, like this with the flat land falling away on either side; and Emily, standing beside her, was not Emily but Charles. Then they had been going back to the town, not away from it – and somewhere ahead, beyond the horizon that met the sky like the edge of a bowl, there waited, too, another unknown house that she would live in, and a life that she must live ...

'What are you thinking about?' said Binnie, thrusting her head up beside Louise.

'Of a house I used to live in – once.'

'What – here?' asked Binnie.

'Yes,' said Louise.

'What was it like?'

'It was particularly beautiful – to me, because I made it,' Louise answered slowly.

'Where is it now?'

'Broken to pieces long ago,' said Louise. 'Don't talk to me now.' Binnie stared.

Nothing had changed on the river; it might have shifted a little, eaten away a foot or two of earth from the bank, uncovered a new shoal of sand, swept away another, but it was the same; the banks were the same with the same nude brown children running to play in the wash that spread in the same way up the banks as the steamer went along, and the fishing boats moved with the same lilting crescent movement as they passed ... It was the end of our honeymoon, the beginning of my married life with Charles – thought Louise; and suddenly the vibrating of the deck under her feet, the slowly passing scenery, sharpened with a nightmare quality. It was happening over again. ('No!' cried Louise. 'No!')

She was wearing a narrow veil tied over her hat and the two ends blown back resolved into the two long ribbons of the steamer wash, and for her, unlike Emily, they broke the quiet of the river with a sustained inexorable break.

('Stop!' she cried. 'Stop. Please stop. I must go back!' But this was a nightmare and her cry had not made a sound.) The steamer went on. It had started, it would arrive at the terminus. It might stick on a sandbank, but that would only be a delay. It would arrive.

Louise had lately been having a dream. It was a dream in which a man rode on a horse, and the man was Pestilence or Famine or Death or simply a rider, an ordinary man, but Louise did not know what he was because she would not look at him. That was the dream; she knew that if she looked at him she might be saved, but she refused to look till he was close, riding her down, and then it was too late. The dream was a symbol for what was happening now, in this terrifying repetition that washed away the years and made her catch her breath with panic. It was too late.

Someone else, not Emily, was standing beside her at the rail. She barely came to his shoulder, she could see the outline of his shoulder behind her cheek, his arm by hers on the rail, the wind ruffling the dark hairiness of it . . . She gave a little gasp and put out her hand and touched – Emily.

'Oh, Emily!' she said, 'oh, Emily!' and Emily stiffened as if she had winced. A sulky, almost resentful look came into the child's face.

'What's the matter, Emily?' Her voice was sharp.

'Nothing.'

13

'Then why do you wince away like that?'

'I was thinking.'

After a contact with Emily, Louise often grew angry like this ... Charles ought to have told me, she cried angrily. He should have warned me. Why didn't he warn me? ... And like a cold thought, the answer slid into her mind: 'Why should he warn you? He didn't ask you to come.'

Just before they reached Amorra, the steamer passed a line of buildings along the farther bank: a factory chimney, great sheds of corrugated iron, trucks on rails that ran down to a jetty, and a flotilla of grey launches with a blue-and-white key design round their funnels. Attached to the buildings was a strange yellow house, with gables and turrets and a dark red roof; it had a garden with a row of trees and a jetty of its own. It looked curiously complete: small, foreign and fascinating, like the picture in a French reading book ... I should like to visit it one day, thought Emily.

Then on the jetty she saw two children, waving to the steamer; she could see them quite clearly, they appeared to be wearing dark clothes and dark socks and one had a white pinafore. They did not move but stood and stolidly waved. In the middle, holding a hand of each, was an Indian nurse, an ayah. 'They are too big to have an ayah, holding on to them,' said Binnie scornfully. 'Imagine if we were afraid of tumbling in the water!'

'They are not like us,' said Emily. 'I wonder who they are.'

When Louise's first cable was brought in and he read it, the whole of Charles had been flooded with such a surge of relief that he felt sick. Louise had left Paris at the beginning of the war, he knew that, and he knew she had gone confidently back soon afterwards, but he had not known whether she had been too late to get away again. During all the weeks of desperate anxiety and burning heat, the wirelesses of Amorra had poured out the news; they could be heard blaring in Hindustani and Bengali in the bazaar, in Bengali and English in the College, in Hindustani, Bengali and English in the houses.

Charles went to the Principal's big tall house. It was a blisteringly hot evening. In the College, as he passed, the professors were sitting out on the platform above the tank with small palm-leaf fans in their hands, and the students were walking listlessly in twos or threes or sitting on their beds on the verandahs. The dry nervous heat accelerated the tension, and the loudspeakers still blared.

Sir Monmatha Ghose was in, and he too was listening to the wireless, dressed in a thin muslin vest and beautifully looped *dhoti*, the graceful Hindu nether garment, and toeless slippers, though in College he usually wore European clothes.

'Can I listen to the news with you?' asked Charles.

'Assuredly. Bring a chair for the sahib and bring a whisky peg.'

They listened in silence, smoking. Charles smoked cigarettes, which he stubbed out before they were finished; Sir Monmatha Ghose smoked a hookah with silver chasings and a gay green-and-pink piping to the mouthpiece, and the hookah punctuated the news with a soft hubble-bubble of sound that was echoed by the regular puffing of smoke from Sir Monmatha Ghose's lips.

'May I come again?' said Charles when it was over and he rose to go.

'Come every night.'

Charles hesitated on the step and said suddenly, as if it were torn from him, 'I cannot sit and listen to it alone.'

Sir Monmatha Ghose took out his mouthpiece. 'You need not, I am here.' And he asked, 'Then you think she is in Paris?'

'I don't know!' cried Charles. 'I don't know.'

Louise's cable came a few days later. It had taken nine days on the way. He stared at it and then he realized that he was filled only with triumph that in her desperate moment Louise had wanted him; immediately he crushed that down; it made him faintly pitiful and he had every objection to being pitied. He read the cable again and said definitely and finally 'No,' and crumpled it up and dropped it on the table. 'No, thank you,' said Charles, and then he picked it up and smoothed it out, and said 'Why not?' He answered: 'MAKES NO DIFFERENCE TO ME IF YOU COME.'

After his cable had gone he would have given anything to get it back. 'She won't come,' said Charles, 'it was only panic.'

(Louise's panic came up like wings out of the grass before the footstep was anywhere near. He had cause to remember that, and he cried, 'I can't start that again!')

('I shall not start it again, whatever happens,' said Charles; 'I could not. It is over and it is dead. It can't begin again.')

The last words Louise had written came to him now. 'Understand; nothing – nothing – will make me alter my mind. You have finished this for us, for ever.' He wrote them now, in a letter to meet her in Calcutta. 'This is what you said when you went away. This is what I say now. Nothing shall make me alter my mind or anything else about me. You can go or you can stay. It makes no difference to me. Nothing can alter me now.' As he wrote it he had altered already.

He had grown a certain laziness in these years; perhaps, like most Indians, he wished more than he did – hoping, almost believing, that wishing is the same as thinking, and thinking is tantamount to doing. He had been contented and that had made him lazier still; laziness, dilatoriness, is natural to India; the sun steals the marrow from the bones, and Charles had worked for eight years out under the sun in the fields, in the lazy certain rhythm of the land, and he had not finished yet ... Because I believe in it, said Charles. Why? Because this is my work that I have found for myself, and I shall not finish it till I die; because I believe that India is one of the new countries; like China and like Russia it is so old that it is beginning to be new. I am of the country now, I am not an exile, I am not even an alien. When I pick up a handful of earth to feel its quality, I know it as I crumble it. I know it better than the Indians them-selves. I have studied it, tested it, doctored it, made it better than itself. My results are creeping like a tide across the land – no, they are coming out of the land, because they come from the soil – and when I die, said Charles, don't let anyone have me cremated. Put me into the soil where I belong, where I may do some final good to a patch of wheat or a mango-tree. Louise called me a clod. Well, so I am; and I shall stay a clod, come or stay as you like. There's nothing you can do to me now ...

In all his calculations he had forgotten the children. For the children, their father was a little far-away man on the part of the map that was shaped like a deep pink teardrop. Emily, it was true, had invested him with a personality from a picture she had seen in the *Illustré*, a picture of the Patagonian Consul in a white pressed suit, white sun-hat, dark face and beard. No one knew how Binnie had imagined him, but she was certainly as surprised as Emily when Louise pointed down from the deck of the steamer and said, 'That's Charles,' and added as if it were an unfamiliar word, 'that's your father.'

'*Father?*' said Binnie, and she and Emily looked down at the man standing on the wharf among the coolies. Emily knew that the same dreadful thought had struck them both. 'Is he – black?' Binnie was just going to ask it when he looked up at them and they saw the blueness of his eyes. He stood on the wharf in the midday sun without a hat, in shorts and a khaki shirt, no coat and no collar or tie or socks. He looked to them wild, not at all their idea of a father, and Emily felt a little stir of excitement and anticipation as she watched him; he was totally unexpected and new. He did not wave or smile. 'Isn't he expecting us?' said Binnie.

He came up on the deck of the steamer that made a stage high up above the town, and Louise stood up like a child to meet him. In her white cheeks there was a hot flood of colour. Emily watched them from the rail; Louise, who had always seemed tall to her, looked quite small, and the sun striking across the deck made her skirts transparent, showing her legs, and thighs, making her look flimsy. They did not kiss. They stood with those few yards of deck between them and looked at one another and there was a pricking silence as they looked. Charles spoke first. 'How do you do, Louise?'

Emily savoured the oddness of that. She looked at Louise, but Louise said nothing and the moment seemed to be given to Charles. He said, 'You look very well – after all these years.'

'So do you.'

'You are prettier than ever, but you know that of course.'

Why did he speak to her in that curious taunting way? Emily and Binnie were staring in surprise. He did not look at them. It seemed to Emily he would not look at them.

'You haven't seen the children,' said Louise.

'You can hardly expect me to recognize them, can you?' He spoke roughly and, as he said it, Emily with a peculiar little shock recognized herself: that was just how she herself spoke when she had something unbearable she wanted to hide.

Then Binnie walked straight across the deck and shook hands. She looked up at him and he, very slowly, looked down at her. 'How do you do, Father?' said Binnie.

He stood, swinging her hand a little in his, and his face had altered ... He was – frightened – before, thought Emily. Why should he be frightened of Binnie? ...

'I don't remember hearing an English child's voice before,' said Charles. 'Funny.' And he looked over Binnie's head to Emily. 'Can't Emily say something too?' Emily was hotly embarrassed, but under the mockery in his voice she thought he sounded eager. 'Emily—' he said again as if he liked to say it, then his eyes came back to Binnie. 'What's your name?' he asked.

'You don't know my *name?*' Binnie was shocked.

'I haven't seen you before,' said Charles, and he said to Louise a little triumphantly, 'She gets her eyes from me,' and immediately he dropped back into his bantering. 'But of course, hers are steadier than mine.'

Emily had a sudden unaccountable pang of pity.

They drove through the bazaar to the house, and as they turned in at the gate, a young Indian, dressed like a soldier in khaki with a puggaree and a polished belt and a cane, clicked his heels and saluted. 'That's Mahomed Shah,' said Charles to the children. 'He used to be a sepoy, now he's our porter. You'll like him.'

'Are there any other Europeans here?' Louise asked, and her voice was tense.

'None,' said Charles, 'except the Nikolides.'

'What a funny name,' said Binnie.

'There are Mr and Mrs Nikolides,' said Charles, 'and they have two funny children, funnier than you. Their names are Alexandra and Jason.'

'They sound funny,' said Binnie, 'but I like the sound of them.'

'Those must be the children we saw on the jetty as we came,' said Emily.

The car drove under the porch where the servants were standing in clean white clothes. As they came into the hall, Louise stopped with a sharp catch of her breath and put out her hand as if she were giddy; her hand found Emily's shoulder and tightened on it so that it hurt, but Emily, with her new awareness, said nothing. She looked round the hall; it was exceptionally pretty and she could see nothing in it to startle Louise. It was panelled in white, and the stairs leading up were stone with a solid side instead of a banister rail and a shelf where a row of Canton enamels, like the ones Louise collected, shone with coloured flowers and birds. 'Remember those?' asked Charles pleasantly.

The dining-room had white furniture, with a deep red floor and curtains of patterned red and gold leaves on white silk. 'That material has worn wonderfully well, hasn't it?' said Charles. Over the fireplace was a curious huge axe, with a handle of wood carved with a crest and a blade-edge that looked sharp and clean.

'Does it really cut?' asked Binnie.

'Does it, Louise?' asked Charles; and then he said, 'Of course it does. It's Dutch; did you know you had a Dutch great-grandfather? He built his house with that.'

'And what do you use it for?'

'Now I have decided to keep it up here,' said Charles.

Upstairs was the drawing-room stretching away to the windows in a high curved bay. 'Some of the pictures are new, of course. I couldn't save those, but this is your piano—' he ran his fingers down the notes – 'you see it's managed to keep its tune without you.'

Louise said nothing at all; she still held Emily's shoulder and she looked suddenly exhausted. 'You want to go to your room,' said Charles; 'I've put the children in the spare room. This is yours—' and they followed him across the passage. Emily thought Louise did not want to come, but Charles led the way in through double white doors.

'What a lovely room!' said Binnie.

'Like it, Louise?' asked Charles.

'Why did you keep it – exactly the same?' Louise cried, and her voice was breaking. 'How could you? It was broken for ever.'

'It's still broken,' said Charles.

'It isn't, it's lovely,' said Binnie. 'Look at the lovely table and the brushes. Whose are they? These are not your brushes, are they, Mother? Three mirrors and lights! Look at the light in the bed. Mother, is that your bed? Are you going to sleep in it?'

'She has made it, so she's going to lie in it, isn't that it, Louise?' said Charles, and, as if he could no longer bear the sight of them, he shook his shoulders and went out and downstairs. Louise went slowly across the room as if a weight were dragging at her knees and sat down. Emily watched, standing still and clumsy and cold in the middle of the floor. She was beginning to feel sick.

'What nonsense,' said Binnie cheerfully, bouncing up and down on the bed. 'You didn't make it, did you, Mother? You needn't ever make your beds in India, need you?'

In the night Louise lay and listened to the drums. The bazaar lay close beside the garden walls and the drums and cymbals in the temple by the banyan tree were very constantly beaten. It was a harmless cheerful little temple; it was lined inside with bathroom tiles, and the roots of the grey old tree appeared surprisingly among them. It was used chiefly as a meeting place, for argument or gossip, but in the night its drums had a baleful throbbing sound. Louise had never noticed the life of the temple and the tom-toms started in her the beating of panic in her heart. She lay and listened, her heart beating, beating, and painfully awake ...

If I go to sleep I shall dream. I shall have my dream again and I shall dream we are not safe. But are we safe? Is anything safe? Why did I come? Oh why, why did I come? What have I done? But what else could I do? I didn't know what to do. And, what else was there to do? It was mad, an impulse; a silly impulse, but anything then had to be an impulse. There was no time for anything else. No time to think. Every night I see again that road we drove along. The car went slowly, so slowly; I was faster than the wheels all the way, trying to urge them on. Why was it so dreadful? Dreadful – so that it will be with me to the end of my days. There was nothing spectacular. The only fear all the way was the petrol. I had forgotten the petrol. We nearly ran out of petrol and I saw those two British officers in the square – where? I don't know where – and they gave me a five-gallon tin. Later on we found one petrol pump that was working, but they would only part with ten litres. No one stopped us or questioned us. We were not alone. Cars passed us, or we passed them all the way, and pony-carts and bicycles and horses, and people walking and people with wheelbarrows and perambulators. The children seemed sunk away to nothing, with small tired faces, and Emily was abominably cross. Then she was carsick and I had to keep stopping the car for her. Binnie said nothing but Emily kept asking why we didn't stay where we were ...

('Because the Germans are coming.')

('Oh. Have they come? Will they kill us?')

('Of course not' – hastily.)

('Then why didn't we stay where we were?')

Emily's face was green-white, and she had on her new winter coat, black-and-white check; its smartness was all crumpled by her sleepy sitting. So was Binnie's ... Now in the night it seemed to Louise that she had dragged them in those coats across the world, by sea and by land and by road, by Europe and Africa and Asia – to safety. Safety. Was it safety? ... It must be, cried Louise. I am so tired, she said. If only the drums would stop beating I would go to sleep. But – if I go to sleep I shall dream ... She lay on her side and listened to the drums and presently she went to sleep and presently she did begin to dream.

The last house on the New Road along the river the coolie lines fires were still burning, with the men squatting round them to smoke and talk and play cards on a mat spread out on the ground. They would burn till long past midnight. In the Hostels the Superintendent had made a perfunctory round and the lights in the windows went out one by one. The staff quarters were silent long ago. On verandahs were the shapes of beds under mosquito-nets, and in handy places, on porch steps, beside the kitchens, the servants carried out their beds or their bedding to sleep in the cool. Some lay simply on the ground with quilts wrapped round their heads and looked like bodies wrapped in shrouds, and others lay on the steps or the shelves of the verandah rails; the watchman stood his lantern in the middle of the drive to keep watch by itself and fell into profound slumber standing up against a wall.

Mahomed Shah put his hurricane lantern inside his door,

where it turned his room into a cave of deep soft yellow light. The room was a hut beside the gate, so small that he could not stand up in it, and he could touch from wall to wall without stretching his arms. It had a floor of beaten dried mud, a few pots and *lotas*, and an earthenware pitcher of water in the corner and a shelf with a broken mirror and a comb. He kept his clothes in a tin trunk painted with roses that usually stood under the bed, but tonight he had carried the bed outside. The walls were plastered with pictures from the European papers, *Post* and *Bystander* and *Illustrated London News*; in the night it was singularly inviting.

He sat down on his bed and took off his twisted soldier's turban with its falling end and pointed centre cap and placed it whole on the end; he leant his *lathee* against the head and drew up his legs, dropping off his wooden pattens that stayed on because they had a peg to hold between the toes. He sat for a few moments staring into the garden where the moon was advancing up the sky, and then he lay down and went to sleep.

The last house on the New Road along the river belonged to Narayan Das, the new young veterinary surgeon. It lay outside the limits of the Amorra Electric Company, and in the night it was lit by oil lamps; each room was filled with a soft bubble of light, the same refulgence that Shah's hut walls had. The garden of the house was only half made, but it had been the garden of an old pavilion on the river, and the light fell from the windows across a square of grass where a pillar had fallen down and was slowly crumbling away. Now it made a seat with a flowering creeper growing over it. Narayan's young wife, Shila, stood beside it and listened to his footsteps going away from her down the road with his friend Anil.

She had waited up for him; he had sent her to bed but she waited up, listening to the voices talking and rising, talking and falling in the next room.

Tarala, the maidservant, had come in and sat on her heels on the ground beside her. Tarala was an old widow crone; her face was dark and wrinkled out of all coherence, she had a rag of grey hair on the top of her head and was dressed in a meagre dun-white piece of cotton. She appeared quite garrulous and senseless, but she had two senses left, a sense of scandal and a sense of enjoyment, and occasionally she would delve down into some other former mind and produce a gentle brand of wisdom. She began to press Shila's feet, squeezing them in her hands, pulling out the toes.

'The dinner was beautiful, Ma,' said Tarala.

'Yes,' said Shila.

'Anil Babu said it was beautiful.' She lifted an eyelid to see Shila's answer to this but Shila kept even her foot still in the old woman's hands.

'It was a pity Narayan Babu did not eat the *jilipis* – they are his favourite sweets.'

'He never knows what he eats when he is talking,' said Shila bitterly.

Tarala squeezed and pressed in silence for a minute, a cord with keys on it sliding up and down her forearms that were black and skinny as shin-bones. Then she said, 'It's natural, Ma, for a young man to see his friends.'

'But not only *one* friend; and he is only a boy.'

'Narayan Babu has many friends,' said Tarala, pressing steadily. 'Even the One-Eyed Sahib, Pool Sahib, is his friend. Naturally. He is a very clever man, though some of his ways I *don't* understand,' said Tarala. She, like Shila, had come from an orthodox home, but Shila had been to school and she was young; Tarala clung with obstinate ferocity to all the old cus-toms and beliefs that Narayan condemned as superstition, and she continually combated his ungodliness with private rituals of her own. He would find a pole with a flag tied to it, outside the kitchen door, a marigold and a sprinkling of rice below it, or he would come back to see the courtyard washed over with the cow-dung he had forbidden her to use and, on the ground in front of the door, a fresh line of patterns that she had made with rice flour and the Ganges water; the mixture dried to a creamy white, and the patterns were pleasing, but it infuriated Narayan, and Tarala would silently rub it all out and do it again as soon as he had gone. 'He is a clever young man,' sighed Tarala. 'With a man as clever as that you must expect foolishness, Ma.' She stood, getting straight up from her heels in one movement in spite of her age. 'Well, let God take care of the father,' she said. 'We must take care of the child. Come, let me put you to bed.'

There was the sound of chairs pushed back and Narayan came through the door; his brows came together in quick annoyance when he saw them. 'Shila, I told you to go to bed.' Tarala could not get used to his calling his wife directly by her name. Shila, herself, could hardly force her tongue to use his, but she tried it now, hoping to please him.

'It isn't late. I waited for you – Indro.'

She looked at him pleadingly. She had on a sari of fine blue gauze that almost hid, in its draperies, the present vase shape of her body; the light lay deeply in its folds, turning them deeper blue, her arms and neck were bare in a cut-away bodice edged with silver; the tinsel threads in the silver shone, her skin shone and her hair shone too, glossy blue-black in its coil, and on her forehead, between eyebrows shaped like crescent moons, she had painted a tiny scarlet mark, her *tika* mark that Narayan did not like her to wear.

Narayan did not look at her. He said hastily, 'Go to bed. I am walking home with Anil.'

'But it's late.'

'It's late. It isn't late.' He mocked her. 'You are asleep. You don't know what you say.'

'I'm not asleep.' Her voice burned with feeling, and then she dropped into a pleading whisper. 'Don't go. Stay with me. Just one night.'

'Am I never to be free?' Now he was angry. 'Can I not have one friend or one thought to myself? Leave me alone.'

It was she who was left alone. Neither of them counted Tarala. Shila followed him to the garden door and heard him and Anil go out by the gate in the wall; she heard the pedals of his bicycle ticking as he wheeled it beside Anil; they stopped outside in the road to light the lamp and she heard the match on the box, and then she heard them going away laughing, quite intimate laughter. The child inside her gave a convulsive leap. Did she move or did the child?

The little garden was full of dim moonlight, it brimmed over the walls and above the trees; everything was clear in it, every blade and leaf and stem, dark on pale and pale on dark. She walked out in it, though the grass was wet and chill on her bare feet and Tarala would scold. The river was shining like an unearthly lake, its edges disappearing into mist, and it seemed to Shila to be running extra quietly. She listened to the footsteps going away along the road.

In the distance Anil began to sing; his voice came back to her on the wind.

'I hate him,' whispered Shila.

Anil was a student at the College. Its grounds were lit, too, by the moon as Anil and Narayan walked past the sleeping watchman and in at the gate. It was a Romeo and Juliet moon, and along the path, as separated as those lovers, moonflowers and sunflowers grew together, and though it was late in the year, there were still some flowers on the trees. The lawns unrolled to the verges of the tank, where the steps led down to the water; the water was still and pale and held a long reflection of the moon, and between the darkness of the leaves the sky showed in little brilliant spaces. Near the Hindu Students' Hostel another tree was shaped like a weeping willow and had small scented flowers on its stems.

The College perfectly matched the night – it might have been a palace in Verona; whitened by the moon, its whiteness had a milky lustre as if it had changed to marble, and in its arches and its pinnacles, its balconied verandahs and under its cupolas, were shadows of dim convolvulus blue.

Narayan and Anil walked hand in hand along the path, not to the Hostel but along the lawns. Anil pulled Narayan forward; their figures moved in and out of the shadows that bordered the path, in under the trees, out into the moon again. Narayan had European clothes, but Anil's loose white draperies moulded his thighs and flowed around him. He was still singing, not listening to the words, not even pronouncing them, singing and wandering with Narayan's hand in his, feeling the moonlight, letting it eat into his skin.

Narayan followed, willingly and unwillingly. Anil shared for him the overstudied graces of the night; Anil troubled him as the moon and the scent of the moonflowers troubled him, and the scent of the flowers on the weeping tree that blew into his nostrils with every stir of wind. He enjoyed them but they troubled him and he thought it would be better to be working or to be in bed. He was hot and he had a slight pain of indigestion that came from eating while he talked too much, and his feet in the wet grass were chill. He gave a sad little belch but Anil, singing louder, led him on.

They stopped at the platform by the tank; it was empty, lit softly by the moonlight, so that its edges were indistinct and the canna flowers by it had no colours. It was forbidden to the students, but Anil stepped up on it now. 'Teacher, teacher, do you see me?' he sang.

'Be quiet. We shall be heard. You should have been in an hour ago.'

'Not I,' said Anil. 'I settled that long before. I go and come as I please.'

'Not if you are reported to the Principal.'

'I shall not be reported to the Principal.'

'You have too much money,' said Narayan, suddenly disagreeable. 'You will get into trouble all the same, one of these days.' He sounded as if he wanted it, and in that moment he did.

He loved Anil, he was in love with Anil, but in some way he resented him . . .

I can never see you quite properly, Anil, because you dazzle me. This is ridiculous when I am much older than you, but you dazzle me, Anil. You are something in yourself that has not touched my life before. How did we come to be friends? Really, I do not know. I remember the facts: I came to your rescue when the Police interrupted a meeting – a meeting of the Onward Movement, the Students' League, the Social Reform; you were in all of them, it was any of them – and I interceded for you and undertook to see you to your room. I do not remember what made me do it and it does not explain how the friendship began, but as we walked to the Hostel, both of us silent, you a little sulky, we looked at one another; I talked to you, you answered me, and I think we have been talking ever since. We have not been friends for long, but everything that came before I knew you seems unsatisfactory to me now.

I cannot forget you for a moment, when I am with you I cannot forget myself. I have crossed blood in me that makes me dark and thick and slightly squat; your stride is longer than mine, and your body is built so that you go forward strongly and gracefully; my hair grows close to my head like a Negro's, but yours grows loose and most poetically. When you take my hand I see our wrists together and mine is heavy and dark-looking beside yours. Most of all I am conscious of your family. You are a Bengali Brahmin, the child of tradition that you trace back for twenty-seven generations; the son of a landowner, you will inherit land and wealth. You came to College because you inherit, too, your father's idealistic notions; you came to feed an ideal, not because one day you must feed your mouth or starve. Now you are bored, probably you have forgotten what that particular ideal was; you forget so quickly. You would not stay here except that your father says you must get your B. Ag. degree. The class of student is not high, that is natural in an Agricultural College; young men prefer the Universities, they don't like to dirty themselves with peasants' work. You are bored, and that is why you talk to me.

I stand in a street in the back streets of Calcutta. The street was like any other street in a big commercial city, it had houses far too tall and far too close together, it had noise and smells and its gutters were full of litter and garbage and stray dogs and cats and it was interesting because it was so diverse. A rich street is much the same all down its length, it betrays nothing, but a poor street betrays everything; you cannot be private in hot, small, bug-and-cockroach-infested rooms, so everyone is everyone else's business and there is a kinship that is almost friendliness. I missed it when I was picked out of the garbage and taken to school – and that was done by the detestable British, my dear Anil; the Imperialistic British, who bothered to take up a gutter-boy and give him life.

Am I grateful? I need not be so very; the British have a passion for alteration. I was educated at the Slane Memorial Scottish School for Orphan Boys; they had my mind and my body for seven years, and for seven years I learnt to keep my heart shut away in darkness and starvation. Perhaps that is why it grows such extravagant one-sided branches now I have let it out; I am shamed by it and think I shall put it away again.

Till now I have avoided any kind of friendliness and kept to acquaintance; only this last year since I came here, married to Shila, I seem to be learning friendship – I have even a beginning of friendship with Mr Pool – and through friendship I have learnt to love you, Anil; but you make me feel the marks of that street more than ever; they are on me, I shall never lose them, they are the only caste-marks I shall ever know ... And he thought again of Anil's father ...

What would your father think if he saw us together? I know quite well. I make you describe your father to me over and over again, his stateliness, his rigid orthodoxy; and we laugh at him, but for me it is like pricking at a wound. I have no father. I see your father, as you have told me, on the terrace of your house above the fields; he sits on his bed, his feet drawn up, his shawl hanging in fresh cream folds, his hands and his feet still. He would look at me and his eyes would see at once what kind of a fellow I am and then he would turn his eyes away and not be interested to look at me again, in spite of anything you could tell him. He has retired from the city never to go there again; he hopes, when you have grown wiser and older, to leave his possessions and his family in your hands and retire completely from the world. He holds minutely to the ideal of non-contamination, even a shadow in the street would defile him. Well, it is easy for him; the fields and the land all about him are his, he is the lord of the land and the house where his family and his son's family live, where his son's sons' families shall live. His is the tradition and the heritage of Brahma. It is in him and in you; even if you laugh and are lazy, you cannot deny it.

And I? I am of the city garbage, raised on its litter; my emancipation and position make me accepted here, they allowed me to marry Shila; but if you took me to your home I should contaminate your house. Your young wife and your cousins' wives might peep and stare, but your old aunts, the uncles' wives, would take one look through the curtain and say to your sisters, 'Wherever has Dada picked up such a person?' And they would have my shadow cleaned from the house wherever it had fallen . . .

Narayan sighed and sat down on the balustrade behind Anil. Too many shadows had fallen on him; he was soiled, impure for life; and now everything he had most desired and striven for seemed to him far removed from truth . . .

I have been wrong all this time. I have been going in the wrong direction; all this force and striving, this breaking away and smashing down of obstacles, has been wrong – is still wrong. I should have left it alone. I wish I had left it alone; but what else could I do? I had to make myself, and make myself strong. Now I want to go back, behind that street, behind my birth, accepting them, go back to the only mother I have, to India

herself ... He could not say more than that; an inarticulate longing filled him with humbleness and passion, so that he trembled,
and in that moment he was happy, with a happiness that came
from a sudden rightness of the balance in himself, as if he had
touched truth ... I am, he said, this is myself – and immediately
from habit he began to think of himself and his grievances and
difficulties, and his ambitious discontent swamped and put out
that glimmer of light that was anyhow small as one of the wicks
burning in a little saucer of butter that they sold in the temples ... What was I thinking of? What do I want? And his mind
cried angrily, but still silently: Really, it is impossible for me to
be friends with you, Anil.

And yet – and yet ... To move about the garden as we do
tonight, to talk a little madly and to laugh, to wander in the
light and the darkness with the scents and the still shadows, to
laugh and to talk a little nonsense, to hold your hand, Anil, and
swing it lightly – why should I not do this? It is nothing if not
a waste of time, I am getting nothing for it – and yet ... You sit
turned away, Anil, looking into the water; I see your shoulder,
thin in its fine white muslin shirt; I see the line of your cheek,
thin too, but softly young and dark, and I see the darkness of
your hair. I see you but I don't know what thoughts you are
thinking, I only know that I could never think them and if you
told them to me they would cause surprise and perhaps excitement in my mind. The things you think of and say are often
quite absurd and childish, but they are pristine and curiously
complete and they make my profoundest efforts clumsy and like
a boy's. I don't know what you are thinking ... And aloud he
said, 'What are you thinking, Anil?'

'I was looking into the water and I thought about the river,'
said Anil dreamily. 'Did you see the colour of the river this

evening, Narayan? It was like the inside of a shell. All the colours are deeper when they lie on that mother-of-pearl, the water-lilies are milk-white and crimson instead of pink and cream, and the hyacinth clumps are purple. Didn't you see them like that, Indro?'

'No,' said Narayan sourly. Anil knew very well he did not.

A speck of light sailed across the sky towards them; but it was not a shooting star, it was a firefly.

'I sometimes think my thoughts will end like that,' said Anil: 'Not a star. A very common insect.'

'You only say that to hear me contradict you.'

'Really. Really. You are very cross tonight. What is it? Something, or somebody, has disagreed with you, I think.' He stood up on the edge of the platform and stretched himself, leaning backwards a little so that the line of his body made a taut, clean curve; he looked as if he might fly with the strong springing lines that he made, and his loose clothes fell in long folds, gracefully, as he stood.

Without thinking Narayan followed him and stretched himself as he stood up; but cheap European clothes are not made for stretching – there was the sharp sound of a tear and the back of his coat split and at the same time his collar stud gave way and one side of his collar sprang up against his cheek.

'That comes of wearing what does not suit you,' said Anil, laughing at him. 'You don't look half as much grand as you did.'

An extraordinary wave of temper came over Narayan. Everything was horrible – Anil's bantering, half-sneering laughter, the hot sticky night, his own heat and his wet feet, the fantastic shadow-strewn College, and the long road he must travel home to his house where Shila, if he knew her, would still be waiting up to greet him with reproachful eyes. He hated Anil. 'You damned impertinent boy!' he cried and inexpertly, with a clumsy gesture, he knocked Anil backwards across the chest. Anil was laughing, and he purposely let himself be knocked, still laughing, off the platform, landing lightly on his feet in the grass below it. Immediately there was a howl, and he screamed, a real shrill scream of fear with pain in it, and something ran away in the grass. Anil staggered and fell theatrically against the balustrade, hiding his face.

Narayan did not move; he could not move, he could only stand, watching Anil stagger and fall against the stone. The moment drew out in fantastic coldness and still he could not move and chill drops ran down his neck. When he did speak his voice sounded rusty. 'Anil, Anil,' he rasped, 'Anil, for God's sake what has happened? What is it? Oh, what did you do?' His voice was shriller than Anil's, but Anil still leant on the balustrade, his face hidden and his shoulders shaking. In agony he pulled the hands away from Anil's face and Anil was laughing, and now he laughed aloud. Narayan flung away from him in disgust.

'Another silly trick.'

Anil's face went stiff and furious too. 'Not at all. I thought I had been bitten by a snake. It was not a snake, that is all.'

'You *were* bitten. Show me. Where are you hurt?' There was concern and authority in Narayan's voice. 'You were not play-acting me. Show me where it is.'

Anil stepped back coldly. 'Don't concern yourself. It was not a snake.'

'I know it was not a snake,' said Narayan irritably in his anxiety. 'Other things are dangerous as well. Tell me. I must know.'

'You won't know if I do not choose to tell you.'

'Anil, I am sorry. I was not myself just now.'

'You were very much yourself. Don't mind about it. It does not interest me.'

'Anil, please. Did it touch you?'

'It did or it did not. That is my affair.'

'Please don't take this attitude. Tell me what has happened.'

'Nothing has happened,' said Anil impatiently. 'I thought I had trodden on a snake. It was not a snake. That is all.'

'What was it, then?'

'I don't know. It has gone.'

'Didn't you see it? You must have seen it.'

Anil shrugged. 'It was invisible. Let it remain so. In any case I am a damned impertinent boy. What does it matter what happens to me?' And he turned on his heel, but Narayan saw the flash of tears in his eyes before he had time to turn.

'Anil.' He caught him by the hand, there was a moment's childish struggle and Anil suddenly gave way.

Presently, as they were walking back together, Anil said: 'I am overwrought, I think. I have been working so much, too late for the Examination.'

'You have to work,' said Narayan callously. You have to pass first, with first-class honours; and you will get the Kailash Chandra Prize for Bacteriology, and the MacEwen Purse—'

'So you say.'

'Anil, this is something I want most in the world.'

'But why? For me? I am not your brother.'

'You are more than my brother. You are myself. You are all that I want to be.' And that was true, and though he spoke lightly, Anil's results were desperately important to Narayan. Anil was unreliable. Narayan sighed. 'You must not be too late. You have much to do tomorrow. Professor Dutt is giving you some private coaching, I think.' But still they did not go to bed.

They walked lightly on, while it grew very late. Anil was half touched, half bored; Narayan was blurred with remorse and tenderness. They had both forgotten what had happened, but on Anil's *dhoti* was a trail of small dark spots, bloodstains from a gash across his shin, a small deep gash where the blood had dried already. Anil did not notice it again.

They paused at the door of the Hostel and looked across the College to the outer walls. The moon was sinking in the sky, it was growing darker. In the Pools' house was a light.

'Charlie Chang is working late tonight. He shouldn't be. His wife is here. Why does he need a light?' said Anil; and laughing, sniggering a little, they said good night themselves.

It was not Charles, it was his daughter Emily. Anil's scream had woken her and she put out her hand in the darkness to find her spaniel and he was not there.

The scream woke Emily out of a dream and the voice that had been screaming went on to laugh. It was entirely natural to Emily that screams and laughing should be mingled and entirely natural that on hearing them she should be nipped cold and still with fear. (Louise would not let them scream, nor would Madame Chastel at school in Paris. 'We shall not scream or cry, we shall laugh instead,' and so they did, a high snapping sort of laughing, while fear was naked in Louise's eyes.) Now Emily woke confused. What was that scream and that laughing, high with fright? What was it? . . . ('What was it, Mother?' 'Nothing.' 'What was that?' 'Nothing.' That was a lie, it was almost next door, but Louise told lies. At least she never exactly told the truth.) . . . Will there be a crash? Will there?

Remember, Emily, remember. This is not France, this is India. Remember! India . . . Slowly she began to relax.

She had been born in India; she, Emily – not Binnie ... If you are born in a place does a little of it get into your bones? Yes. I think it does ...

('What do you call people who live in a country always, Charles?')

('Natives, I suppose.')

('No, not natives. People who come to it and want to belong to it and never go away.')

('Domiciled citizens.')

('Then Binnie and I should like to be domiciled citizens of India, please, Charles.')

Why did Emily like it so much? The only way in and out of it was by the river. It had taken ten hours of winding through the plain to reach Amorra from the depot, and all that way they had seen only the fields and the villages and the empty sky; and Amorra was much the same, only a town along the riverbank; the high College buildings that seemed like skyscrapers against the huts looked pygmy against the sky, and all the fields and paddocks were only a little patch upon the plain.

The strange wide land with its heavy weight of sky and water that oppressed Louise was beautiful to Emily; there was more sky here than anywhere she had seen, and the river was a mile wide from bank to bank, swirled with rapids that churned the sand up into yellow-green water, and beyond the river on each side stretched the plain ... We are divided from everything else. We are in another world. Nothing can get at us here ...

And Charles was here. Why had they been without him so long? There had been no one like Charles in the house at Bellevue; none of the men they saw – Félix, dear Félix the cook whom they had laughed at her for loving, or the postman or Madame's nephew Jean André or Louise's friends – were in the least like Charles. Charles was strong and bold and different. Even the smell of him was different; Charles smelled of man; he smelled, too, of tobacco and the grass and herbs he touched all day long, and of soap and eau de cologne, and when he came in from riding he smelled strongly of leather and horse, a good live smell though Louise wrinkled up her nose in disgust . . . I would rather smell of doing things than being clean, said Emily . . . and the smell of Charles seemed to chase the last sickly shadows from her mind.

Now, except when she woke in the night, the life in Paris was like a shadow or a dream; the house with the balconies and paved garden had been the centre of the world, now it was like a dream – all of it; Madame Chastel, the despot whom they thought would go on and on for ever, was gone, left without them; the voices of Félix and the cross old Albertine were speaking where she could not hear them; other people were walking up the road, picking their steps between the *pavé*, walking in and out of the pattern that the chestnut trees threw down on the stones . . . For ten years I lived in that house and walked up and down that road, said Emily, ten times I have seen the leaves change, opening in the spring, spreading a still canopy in summer, drifting in the autumn, rustling along the gutters in the frost of winter – ten times, and all the while Amorra and Charles were here alone.

('Why didn't you bring us out here before, Mother? Why did you keep us at home?')

('I shouldn't have brought you now if it were not for the war. India isn't good for little girls.')

Phaugh! Rubbish!

('Charles, why didn't Mother let us come here before?')

('Because she wanted to keep you at home,' said Charles.)

That was the natural explanation. It did not seem in the least odd to Emily. It had not occurred to her that a father had any rights over his children or could make decisions for them. In Emily's experience Louise was omnipotent. Then, she had listened with close attention to a conversation she overheard between Charles and Louise . . .

'I suppose you will want someone to teach the children,' Charles began it. 'Perhaps one of the professors at the College could do it in his spare time. I'll speak to Ghose.'

'Is it worth it?' answered Louise. 'They won't be staying here for long.'

'Won't they?' asked Charles, and Louise looked at him quickly.

'They can't stay here, Charles.'

'Why not?'

'How can they? It's not – fit for them.'

'I'm afraid it must be,' said Charles crisply. Louise did not answer; she was facing Emily, and Emily saw her hysterical look come into her face; it made her cheeks very white, her eyes very black. 'You came. I didn't ask you to. You came,' said Charles. 'Why did you come?'

'I don't know,' said Louise in a whisper, 'I don't know,' and she cried. 'Can't you understand? It was like being hunted. There was not time to think—'

(Oh, there *was*, Mother, Emily contradicted silently, we were in that nice hotel for days.)

'There seemed nowhere on earth that was safe or quiet—'

(Lisbon was perfectly quiet.)

'I had no one to turn to, no one to help me—'

(Oh, *Mother*!)

'Now – now I know that I was mad.'

'I don't think you were mad at all,' said Charles pleasantly,

40

and all Emily's nerves approved of his light, almost conversational voice, after Louise's overwrought cry. 'I think it was very sensible. My house was half yours even if you didn't care to use it. It's comfortable and it's as safe as any place can be – though naturally you don't like living quite alone, as you have to here. I understand that. I didn't like it either – to begin with—'

'Charles—'

'And we don't need reminding, do we,' asked Charles with a peculiar edge to the words, 'that Emily – and Binnie – are my children?' Louise's answer was silent on her lips. 'I'll ask Ghose to recommend a tutor for them,' said Charles, suddenly, tersely, bringing the subject to an end. 'They have been so well stuffed that it won't hurt them to forget a little.'

Louise still did not answer, and a fear was born in Emily's mind; and now, in the night, it recurred to her . . .

Louise had brought them to Amorra, Louise could take them away. They could not prevent her, children could not be real citizens of any country; they could not choose where they would live. Louise had many weapons and she would use them. Could Charles defend himself against them all? Could Charles? Emily herself constituted one. Emily was delicate and she had an unlucky stomach; often, herself, she had been undone by it. If she should get ill . . . The heat had already made her most unbecomingly pale. She was a pretext Louise had often used before; often she and Binnie had been forced away from a party, an occupation, a holiday or a dream. ('Why?' 'Because I say so.' 'Explain!' And Louise could always explain.) . . . That was it, thought Emily, she had all the reasons, the arguments, all the words and all the power. The only thing Emily had learnt was to make herself expressionless, to give nothing away, above all never to show she liked or loved. Now she set her teeth in her despair ... But one day, Mother, it will be my turn to win. Charles will help me, and I shall win. I shall win over this. I shall stay here – always – with Charles ...

She had grown a violent hero-love for Charles, but Charles, it seemed, was curiously abstracted and had no time to return it. She, the undemonstrative Emily, would push her face against his hot shoulder, tighter and tighter: 'Let me stay with you, always – always.' He said: 'Yes, but not now, that's a good girl' – but sometimes he stroked her hair and turned up her chin and looked into her face, and he had given her a puppy for herself. He had given her Don ...

She put out her hand in the darkness to feel him. Her finger touched the edge of his drinking-bowl, not the top but the side, and her hand found his bed, but it was empty. Shaken out of herself she was able to sit up and switch on the light. The bed was empty and the bowl was turned over, with the water running away across the verandah, and the side of the bed, a wooden frame plaited with webbing, was bitten into splinters all along it and the lead bitten in half. 'Oh, Don!' cried Emily. 'Don!'

Immediately Don appeared like a sprite from under her bed. 'What have you done? Where have you been?' asked Emily sternly, but he showed none of the guilt that customarily filled him at the least tinge of scolding in her voice. He wiped his paws down the side of her net, fawning and leaping and trying to lick her hand with overwhelming love. 'Don't be sloppy,' said Emily sternly again, and at last she coaxed him on to his bed and, leaning on the edge of hers rather than getting out on the floor, though the bed's edge cut across her chest, she managed to tie him up with the end of his bitten lead. She turned out the light and lay down and her hand stroked his warm, sleek-feeling body. Now her hand felt sparser hair and a patch of hot bare skin; he had turned on his back and she was stroking his stomach. 'You're very hot, my love,' she crooned.

If she put her two hands round Don from behind she could feel his heart beating like a little engine; but in some way when he was still and asleep it seemed to be beating all over his body, everywhere except in the rough pads of his feet and in his ears; that was natural, the pads were like shoes and a spaniel's ears were largely ornamental, like long hair. You could not feel much of Emily, could you, in the ends of her hair?

She kept her hand on Don's stomach and the pulse of it seemed to be beating up her arm, very quickly as if it were part of her. But he is quicker than I am. He goes quicker than I do, thought Emily drowsily, but he seems to be going very quickly now ... She was not concerned; with her hand on him all her troubles had gone.

They had never had a dog before ... Of course, Mother had the Pekingese, but they are no more dogs, said Emily, than goldfish are fish; though they are charming, of course. Besides, they are Mother's, and she adores them and they are far removed from us.

On Don's collar she had tied a label—

DON
POOL
Government Farm
Amorra
Bengal
India
Asia
The World
The Universe

—because that seemed to be a satisfactory explanation of her feeling for him. Suddenly, she had entered into richness; she had Don, and, nearly, she had Charles. She was drowsy, she was not afraid any more ... This is India, this is not France. Nothing can happen here. Don is under my hand. He is beating, beating under my hand. Don ... Don ...

Don settled more deeply on his back and sighed. Emily's hand, limp and heavy with sleep, slipped off him to the rug. He started up and began to bite the bed, straining and worrying at his lead.

III

The morning came early to Amorra. First the river began to pale and to look solid against its farther bank where the mist hung down. Soon, beyond the town, the fields seemed to draw them-selves out away from the banks on either side; and this drawing away, this look of stretching, was because the horizon now showed. The sky grew pale too, separated from the earth, divided pale from dark. Soon the fields began to show their shapes – in chequers of pale and dark, in a glimmer of water from the rice-fields, in running criss-crossed paths of white. Now it was possible to pick out the road banked high in case of flood; it looked pale, bleached and colourless; but presently, as the trees changed from dark to green, it changed from a pale thread to a line of pinkish dry brick-dust, with the humped shapes of bridges and the white pepperpot turrets of a country temple beside the road; the railway lines behind it ran on, on and away. Now there were no more stars in the sky, and the sky was grow-ing green and faintly luminous above the plain. Green was the first colour to come, faint green in the sky after the stars, a dark blackish green on the trees and pure bright green, limpid, on the rice-fields. Then appeared the clay colours of the earth, the dry fields and the mud walls and village huts and after them, clear as the rice, the mauve spikes of water hyacinth in the pools. There was a little of that colour in the sky, as in one village and then in another a fire was lit and smoke went up dark into the sky. The sky was soon colourless again with daylight, and white mist chill with dew began to creep across the fields and round the town.

The shaggy old town of Amorra woke before the new.

The first to wake in the bazaar were the cats; they ran along the drains under the steps and leaped over refuse and old tins and heaps of leaves without a sound, skirting the sleeping bodies on beds and mats or on the ground; and as they ran the light ran after them, drawing streaks across the houses. The sun came up and filled the light with warm yellow, and struck across the bathing tanks, where presently the people would go for their ablutions and to clean their cooking-pots.

A dog sitting on a dung-heap stood up and stretched his hind legs; as the sun began to warm the street, a thousand indelicate smells rose to his nostrils. In every tree the crows began their cawing. Someone took the cloth off the cockatoo's cage and it walked backwards and forwards along its perch examining its feathers that were green with purple points.

A thin little boy was the first human to come out; he wore nothing but a coat that came to the top of his stomach and his stomach was blown out into the shape of a melon and his head was newly shaven except for one lock in the middle. He shivered, his eyes were dull with sleep and he went to the tap that stood in the street and began to splash his face. Two other boys ran out from a hut and hailed him; they left the door of the hut open and new smoke and scoldings came out after them and an old woman, bent so that her face was near her knees, brought out a basket. She stepped aside to blow her nose with her fingers, then went to the end wall of the hut and in the sun began to plaster dung cakes on the wall to dry; each cake was patterned with the print of all her fingers and she slapped them on one after the other with a heavy regular rhythm that was soothing in the early morning. The little boys began to play.

Soon after the huts were awake the houses woke too. Soon the families came out on the verandahs.

In a small house a thin old man came out to sit in the sun and near him he had a table of books. He shivered gently and wiped his nose and gathered his grey shawl round him and put on his spectacles and picked up a book. He was Professor Dutt from the College, and he had two extra classes to prepare; after his morning lecture he was to coach that brilliant, uncertain and rather tiresome student, Anil Krishna Banerjee, in his room; and at three o'clock he was to go to Mr Pool's house, where, every afternoon, he taught certain subjects to the Misses Emily and Barbara Pool. That gave him a little welcome extra money every month, but it worried him; he could not decide if it were an honour or an ignominy that Sir Monmatha Ghose had recommended, and Charles had chosen, him; and he could not make up his mind what, and how much, the children ought to know or what, and how much, he ought to teach them, and he varied startlingly between the kindergarten and the academic; also he was terrified by Mrs Pool. She said 'my children' as if they were some rare sort of animal, she attended the lessons and interrupted them and had the effect, he noticed, of nonplussing Miss Emily as well as himself. He sighed as he turned over the pages in search of some small problems that would not harass the brains of the children too much and yet would please and impress Mrs Pool.

A goat and two kids pattered down the road to the bazaar, past houses where oleanders showed in knots between the dusty little gardens, and cows were being milked in front of their suspicious owners. The goat had discharged her milk and now, with her udders done up in a neat white bag, she walked along in front of her disappointed kids. They walked in and out of the legs of fathers coming back from the family shopping, of cake-sellers and bread-sellers and the betel-leaf man. Water dropped on their heads and along their backs as the water-skins and pots were carried in for the day, and from the tanks the sound of splashings and scourings came to their ears.

For the goat the bazaar was a pleasant place to wander, full of pickings and leavings, though her kids became entangled with legs and wheels and the butchers' shops had heads and entrails and whole corpses of little kids hung up on hooks. The live kids filled the air with their hungry bleatings but no one heard them, they were only one more noise in the hubbub of noises; the kids danced on their miniature hooves over leaves and litter and betel stains and droppings and the goat stayed by the side of the road munching a succulent paper. The bull took no notice of any of them, nor of his patient relations the buffaloes, as they walked leadenly along with their carts, overloaded, hot and dusty. The bull swung his dewlap and went off to lick a pile of soft sugar in the sweet-shop; his horns were tipped with brass and he wore a necklace and a hump cap made of blue-and-white beads; and – another side of veneration – a little sick cow stood on three legs and shivered before it limped off starving down the road. Eventually it wandered into the College ground while the porter was round at the kitchens gleaning his morning meal.

Anil saw it as he was getting up. He stood in his room with nothing on his body but a cotton cloth around his thighs. He had just come up from the privy and his Thread, the sacred Thread that hung from his left shoulder to his right thigh, was twisted round his ear. Slowly humming a song, he untwisted it and began to put on his clothes. At home he could not have dressed like this. There he went to wash himself in the tank beside the house; praying, then facing the sun, soaking himself with pourings from his *lota*, saying again the prayers prescribed as he poured, pouring water after he had prayed, thinking of the seven sacred rivers; and as he plunged finally into the water of the tank, as it closed around his shoulders, it was the water of the Mother of All Rivers, the River Ganges; he was bathing by intention in its waters, his spirit floated away to join it in its course.

When he had finished, he turned towards the sun, taking the water in his hands, letting it run off his fingers. He came out of the water putting a pure cloth round his waist and on his shoulders and waited with his face turned to the East for the house priest, the Purohit, to touch his forehead with a paste of sandalwood making the red mark of his caste, and hang round his neck a string of flowers. After saying his last prayers he put on his clean clothes and carrying his *lota* and his flowers went towards the house. That was his morning ritual and now, getting up as he had done this morning, washing himself quickly and putting on his clothes as he looked out of the window, Anil felt slothful and impure ... Why do I not keep to the rites in College? My father thinks I do, I vowed to him I would, then why don't I? I do not know. Why do I think of this now? What suddenly has made me think of this? Narayan is always talking of it. Is it Narayan or is it that little cow tearing up the College grass as if she were in heaven? ...

'*It is acknowledged that the poverty of the Indian breed of cattle is due to the fact that their slaughter is forbidden by ancient Hindu religion; old and useless herds are thus maintained that take from the healthy young animals their share of food.*' That is what Anil himself had written in his essays, but would he have killed the little cow outside? No, he would not ... Would I prevent Narayan from killing it? I do not know. I do not know ... And suddenly he found it was nearly eight o'clock and bent down to pick up his shoes. On his leg the red mark had nearly healed.

Narayan sat in his office and made up his book. It was his case book and though he would not have shown it to Anil or anyone else, or mentioned its existence even, it was precious to him. It was a collection of notes on his cases, not for showing to officials but written for himself; they might even have been called notes on himself. Each one was a record of more than a case, each one was a battle; they were a series of small tough battles in which he had won through from the new deeply inhibited student to Dr Das, the young research man at the Government Farm, the marked-out Government servant ...

And it is quite right, said Narayan, I am good. At present I have to do routine jobs, I have to practise, but I shall get a better post and a better. And I shall deserve it. Each page I turn brings me nearer to that. The pages of the book were deeply serious to him – 'A *bullock* ... *An imported goat* ... *A cow in calf* ... *An infected herd of buffalo*.'

When he was young Narayan had had the thoughtless terrible cruelty of most Indians to animals, a cruelty that reaches from high to low, that runs through high days and ordinary days; it stains the land with the blood of annual sacrifice in temples and holy places; it tortures the cows for their milk and starves their calves to death; it lets sores gather and stream under the yokes of bullocks and buffaloes and on the thin hard-driven tikka gharry ponies; it lets dogs lie out in the road when they have been run over till they die by slow hours, and throws kittens and blind puppies on the rubbish heaps to starve – native, thoughtless cruelty. Now he was not cruel and he was not kind. He was intensely practical and he was a good and skilful doctor; and besides his passionate ambition, and the research that lifted him towards it, lately he had liked his work. Every time he was called to the ordinary and routine work he was conscious of a new deep satisfaction. Even while he grumbled and pulled up his sleeves, the whole of him was filled with a good accustomed feeling of skill and ease.

That was how he had first met Charles; it was soon after he came on the farm, one evening when he had managed to save a calf that might – so easily – have died. It was a hot evening and the shed stank after the calf birth, of blood and urine and soaked stale straw, but as he knelt on one knee over the calf Narayan had been full of ease and quiet peaceful emotion – emotion is too strong a word, happiness too light, but he was filled with serene and utter peace. He, who was usually obsessed with futility, in the shed that evening had a quiet responsible power, reasonable and just, capable of joy and strength and a wisdom of its own. In saving the calf he had in some part saved the world, and his, that evening, were the quiet and the strength of a saviour. At least till Charles came in. When Charles came in Narayan did not move but every hair of him altered and stiffened into defence. He waited for whatever it might be, a question or a criticism or an order, perhaps praise, because no one could deny that he had done good work with the calf – but it was nothing.

Charles, who was smoking a pipe, leaned against the door of

the shed and was completely silent, watching Narayan – watching his hands and watching the calf laid down on the straw and the cow turning her head on the rope to look, watching the sunset through the half-door; and the sun going down seemed to look back at him, winking on his eyeglass; imperceptibly, Narayan relaxed.

The cowsheds were on the edge of the farm buildings; and over the half-door of the shed he could see outside, to the fields where the sun was going down behind the flat plain; the people were going home to their villages along the narrow raised partitions of the fields; they moved to the dim distance – a man driving two bullocks, his plough left standing till tomorrow in the earth; a child, a woman with a bundle on her head, a woman carrying a child; a man, a boy, a child. He could see the village in the distance raised in its clump of trees and the land stretching from it like a sea from an island. The flat land with its bare earth fields, for it was summer then, took for a moment the reflection of the sky; the last light lay on them turning them a deep Indian yellow; it was an unmistakably evening light, and somewhere near the shed, but out of sight, a cowherd began to play a tune upon a flute.

The calf moved, jerking its legs, and Narayan forgot Charles; presently he lifted it and put it by the mother; it was dark cocoa colour streaked with white, it had white on its legs and a white star on its forehead. 'Star of good luck,' said Charles; 'I didn't think it would live.'

'It will do now, I think,' said Narayan.

'It's a good thing we have you and not old Babu Bhobatosh Babbletalk. That is one of our imported Friesians.'

Narayan was so surprised at his knowing and using the students' nickname for old Dr Bhobatosh that he forgot to answer.

Charles was looking at him as Narayan wiped his hands on a towel.

'You should have been a doctor.'

'I should have – did funds permit.' After a moment he added, 'They did not permit.'

'Perhaps that was lucky,' said Charles, and gravely he looked at Narayan. 'You couldn't do any more important work than this.' And he asked, 'You go to the Onward Movement meetings, don't you?'

Narayan flushed. 'I – have gone. But they are silly boys, I think.'

'I wish you would go more often,' said Charles and Narayan stared. 'Tell them – tell them—' said Charles, and his pipe smoked alone in his hand – 'tell them that the future of India may lie in this – in this calf, or a pod, or a bud, or a healthy blade of rice. Tell them not to talk so much. Politicians talk, and they start at the top and they never reach bottom, or earth – or truth. Young men are talkative and they like to be politicians – tell them to forbear,' said Charles; 'tell them to start at the bottom with the soil. They have inherited it. It is theirs. They are always telling us that. Tell them they should learn how to use it.'

That was what Charles had said – and each word struck a note from another world like it in Narayan. It was as if he had been tuned; and he flushed and cried, 'I will tell them to hold their tongues and use their hands!' As soon as he had said it, he saw the absurdity of what he had said and he burned with the ridicule of it so painfully that his eyes and his throat hurt him almost to tears; but Charles did not appear to have heard and presently Narayan was able to stammer: 'That is – I – I think you should tell them yourself, Sir.'

'I?' said Charles and laughed. 'They are frightened of me.'

That was true. They found Charles disconcerting. He had a way, not of tripping them up, but of making them give an exact attention to everything they said; the mind of Narayan appreciated that, while his own cheeks burned, but the students were not robust enough for it, and those who loved hyperbole and smartness disliked Charles. Narayan had heard him in conference and debate and, from curiosity, had gone to hear him lecture; the lecture was vigorous and engrossing, Charles was magnetic and he had fired some of the students into action.

They came to Charles after the lecture. 'You need voluntary workers,' they said grandly. 'We shall go.'

'Very well, go,' said Charles.

That left them in the air. They felt snubbed and they resented it. They felt entitled to his consideration; they had offered their services, free. 'We said *voluntary* workers,' they reminded him.

'I said voluntary workers too,' said Charles. 'You know where the organization is. If you want to work, go there.'

'Sir, if you do not want us—'

Charles's answer came swiftly and hard. '*I* don't want you. *It* wants you. Don't make it anything to do with me.' But they did not understand and they were offended.

Narayan wondered over this: Charles knew the young Bengalis; under their buoyancy they were deeply sensitive, and if he had been more gentle with his words would have gone twice as far. Narayan was certain he knew this, himself; then why was he not more gentle? He deliberately discouraged affection and Narayan, who had just begun to cultivate it, found this hard to accept. Charles was friendly to him, Charles was interested in his work, but Narayan felt that they were still waiting for their intimacy. He knew it was most unlikely that Charles should be his friend, but he felt, quite certainly, that presently this would be.

He tried to interest him in Anil. 'No, thanks, Das,' said Charles, 'I haven't time for protégés,' and Anil refused most firmly to further it either.

'Let me show your poems to Pool, Anil?'

'To *Pool*? To Charlie Chang? What a foolman you are, Indro. He only deals in seeds and cattle breeds' – but under his lofty derision was the same note of fear.

He had once encountered Charles; Narayan did not know that. It was at another lecture that Charles had given in the College. 'And we must take a wider, broader view of what agriculture means to India,' said Charles, concluding. And he asked, 'Has anybody anything to say?'

Anil always had something to say. 'Sir,' said Anil, standing up, 'I see the whole pattern of agriculture as a circle ... '

Charles had never thought of it, but now he was suddenly and most definitely against that; if he saw a pattern at all, he saw it as a long, long line, like a road beginning far back out of vision, continuing broader and broader out of sight.

Anil was still speaking: '... Everything is a circle,' said Anil. 'The rhythm of the year, the season, make a rhythm of the land – the preparing of the land, the seeding, germination, ripening, harvest, the return to earth as seed again – full circle is come; and is it not strange,' said Anil, waxing louder, 'is it not strange that everything that is symbolic of the life of the people is also the shape of a circle? The grindstone, the feeding bowl, the basket, the wheel—'

'What about a plough?' asked Charles.

No. Anil would not come and speak to Charles. But one day,

thought Narayan that morning in his study, I shall ask him to dinner, and Anil too, and they shall learn to know one another under my roof. We shall have a charming dinner, we shall talk. And he shut his book and called, 'Shila!'

Shila came to the door.

'One day I shall ask Charles Pool to dinner,' said Narayan.

'Mr Pool – to *dinner*? But – but – what does he eat? What could we do? How shall we do it?' Her eyes widened and then she said, 'He will never come.'

'Certainly he will come and we shall give him dinner.' They would sit in the study, though they must borrow another chair, for the study only had two chairs, and Shila should send in a tray of sweets and they would sit talking while the light died on the river and Shila came softly in and trimmed the lamps; talking in friendly understanding talk. 'Certainly he will come.' And at Shila's dismayed face he laughed in good spirits and said, 'Tell Tarala.'

'Tarala has gone to the bazaar.'

'And you? What do you do?' he teased.

'There is plenty to do in the house.' She was delighted that he was in this mood and talking to her. 'What do you think I should do?'

'Sit by the river and dream,' said Narayan.

Much of that was true. On the tumbledown pillar in the garden Shila would sit while minutes and whole half-hours slid away. 'Where is the knitting they taught you at school? Where are the books I like you to read?' They lay forgotten, and the small red ants that inhabited the pillar came out and ran across them. The sun lay hot there, and in the evening there was a breeze warm from the river, and Shila like one of the ants or a little lizard could never have enough of warmth and sun. The creeper by the pillar was an allamanda with big trumpet-shaped flowers of bright yellow and a heavy scent of honey – and all the time the river ran below and she watched the water running, running past.

'You sit there and dream of all the things you wish for,' teased Narayan.

'No, I dream of all the things I have,' said Shila softly, and she shut her eyes to see them ...

When I am too happy and when I am too miserable I come and sit beside the river and a little of the sorrow or the joy is drained off by the flowing water and runs away with it; then I can go into the house again and no one will see anything unusual in me. No one knows I have to do this but the river. I should not do it, I am a wife and a wife should spend her days evenly; if she has moods they should reflect her husband's; when he is glad, she is glad and when he is unhappy, she is unhappy too. My mother taught me this, but she was not married to Narayan.

Narayan has so many moods and he does not like me to watch him, it irritates him, and still I cannot help watching him. He does not want a wife like the wife I have been taught to be; he calls her a slave and a shadow, and he says he wants me to be myself. He makes me call him Narayan or Indro, as if he were not my husband at all; he makes me sit down in the room with his friend and he has asked me to eat with him, but this I cannot learn to do.

I am not clever enough for him; I was sent to school but I did not pay much attention; the bus used to call for me with the other girls and we sat in it, in two rows, facing each other behind drawn curtains and from that moment we began to giggle and we giggled till we came home. There were serious girls, and girls who used really to study; I laughed at them but now I wish I had been with them. Narayan likes mixed schools for girls and boys; what would my mother say to that? He says that girls can learn as well as men, but I have not found that yet; I find the books so very hard to learn, I cannot talk about them – like Anil Banerjee.

Don't think I am unhappy. I am the luckiest girl in the world. I only wish I was clever and not shy and then I could amuse Narayan – like Anil.

I have so much. I never thought, for instance, that when I was married Narayan would have a home of his own. The house is small, the little rooms lead out of one another, but it is all ours; the study is larger and has a window facing the court, and a door facing the steps; it has a desk and two chairs and a book-case with all Narayan's books and a cabinet for his instruments. I should like our friends to see it, but would they come to see us now? I dare not ask them; they might say 'No.' Narayan is not orthodox; he is not even Hindu nor is he Christian; he is against religion. He says it is superstition, he says it is nothing and he will talk against it for hours. He forbade me to go to the temple or to keep the Holy Days or to fast – and yet I think he wanted me to go. At first – I obeyed him and said nothing.

('Why don't you answer?' he asked. 'Don't you want to go to the temple?')

('Yes.')

('Why don't you go?')

('Because you tell me not to go.')

('Oh, Go! Go! Go! Go! How many times have I told you not to do everything I say?')

Now I don't know whether to go or not to go; neither will please him; but there is one day that I must go. I must make my

puja to Shasti ... Her lips curved of themselves into a smile ...
I shall pray to the goddess of all children and she will keep my
child.

It is not long to wait now. I sit out in the sun and the sun
shines on me warming me all through and the river runs very
softly and the sound of it goes in at my ear through all my body.
My baby stirs and moves gently at the warmth and sound. He
will be plump like a little pigeon and his skin will be soft like the
petal of a champac flower to touch. Narayan says it will be a girl.
He will be delighted with the baby. Will he? Will he? I am not
sure. I am never quite sure of Narayan ...

She opened her eyes and asked Narayan timidly, 'Has Anil
Banerjee's wife a son?'

'I do not think so.'

'Ah!' said Shila softly, and she asked, 'He has been married –
how long?'

'He has been married for nearly two years,' said Narayan
crossly. 'The marriage was consummated ten months ago. I have
told him it is absurd. The girl is not fully developed. She is only
fourteen.'

'Fourteen is developed,' said Shila suddenly and boldly; there
was a distinct gleam in her eyes. 'And he – what does he say?'

'He does not say anything at all. It is not his fault. He married her to please his father; if his father tells him, he will send
her away. Meanwhile she is his wife, a little girl. It is a good
thing he has to leave her and come to College.'

'All the same,' said Shila softly, 'he must want a son.'

Narayan was tired of it. He said, 'Here is Tarala, come back
from the bazaar. Shouldn't you go and see what she has brought?'
But Shila had already gone.

Shila saw the bazaar through Tarala's basket; everything that was important to her in the bazaar was in it. At the beginning of the month the stores were brought; sugar, rice, oil, spices and grain to last the month; but every day Tarala went down and came back with a triumphant expression on her face and a coolie boy carrying her basket. 'What have you brought, Tarala?'

Vegetables – young sweet carrots, and glossy purple knobs of brinjals, and a pomelo that opened like a big pink-fleshed orange; sour-milk curd in an earthenware pot, some fresh firm hilsa fish.

'Is that all?'

'Yes, Ma.'

Neither Shila nor Tarala would look at one another. At last Shila spoke. 'Was there – no mutton?'

'No, Ma, none.'

'Tarala – did you look?'

(Looked, and turned my head away quickly!) And aloud Tarala cried: 'None, Ma, anywhere. Narayan Babu must have fish for his dinner.' ('And that is bad enough, God knows!' she said under her breath.) 'But we shall make it so good,' she reassured Shila, 'you will see he is pleased. Narayan Babu likes hilsa fish, Ma.'

'He likes mutton,' said Shila, and as firmly as she could make herself say the horrible word, she said: 'There must be mutton tomorrow.'

Before she woke, Louise saw the horse and the rider going along behind the hedge, a tall white horse with a dreadful boniness that she most strangely knew; the rider's face was turned away from her, hidden by a hat with a long plume that trailed into lines of mist and lay on hedges and trees; a dim half-white, half-hidden landscape, where any noise was muffled in the mist. She stood in long grass wet above her knees and, as she stepped back, the grass drew after her drawing all the landscape with it, the hedge and the horse and the rider. To stop it she must stand still and look at the rider and then he would turn his head and she would see – she would see ... But she would not look; she stepped back and back, though the grass grew heavier and wetter and the mist was lapping round her in tenuous spirals and folds ... *Look at the rider! Look him in the face. Look. Look. Look!* ... And she screamed dreadfully and silently, and the trees were immediately distorted and the mist changed to smoke that was coming to scorch and burn her. It was in her tongue and her throat, burning, tasteless, burning, and her throat began to swell. The swelling rose in her mouth and the landscape began to swell as well, swollen trees and leaves and hedge, and the malformed horse came backwards towards her, bearing its rider backwards while it went stepping on in a terrible duplication of itself. There was a bony grating – Ah! *crepitus!* She recognized it from the First Aid Lectures – but that meant the rider was turning his head ... I must look. I must look. *Look. Look. Look!* And the swelling choked her and before she died, she woke.

The room was full of pale light and the grating, the *crepitus*, was the noise of the bee-catcher birds walking in the garden. It was hardly morning, but to Louise the room was full of heat; it ached with heat like her head, and her eyelids felt like eggshells, brittle and dry. Through the windows she could see the sky turning from grey to white with a line of hyacinth above the dark dusty tops of trees. Everything was dry, hot, dusty; and the dream filled her mind with a sharp horror of fear. She picked up a glass of water that was on the table by her bed and drank, but the water had been standing and was warm with a horrible body warmth, and she retched and in spite of the heat her skin was suddenly goose-fleshed and cold. She trembled so that the whole bed trembled too – and snatched up her dressing-gown and went out on the verandah.

After her padded the Pekingese, Sun and Picotee, that she had snatched with the children from France. She had refused to leave them behind – she bullied and cajoled to get them on the steamer; her love for them, for all animals, was touched with fanaticism, and now she lived in continual fear that they would pick up something from the bazaar.

Louise saw the bazaar as a patch like plague against the walls of the house ... I see the bazaar, she said – at least I am prevented for ever from seeing it by smelling it first. I smell the street and the nest of lanes behind it as one foul latrine. I swear the Indians can have no sense of smell. If I walk through it I am contaminated even through my shoes, even through the high heels of them – soiled and contaminated. It is filthy, unhealthy, dangerous; there is cess in the gutters where the men squat down even while I am passing, there are stains and patches where betel-nut and cough-phlegm are spat out on the stones, there are flies that rise up from litter heaps and settle on the sweets and foodstuff in the shops. I smell the rancid ghee in these shops and the smell of mustard oil and garlic and rotting fruit and meat that has hung too long, and in the road all round me is the smell of refuse and the smell of unwashed sweat and oil from the coolies, the smell of musk and sandalwood from the cleanest white-clad clerk; and on some days I smell the burning of a body from the burning *ghat* and that I cannot bear. Charles, I cannot bear to go into the bazaar. I cannot bear to stay here when I must see it and hear it all day long.

It is hideous and cruel. I see the woman with elephantiasis, and the beggars withered, distorted, deformed, and among them the leper who is allowed to wander here for begging. The children's stomachs are swollen with fever and spleen, and the babies have flyblown ophthalmic eyes. The dogs have mangy backs and bruised outstanding ribs, the buffaloes pull the carts in the sun all day long – buffaloes, that are water beasts and meant for water and for coolness; the iron bullock-wheels turn and creak along the road, so that I cannot forget them. I see a kitten lying where a crow has pecked its eyes, and the men are as cruel as the crows, they have birds hung in tiny cruel cages and sometimes they have put out their eyes to make them sing. I can forgive them their babies but I cannot forgive them the birds.

There is nothing picturesque or attractive in the bazaar, it is sordid and poor, it has no products of its own; it has no muslins or silk or pottery or weaving or rugs or ivory. Even the temple is hideous and cheap, even the sacred bull has a sore on its rump and filth on its tail. There is nothing but filth and squalor and misery in the bazaar. I hate to go there, I hate the children to go there and I am terrified the dogs will stray and catch some disease in the bazaar.

I asked Charles not to give the children a dog. I asked him not to give them Don. He gave them Don . . .

He gave him to Emily.

'Why Emily? Why not Binnie? Why Emily?'

'I think,' he said, 'that that little girl needs love.'

In her surprise Louise had stared. 'Emily! Why, Emily won't have love. That shows how little you know of her. She is hard. She is completely oblivious of everyone but herself. She doesn't care an atom for anyone. She is almost unnatural.'

'You don't like her, do you?'

She answered icily, 'I love Emily more than you could begin to understand.'

'You may love her. You don't like her.'

'I love her and I know her better than she knows herself.' And she said, 'I must ask you not to interfere with the children.'

Charles's eyes went dark and the cast in them showed plainly. 'If you didn't want me to interfere, why did you bring them here?' he asked. 'Did it never occur to you that I might get interested – in the children?'

'You are – insufferable,' said Louise, and she cried: 'You know nothing about children. You don't like children. You don't know them. Why should you interfere?'

He said nothing to that. He gave Don to Emily . . .

Now, as the Pekingese poured in a wave of tails and feathers down the stairs, Don whined from between the children's beds. Louise went quickly up the verandah where the two white-netted beds stood. Under Emily's on the floor lay a watch face downwards.

('Emily, don't take your watch to bed.')

('I will put it under my pillow.')

('If you do, you will break it. If it falls on the stone floor it will break. You know how you toss and turn. Don't take your watch to bed.')

Louise set her lips and picked up the watch. It was not broken.

Don was tearing at his rug and whining. She went round Emily's bed to set him free and she stopped. She bent down to look at him, and looked again. For a long while she stood there looking down at him. Then she ran down the verandah calling for Charles and Kokil, the sweeper.

*

The world is square, said Charles in his sleep, and I shall have it square ... That was the last moment he slept. He was awake; he still lay with his eyes shut, but he was awake, aware of the light on the outer side of his lids, and the hardness of the bed under him where before he had been floating – floating – floating ... He was nearly asleep again and again he was awake. He stretched a little and yawned.

He began to consider the day. Before he went to sleep Charles added up his day, as soon as he woke up he forecast it, and tried to read it out. It was one of his fixed, lonely habits; he knew exactly what he would do in the day and he liked to know; but now, since Louise had come, it was not as clear and not as easy to read. Anything might happen in the day ... And I can't predict, said Charles, how well I can behave. He felt tired ... Lying in bed is easy; to get up and face the day is not. I shall not get up – just yet ... And he turned resolutely on his face, but a little pulse beating against his pillow, somewhere in his head, seemed to beat Louise ... Louise ... Louise – and impatiently he sat up.

The morning had a milky coolness under its promise of heat, the wind blew across the garden that still had dew in all its shady places. There still was freshness in the wind, there still was dew and freshness in the garden, on the lawns under the trees, on the underside of leaves, between the shafts of the bamboo, inside the striped cyclamen trumpets of the blue convolvulus, in the lemon-yellow allamandas. His skin felt cool and dewy, he was strong and he moved in bed stretching, sending the sleep from his bones as he stretched and stretched, stretching his annoyance away. There was the sound of someone running and Louise herself came in without knocking, swinging the door back. 'Charles! Charles! Charles!'

'I'm here,' said Charles quietly.

She stopped abruptly and the urgency faded on her face. She looked at the room: his clothes put out on a chair, the bath running in the bathroom, his dressing-table and shoe-stands, his crop and hat on the table, a row of photographs on the wall, cups on a shelf, a pile of papers; Charles's room that she had not seen for years. It arranged itself in front of her eyes with a series of pricking shocks – and Charles was lying on the bed watching her, raised on one elbow, wearing nothing but a *lungi* wound round his waist. His chest and legs and arms seemed brilliantly brown and strong on the white sheet, and the sun shone on his head and made hundreds of dark bright points on the hair on his legs and arms and chest. 'Haven't you a dressing-gown?' cried Louise.

'You didn't knock,' said Charles, and she blushed. He made no attempt to get up; he lay there looking at her and his gaze went slowly down from her face over her body to the hem of her skirt. She wore a wrapper of thin white silk, tied at the wrists and neck and waist with rose-coloured woollen cords; it swung open at the hem to show the chiffon nightgown and her bare feet in mules. Her hair was down, loose on her shoulders; she tried to stem the hot colour that flooded her cheeks and neck but it grew hotter. 'This is quite like old times, isn't it?' he said pleasantly.

For a moment he thought she would go, but she controlled herself. 'You know I shouldn't have come if . . . ' Her voice broke into genuine panic. 'Charles. Please come quickly. It's Don. Oh, Charles. Please come.'

They took Don downstairs while the children were still asleep.

For Emily the morning broke in streaks of green and white: white on sunlight, and flying bands of green; and she woke in her bed under the white net high above the garden. In the garden on the trees every tip and frond was waving in the morning light; there were the tall exciting shapes of palms, petrified, in colours of greys and greens like palm-trees in old prints; there were the emerald diaphanous sprays of the cassias, and another tree whose leaves were like countless little coins or seals moving in the sun. The sun spread like a fan over the garden, the same shape but upside down as the tails of the cook's pigeons that sat on the roof and round the stables; one fan-stick of sunlight lay across Emily's bed and touched her cheek, it had not touched Binnie or anyone else, it touched only Emily. It altered as the sun came up, now it was long and thin like a spear. A golden spear.

'Bring me my spear. O clouds unfold ...'

Charles sang that. Charles's voice was big and rather rough and it had notes that were so deep and vibrant that they woke a literal echo in Emily, as if she had harpstrings inside her.

'He makes an awful noise,' said Binnie, her head cocked to listen. 'It's like listening to a whole band.'

'I like it,' said Emily.

In the early morning, waiting for his horse, he always stood on the steps above the garden and sang 'Jerusalem.'

'Bring me my bow of burning gold,
Bring me my arrow of desire,
Bring me my spear. O clouds unfold,
Bring me my chariot of fire ...'

'Oh, hush!' said Binnie, scandalized. 'They'll hear you the other side of the river.'

'It will do them good,' said Charles. 'It's the most beautiful song in the world.'

'Mother doesn't think so,' said Binnie.

What possessed her to say that? Charles sang no more and called for his pony and Emily beat at the plumbago bushes with the switch that she was carrying. They went a little way with Charles and then suddenly, over some stupidity like this, they lost him; always Emily was turning up, from him or from Louise, continual proof of what she did not want to know.

'*There are circumstances over which we have no control.*' Louise said that often, but Emily had never quite believed her ... I shall *not* let them spoil it. I shall stay here, said Emily. Nothing, nothing must happen here to spoil it.

'Jerusalem,' Binnie was saying, 'is a place in Palestine. How could it be in England too?'

She spoke to Charles, and Charles, who had one foot in the stirrup of his nervous and very lively little country-bred, before he mounted paused to answer her; at however inconvenient a time, Charles always answered, '*That* Jerusalem wasn't a place,' said Charles, and swung himself up.

Delilah, the pony, went dancing away, sending up the gravel in a cloud of red dust. Presently she came fidgeting back again.

'What was it then?' asked Binnie.

Emily waited for his answer. He hesitated, looking down at Binnie who stood by his foot; from Emily's view she looked foreshortened, all gathered frock and round pink face and a neat little pate of curls, and her heart gave a jealous pang at the tenderness of Charles's face. They did – they did like Binnie best.

'What was it then?' asked Binnie.

'Your heart's desire,' said Charles, and Emily forgot her jealousy in her interest. That was the first question he had not

68

answered properly, he seemed to feel that; he was looking not at Binnie but over Emily's head. 'Your heart's desire,' he repeated, and he said it with a mocking bitterness that appalled her. 'And if you can't get it,' said Charles, 'don't lose your temper. Be reasonable. Take something else instead.'

Emily knew, without turning, that Louise was standing behind her.

Lying in bed, thinking of that, she shut it quickly out of her mind . . .

This is how I used to wake when I was a baby, thought Emily hastily, in another house that seems in some way joined to this. Now I am back again as if I had never been away. I am back again exactly where I started from. I am back. I am back . . . But was she? Could she be? Was she? . . . Yes I *am*, insisted Emily, I have forgotten I have ever been away . . . But she said it as Charles said the world was square – for Emily had been away . . .

She had been in the school room at Bellevue, for instance, where the vine hung over the balcony making a peaceful green light over the little boys and girls. Madame Chastel said, '*Ecrivez la moitié, jusqu'à: "Hannibal était parti pour les Alpes . . ."*' when the alarm went and Madame stood up, her dark moustache trembling slightly above her lips and cried, '*Attention. Marchons!*' And they marched between the desks across the parquet in the hall into the panelled cupboard that led under the stairs to the cellar.

Emily had been in the cellar. The concrete reinforcements made twisting shapes on the walls, there were dim piles of sandbags, and benches where they sat. Once the light went out and it had been quite dark. Emily sat on her bench and felt a sliding trickle run behind her ears. Somewhere a little girl began to sob, a little girl that might be Binnie. 'We are not afraid,' said Madame, 'we think of our brave airmen, of our soldiers and our nurses and our ships – we are not afraid' . . .

('Mother, need we, need we go to school?')

('Why?')

('Because of – raids.')

('Why, Emily, you ought to be ashamed, *everyone* is carrying on their work! You mustn't be afraid of raids.')

('I'm not afraid of raids, I'm afraid of the cellar.' But it was no use telling that to Louise.)

Louise approved of the cellar. 'There is no immediate danger,' said Louise; but she hurried them into the cellar and she snatched them away in one push from Paris to Louvain. 'No danger' – in that clear and perfectly toneless voice, when she laid out in the cabin every night their warm coats and their life-belts; when with trembling fingers she tied the life-belts on them up on the deck.

('What is it? Is it a wreck? Is it a mine, or a submarine? Have we been hit?')

('Nothing. Only a practice.')

('*What?* In the middle of the night?')

It was a submarine, Emily heard that afterwards. The submarine had missed them. Why couldn't Louise have said it was a submarine?

Emily stirred and turned impatiently in bed . . . Whenever I start to think, said Emily, I come back to Louise. Now – I shall teach myself to stop thinking of you, Mother. I am here, now, safe, away in this place, away from the world, with Charles. Soon, soon I shall think of myself and not of you, and I shall be free. I shall stay here and you cannot touch me here. Nothing, nothing shall happen here . . .

She lay and listened to the noise coming up from the bazaar where the day was well upon its way ... I see the bazaar, said Emily as she lay; it is interesting and exciting. The first shop you come to is the shop where they make kites; you can buy twelve kites for three annas in colours of pink and green and white and red, and a wicker spool to fly them with, and a pound of thread. The thread is glassed, and – only don't tell Mother – we fly them with Shah off our roof and challenge other kites and cross strings with them and cut them adrift and then we can put another bob on our kite's tail.

The front of the money-changer's shop is barred, and he sits on a red cloth quilted with black and white flowers – and he is a Marwari with a small orange turban like a doughnut twisted on his head. He has nothing in his shop but a safe, a pair of scales and a table a few inches high. In India jewellery is sold by weight, and the jewellery is made of silver threads woven into patterns and flowers. The moneylender tests every piece of money he is given by weighing it before he takes it, and I think that that is sense. Shah does it too, only he bites the money instead.

The cloth-shop is inviting with rolls of cloth on the shelves all open to the street; cottons and prints with patterns, and new crisp sari cloth, and children's dresses with low waists, cut square and flat like paper dresses, hanging outside in the street. The grain-shops have grain set out in different colours in black wicker baskets, and with them are sold great purple roots and knots of ginger and chillies and spice. The sweet-shops have balls like American popcorn and other balls that are like marsh-mallows, and clear toffee sweets that are made in beautiful spiralled rings. Mother says we must never taste them but we have.

The temple is very clever and interesting because its outside walls and its floor are mosaic made from broken pieces of china. In one little patch on the floor we counted a hundred and seventeen pieces; the banyan tree grows right down through the roof of the temple; a banyan tree grows out of the earth and sends some of its branches back into the earth again – it sounds like dust to dust – and the walls of the temple are tiled with the same sort of tiles that we had in the bathroom at Bellevue. On the platform are the images of Rada and Krishna, made of two jointed dolls with tinselled clothes, and in front of them a table with offerings of sweets and flowers. A woman came to pray – on the brass tray she put a little powdered sugar and with her thumb she made on it the pattern of the sun for luck.

There is a mosque in the bazaar too, and it has a minaret shaped like a lighthouse beside it, only instead of a light, the priest goes there to call the people when it is time to come and pray.

There is such a good idea in the bazaar. There are rickshaws, but instead of men to pull them they are joined to bicycles and pulled along like that.

We buy bangles in the bazaar, glass ones, and the shop is full of their clear glass goblin colours. Mother forbids us to wear them because she says they are dangerous. They are dangerous; Binnie cut herself to the bone wearing hers – she had to have three stitches in her wrist.

('That's your fault, Emily. You take no care of Binnie. You are the eldest but you never think of her. You never think of anybody but yourself.')

Now Emily called across to Binnie's bed to see if she were awake.

The morning did not break for Binnie; there were simply the morning and evening of the next day.

'What are you going to do today, Bin?'

Binnie answered promptly. 'I shall go fishing for pearls.'

This was not such an incredible pastime as it sounded. On the edges of the river, in certain places, were beds of a curious deep-blue river-shellfish, more like a mussel than an oyster, and they could be dislodged and floated up by a hook on a string, sometimes – not very often. The native divers went down for them, naked and unprotected, and they could walk about below the water for minutes together without anything to help them but their muscles. Sometimes, not very often, just occasionally, the shells held a pearl, a real pearl with a gold sheen that was almost apricot. Charles had two in a pillbox on his desk ... Why doesn't he give them to Louise? ... Don't think of that. We shall go fishing for pearls ...

'We'll take Shah and a fisherman,' said Emily. 'We'll take the fisherman's boat—'

('We shall float down on the sun-green water, trailing our hooks past little bays and promontories in the hard white sand; there will be no sound but the sounds of the boat and the voices of Shah and the fisherman.') Other boats, the same as theirs, crescent-shaped with a wicker cowl in the middle, would float down past them with dark-skinned crews who did not know their language and could not speak to them any more than the floating clumps of water hyacinth could speak. No one would talk to them or ask them questions; there would be nothing to listen to or to watch, everything would be wrapped in sun and silence, quietness and sun.

Binnie sat up in bed. 'Why, where's Don?' she said.

At that moment Louise came lightly down the verandah. 'Children! Children! You have been asked to go to breakfast with the Nikolides.'

IV

For Emily, the Nikolides were as desirable and nearly as distant as on the first day she had seen them. She had met them; they had come; and the Pools had been to their house for tea and to spend the day; but Louise did not approve of Mrs Nikolides nor Mrs Nikolides of Louise.

('Mother, can't we go and see the Nikolides?')

('Every time you go there you are upset. Their food is so ridiculously rich.' And when they did go Mrs Nikolides would feel their elbows and shoulders bare in their sundresses and say, 'You'll catch a chill, poor children. I wonder your mother can let you out in the river breeze, without so much as a coat on, or a vest.')

Now, direct visits were rare, but the children saw one another occasionally, passing in launches up- and downstream, or in cars on the road; but always they were separated, and in the presence of their mothers only sent small reserved smiles and the wave of a hand across the air or water. Emily did not know whether or not the Nikolides family would have sent more if they could; it was probable that their desires were as well schooled as themselves.

They were distinguished by their beauty, their obedience and their bravery. Emily felt that she and Binnie were not distinguished in any way at all.

Alexandra, the girl, was beautiful and dignified; there was beauty in her straight chiselled nose and curved chiselled mouth, and dignity even in the fall of her hair, curling black on a very white neck, and in her grave dark eyes; and her smile was like a queen's. She bore the weight of clothes with which her mother loaded her without complaining, only keeping still so that she should not feel their heat; and she was perfectly sweet-tempered with the ayahs and governess who followed her everywhere she went; she had beautiful unusual manners and once, when a car door was slammed upon her fingers, she had neither screamed nor cried, but simply fainted.

Her brother Jason was like her, but more sallow, completely stoical and biddable to the point of death. Binnie, in the rare moments when she had him to herself, liked to find out how far he would go; he had never yet refused her. He would, when she told him, climb out to the end of a branch of a tree, walk on the roof parapet, be pushed out in a tub on the tank – and was rescued each time, just in time, by Shah. It was fortunate perhaps for Jason that the friendship was not encouraged.

('No *wonder*,' mourned Emily. 'Why do you make him do it, Bin?')

('He never answers back,' said Binnie with a slow smile. 'He says nothing; he does it.')

So the Nikolides children remained as they first had looked for Emily, like those in a book, all that she herself was not, in another world, unattainable; and when Louise came down the verandah and said, 'Breakfast with the Nikolides,' surprise, excitement and delight swept every other thought out of her mind.

'Be quick. Hurry!' said Louise. 'I've put your clean dresses ready, your spotted cottons and your sandals. The launch is waiting to take you.'

They ought to have heard the smoothness in her voice, it was much too smooth to be natural; they ought to have seen her hands trembling against her dress; but they leapt out of bed, and cried 'The Nikolides!' Without a look or thought they raced away to dress.

They met Charles on the steps downstairs. 'Why haven't you gone riding?' asked Binnie in surprise.

Charles, as soon as it was daylight, went out riding – they were not often up early enough to catch him.

'Why do you go so early?' they had once asked him.

'Because that's the best of the morning.'

'But it isn't really morning, it's hardly even day,' Binnie objected.

'What is the day like then?' asked Emily.

'Like a violet,' said Charles.

Binnie laughed, but Emily knew what he meant. She had seen the day opening as they came in on the river; the sky opening above the flat land in violet curves with a glimmer of that colour in the water and in the freshness of the dew. Charles said things like that and Emily knew what he meant when no one else did, and he was looking at her now in a way that made her pause.

'Why haven't you gone riding?' she asked, and the question made a rift for a moment in the excitement that filled her mind; but it was only for a moment, she did not even hear his answer.

'He is taking you to the jetty in the car,' Louise said hurriedly.

'*That* little way?' said Binnie.

It arrested Emily too; it was strange that Charles should stay in to drive them a few hundred yards; it was out of order, but the morning was already and delightfully out of order and Binnie was in the car. Emily ran down the steps forgetting to say good-bye to Louise, and Charles silently followed her and drove them in a few minutes through the bazaar to the jetty where the launch was waiting.

'Emily, wait—' he said, but the launch had a feather of steam, like a breath blowing out of its funnel, and it rocked on the water as if it really were alive; and beyond it the green spaces of the river were bright with pin-points of sun. Emily could not possibly wait. She ran in front of Binnie down the jetty planks and jumped down on the deck; Shah saluted and walked down after them, and the loop of rope was lifted from the jetty post, the launch backed away into the stream and turned in a half-circle bearing them away. They saw Charles walk back to the car.

Something in the way he walked made Emily look again. 'Binnie,' she said, 'there is something wrong.'

'Oh, *Emily!*' cried Binnie impatiently; and after a moment she said, 'If there were anything wrong, would Mother have let us go out? You know she wouldn't.'

Emily longed to be convinced but she demurred. 'Why did Charles take us down in the car?'

'I expect there is something she didn't want us to see in the bazaar,' said Binnie practically. 'Perhaps there is another leper. You remember the fuss she made about the last ... I remember him well,' said Binnie with dispassionate interest, 'he hadn't a nose. His nose had quite gone. Mother thought it was dreadful, but I didn't mind seeing him at all, did you?'

'Not in the least,' said Emily proudly, but she had to press herself down in her chair and fortify herself by pushing out her ribs and making herself hard and strong, and a comfortable peace replaced the trouble in her mind.

The launch went on towards the Nikolides' house, which could be seen with the mill chimney and the sheds at a great distance down the river. The river traffic grew thinner; soon they were quite alone on the expanse of water, and it seemed that the house and the chimney were coming gradually and inevitably towards them while they on the launch were still; now they could see and separate the colours; the chimney and the sheds were red like the house-roof, and the house walls were yellow; and presently they could see the line of trees and the fleet of launches moored there like grey ducks on the water. Emily was looking at them, excitement beating in her chest, but she still saw the figure of Charles walking away from the jetty and the sudden fear started up in her ... What is it? What can it be? ... And immediately she asked, What has Mother done? And clearly she saw Louise ...

I see you, Mother. I cannot help it. Everything I know, I know from you. You have been there as long as I can remember. As soon as I come near you I am stupid and stiff and I cannot think properly and I cannot say even what I think. I can arrange words clearly in my mind so that they would astonish you, and as soon as I come to you to tell them, I cannot say any of them; but perhaps I am not quite as stupid over this as I used to be. You are so beautiful, so utterly quick and clever; your eyes are dark and your lashes make them look darker still and very very large, but I have discovered something: they are not as big as we think and they move quickly like a bird's; birds' eyes have no lashes and if yours had none, they would be exactly like a bird's, and your fingers are like your eyes, quick and busy ... Her mind broke into panic ... Mother, please be still. Don't do anything, don't let anything happen here! . . . And she grew angry . . . I am warning you, Mother. I see you. One day, you will do more than you mean . . .

'There they are,' said Binnie, and on the edge of the jetty they could see far-away figures standing and waiting. 'I should be jumping up and down,' said Binnie, and she added, 'but of course the Nikolides don't jump if they can help it.'

Emily straightened herself . . . I shall *not* think now. If anything has happened it can wait . . . And replacing Louise in her mind came the figures of three little monkeys that Charles had given her. 'They are Japanese,' said Charles. 'Sensible people have them all over the world, not to emulate altogether, but there are times when it's good to be like them.' 'See nothing, hear nothing, say nothing,' said the monkeys, and as Emily thought of them Louise seemed to dwindle back across the water; and the jetty and the Nikolides grew every moment larger and more clear.

Louise that very second was thinking of Emily . . . I see you too. I see you, Emily. You always do all you possibly can to upset me. All this trouble has come from you and Charles. What did I say? What did I beg? 'Don't give Emily a dog. Don't take Don into the bazaar.' You never listen to me – you never think of me. When you went this morning you pushed and rushed into the car. You did not say goodbye to me like Binnie. You did not wave and smile. That was so like you. You forgot all about me. You forgot all about Don.

Don was shut up where you could not hear him cry. I need not have bothered. You never asked for Don. All that you thought of was yourself. You see I am right; I know you and I can turn your thoughts like the wind on a paper streamer . . . And suddenly, into Louise's mind came a remembrance like a prick. Was she so sure? She remembered something that Emily had said a day or two ago. 'Mother, if I have two children, do you know what I'm going to call them? Willy and Nilly, Mother. Isn't that a good name for two children like us?'

Emily could not have thought of that for herself; it must have been coincidence – or Charles. She could not have thought that for herself . . .

You have not improved, Emily, since I brought you out. You have gone unbecomingly sallow and you have grown too much, outgrown grace like a weed, though you have never been pretty like Binnie. You have a long face, not like a little girl's, with flattened cheekbones that give your eyes a slant as if you were keeping a secret, and usually you are; you are deceitful and you have a way of keeping your elbows out defensively, and you are very very obstinate and you are one continual worry about your health. You looked well yesterday, today you are suddenly more sallow than ever. I have bought you so many ribbons for your hair, I like it plaited and turned up in coils, it makes your face look longer to have it hanging down like that; it is so fair and so limp it looks quite greenish, and when you shut your eyes it gives you the look of a girl that is drowned; it makes my heart turn over. But I am foolish to agonize over you, Emily. You think of nothing and no one but yourself. It is strange that I should have so insensitive a child. I am foolish to save your feelings, you have none to save . . . A brisk stir filled Louise . . . She has gone, gone to breakfast with the Nikolides; she took that without one question. When she comes back it will all be over, and she will never know what has come near her . . . And dramatically Louise cried: This threat will have been wiped out of their lives! . . . And then a small, familiar worry nagged her . . . 'I hope you will be careful what you eat, Emily. I have had to leave that to you. Charles is so odd, he refused to let me warn Mrs Nikolides about your stomach.'

'You shall not shame Emily like that,' said Charles.

'Don't be absurd. You know how greedy she is. She will eat anything, and then she will be upset.'

'Better to upset her stomach and save her face,' said Charles.

'We saw you from the distance,' said Jason as the launch touched the jetty. 'How do you do, Emily? How do you do, Binnie? What a long time you have taken in getting here!'

'How do you do? How do you do?' said Alexandra gravely. 'No, you are not late. It's half-past ten. You are just in time for breakfast.'

'What is there for breakfast?' asked Binnie as she stepped ashore.

There would be queer, rather greasy things for the breakfast that the Nikolides had at this enchanting hour; perhaps mulligatawny soup with rice, fish balls, stewed fruit and cake. Emily knew with certainty what would befall her later in the day. Never mind, 'See nothing, hear nothing, say nothing.'

A warm wind blew down the Nikolides' garden, bringing the smell not of breakfast, but of scent from the flowers on the row of trees that were champac trees – queer bare thick polished branches, no leaves and white chiselled cups of flowers touched with gold, as strange and exotic as the Nikolides themselves. Through the cracks in the jetty the water looked miraculously, clearly green, and Emily's stomach gave a delicious little rumble.

First Binnie, then Emily, then Shah, passed inside the house to breakfast with the Nikolides.

V

The telephone rang in the Das house while Narayan was dress-ing; he called, 'Shila, answer that.'

Shila was dusting the study and when Narayan called she stayed there, rooted by his desk, the duster in her hand and a piteous expression on her face. The bell continued to ring. 'Shila. Shila, where are you? Answer the phone.'

She took one step towards it and, as if it knew she was coming, it gave another peremptory ring. '*Shila!*'

In a rush she took the receiver off and held it. There was a prolonged silence. Narayan came in fastening his collar. 'Well, who is it?'

She shook her head and offered him the receiver.

'Who? Who is speaking?'

'I – don't know.'

'You have taken if off and you have not answered it? What is the matter with you? Are you dumb? Are you mad? ... What have you been doing?'

'I have ... not listened to it ... Indro.'

'Why not? Why not? All this time we have had the telephone

and you are still afraid of it. Other girls use the telephone, why not you? What is the matter with you?' She twisted her fingers and said nothing, though her lips trembled.

'Answer. Answer me,' shouted Narayan. 'How many times have I told you to answer me?' He stopped, trying to control himself, and he said more gently, 'You make me speak and behave to you in a way I have sworn not to speak or behave. Why are you afraid to answer the telephone, Shila?'

'Suppose – suppose it should be – Mr Pool.'

'And if it is – you can speak to him as well as I. Why should it be Mr Pool? He has never telephoned me here, and at this hour he goes riding.'

'Suppose he did not go. Suppose he has come back.'

'Suppose! Suppose! I tell you, it won't be Mr Pool. Answer it at once.'

From the telephone impatient buzzing noises were coming; her eyes bright with tears, Shila held the receiver up and whispered down it, 'Ah?'

'Louder. Much more louder than that.'

'Ah?'

Narayan heard a second voice. It sounded impatient.

'Ah?'

The voice went on, a long speech, and her eyes slid to Narayan in anguish. 'Ah?'

'Oh, give it to me,' cried Narayan and seized it out of her hand. 'Who is it? Who is it?' he barked.

'It – it is Mr Pool . . . Indro.'

He was intensely irritated. 'And he will think I'm married to a fool,' he cried bitterly. 'You do not try, you do not care. You do nothing for me that I ask you. What use are you to me?' He turned his back on her and said, 'Good morning, Mr Pool. I am sorry I have kept you; my wife is an ignorant girl and not accustomed yet to answer the telephone.'

Shamed to the quick Shila stood behind him; her head was bowed and her hands pressed together in an effort not to cry, but in spite of that two lines of tears slid down her cheeks and dropped on to her skirts; she was wearing a sari of white, dotted in a pattern of green; and between the green flowers the teardrops fell and shone for a moment and sank away into the muslin. Narayan turned his head to make a note and she quickly bowed her head still lower and made the quick age-old gesture of drawing her sari across her face so that he should not see it, and ran out of the room; he heard her crying break as soon as she was outside the door.

He could not wait, he had to answer Charles's call, and he hurried off on his bicycle – but as he went, the sound of his voice, not Shila's, came back to his ears; and it sounded unnecessarily violent and a little pedantic, and from that violence came a sense of shame: he felt jarred, out of content, and though he tried to blame Shila the blame fastened on him and the sound of his angry voice seemed to follow him as he rode along the road. 'A *woman's tears in the morning bring bad luck.*' That was superstition, told by old women like Tarala; but he almost turned and rode back to tell Shila – What could he tell her? Only that he was sorry and she would not understand that; she thought only that she had offended and that his right to punish was divine; besides, Charles had already been kept waiting and Narayan bicycled on, though he knew it would not have been necessary to say a word: to go back was enough ... Later, later. I will comfort her later, said Narayan, and turned in through the Pools' gate.

He was riding up the drive where the poinsettias dipped their scarlet beads when Charles, riding the little mare, passed him almost at a gallop and flashed out of the gate with nothing to show they had gone but a cloud of dust and kicked gravel, the servants who had run out of the house at the noise, and the noise of hoof-beats dying away on the road.

'What in the world?' cried Narayan, who had fallen off his bicycle. He was furious. 'He nearly rode me down. I shall certainly go away.' He did not mean that; he was far too curious, and when the servants salaamed him with a civility that came from important happenings, he followed them at once to the stables. 'What is up? Something is very much up.' He was ushered through the stables to a loose-box, and there was Mrs Pool in tears.

This morning will never pass, Louise had said dramatically ... Days may be all the same in the sight of God but for us some are over before they have come, some go on for ever; the days of misery and suspense go on, days like this ...

(And interrupting her was a voice that was like Charles's, like all the unsympathetic people in the world: 'You invented a dream for yourself ...')

('I did not invent it. I dreamt it.')

('You invented a dream for yourself' said the inexorable voice. 'Take care. You started more than you knew.')

('I can't stop it. I can't stop it!' screamed Louise.)

('You could have stopped it. Why didn't you look at the rider's face?')

Louise shut her eyes and her ears and turned her head away ...

She was in the long line of stables behind the house where Delilah and a Bhutia pony and the pigeons lived. In an empty stall Don lay on the floor and Louise watched beside him, and Charles stayed there watching Louise. 'Why don't you go away,' said Charles, 'and leave the poor little brute alone?'

'I want to be *sure*.'

'You have made up your mind already. Why do you have to pretend?'

She did not deny it and he could have predicted the justification she made – 'With children we must not take the faintest risk.'

'Not we – you,' said Charles. 'I will take risks – in proportion – even for them. But you have no sense of proportion. You won't; not if Don and I and everyone in Amorra have to die for it.'

'Oh, why don't you go away?' cried Louise.

Why did he stay? Why did he stay there, still and gloomy, watching her? The truth was that it was no good Charles going away; in the day and in the night and the next day and every day Charles was conscious of Louise and Louise was conscious of Charles.

In the evening he worked late in his office and he could hear Louise in the drawing-room above; her heels made a tattoo on the stone floor, a tattoo that filtered down through the thick ceiling so lightly that he had to listen for it. He listened for her playing too, and it was either so restless or so passionate that it was infuriating; she played too softly, beginning something, wandering off into something else, or else she filled the whole house with a torrent of sound.

'Surely Mrs Pool plays the piano a great deal,' said the resident professors in the evening. 'Is Mr Pool so fond of music?' asked another. The students laughed and said, 'She gets from the piano what she can't get from Charlie.' There were rude rumours current in the College because Charles had lived eight years in Amorra and kept alone.

In the evenings when he came upstairs he would not find Louise playing; she was silent, usually embroidering a small canvas on a frame. Charles hated fine useless work.

'That is bad for your eyes, and for you. It's too fine.'

'I don't find it fine.'

It gave her hands something to do. Charles smoked cigarettes which he disliked and poured out drinks. Each time he touched the bottles on the tray he saw her watching.

'I don't get drunk, you know,' said Charles. 'That wasn't one of my failings.'

Louise did not answer; her needle went a little more quickly in and out.

'Don't say you have forgotten.'

She lifted her head and said with the direct intentness of a little coiled snake, 'I shall never forget.'

But Charles was not stung. He smiled and looked down at her easily, as if she were a small, pretty thing, harmless to him. She was very pretty; she was dressed as if it might have been a party, her wide spreading skirts were chiffon, dead-leaf brown with a tinge of squirrel colour in the folds, and the brilliant colour of her hair with its knot shadowing her neck made her skin look cream and warm, and she wore two studs of earrings, tortoise-shell, that had all the colours of her dress, her eyes, her hair. 'You always did know how to dress, didn't you?' said Charles.

Her look was almost a glare and he laughed and said: 'Don't be afraid. I mean nothing more than I say. I do admire – the dress.'

The evenings passed in silence and constraint until one night when Charles came up in an old pair of shorts stained with oil

87

and chemicals and a shirt frayed, with all its buttons gone, and bare legs, native sandals and an old checked coat.

Louise stared. 'I'm not going to dine with you like that.'

'I fail to see your objection.'

'In those clothes—'

'I put them on to match you.'

'What do you mean?'

'You put on your worst mind to dine with me,' said Charles mildly, 'so I put on my worst clothes to dine with you.'

She gave in with a sudden grace, and on the rare occasions that Louise chose to do that she could be very graceful indeed; and she found, now that she had allowed herself to talk to Charles, that it was a relief, it was even a pleasure; the evenings wound away smoothly with sudden little surprises of unexpected thought, like islands in a river. Charles was unusual, Louise found herself remembering and thinking of the things he said. He had changed; he was courteous and cultured; and another question came up in her mind with the uneasiness of one of Emily's pricks – had Charles always been courteous and cultured? Could it be – Louise who had changed?

I think about him because I am homesick and lonely, she told herself. It is because he is the only person here – that makes him seem important ... Louise, quite naturally, did not count eleven thousand Indians. To her an Indian was not a person. She tried not to think of Charles, but she was so much alone. Everyone else in Amorra seemed to lead a teeming busy life; Charles had his work; the children had their lessons, and for the rest of the day they were curiously absent. They had always some perfect plan of their own and, even when they were with her, they talked of things she could not talk of. They were immersed in their own occupations, trust Emily for that, and Louise was left alone.

Charles had a picture in the drawing-room, a new one that she had not seen; it was the Chinese, of flake-white pigeons on a green background the colour of poppy stems. Most Chinese pictures are still, but this was full of movement, full of white wings beating upon the green, beating out of the picture ... Does Charles know the feeling of that? asked Louise. Is that why he bought it? ... She would look at it with her hands pressed down on the keys of the piano, staring at it while the notes, held down, vibrated on and on until the room was full of them; they would not escape until they died, and the pigeons could not escape however they beat their wings. Did Charles feel that? No, probably not.

It was probable that he had not even bought the picture, it had probably been given to him by one of his Indian friends.

('Graft,' said Louise scornfully.)

('Gifts,' corrected Charles.)

They quarrelled over Charles's Indian friends. Louise could not understand how an Indian could be a real friend. 'Naturally,' said Louise, 'we must be prepared to meet them in society now, and in the cities and larger places there are cultured Westernized people, like Sir Monmatha Ghose—'

'Monmatha isn't Westernized, thank God,' said Charles. 'He adopts certain customs and manners that are now more universal than Western, but he keeps himself quite integrate.'

Louise did not understand what he meant. She hardly saw Sir Monmatha, though she had met and dined with him often. The students who worked and played and lived next door to her were quite unnoticeable unless they made too much noise; when, if Charles were out, she would send Shah to stop them as if they were street boys. If one of them had spoken to her she would have called it impertinence and she would not leave the children alone even with the venerable Professor Dutt. She hated it that Charles refused to have an ayah for them but sent them out attended by Mahomed Shah. She had a peculiar, distorted, almost diseased idea of the Indian, of his life and his religion, particularly if he were a Hindu. Nothing Charles could say would shake her.

They quarrelled over many things. They seemed to make a point of quarrelling; in Amorra that was easy; they were like two people on a stage – as they had been from that first moment on the deck of the steamer – held there in the limelight as husband and wife, with all that the audience did not know between them; and the situation was complicated by two of the audience being there on the stage with them, Emily and Binnie. They would not keep an armistice for long ... We have not quarrelled for two whole days, they said. I was forgetting. I am being far too amiable. I must start a quarrel at once ... If it was not Louise it was Charles. If it was not Charles it was Louise.

('Why don't you ride, Louise?')

('Isn't there only one horse?')

('I can use the Bhutia more. You can have Delilah in the mornings.')

('Thank you. I prefer not to share your horse.')

She regretted that. The days were still long and empty and though they were empty they were oppressive; she felt herself crushed under them, shut away from a world that was up and vitally alive. When I go back, said Louise, I shall now be a stranger. I shall be foreign for ever and ever. I have lived out of time ... She could only read and listen and ponder and wonder; but the wireless news reports had the unreality that they might have had for a child, a little voice speaking out of a box, and the daily paper by the time it reached Amorra was thirty hours old;

papers from Europe came far apart in a deluge of deliveries held up together, sometimes three months old; books and letters were rare and precious; and from Paris, from Bellevue, was silence … I have no mother or father, said Louise, no one nearer than my old governess, though she is very dear. Grief for a people is sharp, grief for a place is sharper and has a peculiar bitterness that can never be wiped away. It is the place I mourn most – and that at this time, I should be shut away, a prisoner. That is what I am – a prisoner. ('Nothing of the sort,' the voice answered clearly and precisely. 'You chose to come – you came. What did you expect?')

Louise did not listen. She asked aloud, 'But what can I do? How can I keep with them at home – what can I do?'

'What everyone else is doing,' said Charles, 'go on.'

But Louise only felt herself crushed, a prisoner dulled and tormented by loneliness and fear. She was afraid; she was in danger of dying, of losing herself – Louise. ('And it has taken you such a long time to build yourself up, hasn't it? No wonder you can't bear to knock it all down.') And two lines of newsprint that she had seen in some paper came inexplicably into her mind: *There are some preposterous edifices*, said the paper, *that the war has brought to light … At least these will be better cleared away*. Louise checked herself sharply. Where was she drifting? And she tried to break free in paroxysms of temper that were not temper, but fear.

It was worst in the evenings, after the children were in bed; Emily went to bed with Binnie. Even in her loneliness and need Louise would not allow her to stay up; Emily because of her health must be sent to bed early.

'But I'm nearly twelve,' Emily protested.

'You are still only a little girl.'

'Indian girls can be mothers at my age.'

'You are not an Indian girl.'

'I'm not a little girl either,' muttered Emily rebelliously; but she was still young enough to be sent to bed and she was sent to bed! Louise was left alone.

And as she sat alone Charles was working, she could see him, imperturbable and cheerfully busy . . . There are two worlds, said Louise. There is one – reasonable, positive; some people are lucky, they live only in that. There is another, the limitless height of the first, like a mirage, a mad distorted mirage, and sometimes it blots out the other and the sky. You don't know what it is like, Charles. You have never seen it. You think I invent it, to bend the first world to my will, but it is there – it is there. I try to be reasonable – but it is there. You think I invent it, but I don't . . .

Charles had very little time to think, to reason or to talk; he had to act, and arrange and settle; he had to create. The lights fell till late from the office windows across the lawn below, and there was a continual coming and going on the drive; white figures disappeared into the dusk, there were continuous bright stars of light from bicycles coming, and red stars of light from bicycles going away. Did everyone in Amorra have a bicycle? Did everyone in Amorra come and see Charles on business in the evening? It looked, she had to admit from the loneliness of the drawing-room, strangely attractive – friendly – busy and important.

Once she went as far as to say, 'You work from five in the morning, Charles, till nine or ten at night.'

'There is all that work to do,' he said defensively.

'I – I know. Would it help you – Charles – if someone took part of – the correspondence for instance – from you? There must be a great many letters to write – someone with English at least that you need not supervise . . . '

'Meaning you?' asked Charles. For a moment she thought he was pleased, eager to accept; then he said, 'No, thank you. My work belongs to me. That is one thing you won't get your hands on.'

Now, this morning, they were violently opposed; Louise refused to leave Don, Charles sat and watched her, miserable and angry.

Don lay on the floor and all the exhibits were there: the bed with the gnawed wooden sides, the leash bitten through; and he had had a sudden choking fit like a convulsion, and he lay panting quietly on the floor.

'You did send for the vet?'

'I told you so.'

'Why doesn't he come? Oh, why doesn't he come?'

'Because he can't fly,' said Charles irritably. 'He has to bicycle.'

The Pekingese pressed their faces against the netting that had been nailed across the door and uneasily moved their tails; their tails were their barometers, they went down as they watched Don, up as Louise spoke or stirred; they made questioning marmoset noises in their throats, while the same question was going round and round in Louise's mind . . . What am I going to do? What else is there to be done? This is hydrophobia. Hydrophobia. The whispered word is like a spark, a tongue of fear licks up from it and runs and flames and flares into a conflagration. That is no exaggeration, Charles . . . In her mind Louise perpetually defended herself against Charles . . . Hydrophobia is like that; it starts, no one knows where, it spreads and spreads away from its spark – anyone can get it – you, Charles, Emily, Binnie, the Pekingese, the servants; any of them, anyone outside them. We don't know if Don has been out of the grounds, we don't know where he has been. Did he go out? Where would he be likely to go if he had? Anywhere. Nowhere. Everywhere. He has shown no sign of biting but he is affectionate – to be more than usually affectionate is a symptom – he jumps up and fawns like all spaniels, he might lick, he might scratch. Affection can become a horror – I, who worship dogs, have to steel myself not to recoil from him. The virus runs from the spark of the bite, along the nerves, to the brain – sometimes it is quick, sometimes it can smoulder and smoulder along – and it is madness that kills in agony, for which there is no cure. Madness . . .

'If it is hydrophobia—' said Charles suddenly.

'You think it is. You think so yourself.'

'I think it is – but it might be hysteria.'

'Hysteria! Do you think I would not recognize hysteria?'

'I don't see why you should,' said Charles, and he added quietly, 'I have mistaken it for truth myself.'

She turned her back on him . . . It is like a plague, her thought raced on, we don't know where it will break out next. Don has been brought up with children, he may have jumped up and licked a child's face, a hand that had a scratch on it; I can examine Emily and Binnie for scratches – I am powerless to find and save those children . . . And at the thought of the children, a sob rose in her throat.

('Why is it worse for children to die than grown-ups, Mother?')

('They are at the very beginning of things – they are little – unprotected.')

('Yes, but it's easy to make them again. It takes ages to make a grown-up.')

Louise moved impatiently. Why must she think of Emily's arguments now? Emily was a perpetual annoyance. They had questioned the servants that morning – 'Who has been near to Don in the last few days? Who has been to the house?'

'No one but the men who come to the office.'

'The Babu shall warn them. Anyone else?'

'The man with the cows—'

'The peon with the letters—'

'And—' Kokil the sweeper shifted his feet – 'yesterday, the monkey man was here.'

'The *monkey man*? You know I have given orders never to let him in!'

The monkey man had a drum, a miniature tom-tom with weighted strings, that beat as he twirled it in a little rattling rhythm; it sounded like the chattering of a monkey. He had a large male monkey and a little female dressed in patchwork clothes, and they all sat down together in the hot shade of a tree and the monkeys did their acts and dances, which towards the end of the performance grew candidly obscene.

'Why did you let him in?'

'Emily baba said—'

'Whose orders do you take, Emily baba's or mine?'

They were silent; they took Emily baba's. It was easier. Louise cried, 'You must go into the bazaar and tell everyone. Everyone! Do you understand? Charles, you must see – you must insist—'

But there was no answering certainty on Charles's face.

'You must. You must.'

'I'll try.'

Charles was not at all helpful. Now he said, looking down at Don, 'Louise, you must wait.'

'We dare not risk it. He might escape – suppose he did? We

shouldn't know where he had been or what he had done. Think of the havoc he might cause.'

'He couldn't cause havoc, he wouldn't have a chance.'

'He might. He might easily.'

'The moon might turn to cheese,' said Charles rudely.

'I don't understand you. How can you hesitate? No one else would wait a minute.'

'Oh, I know. There are plenty of good fellows who will let down their dogs,' said Charles with venom. 'Deserters. Judases.'

'Charles! Don't. Please don't.'

'Why worry? You'll have your bloody way,' said Charles and then he said more quietly, 'Louise, at least don't do it while Emily's away.'

'But that's why I sent her out. What do you mean?'

'Don't do it. Wait for her. Tell her and then do it.'

'But why?'

'Because I ask it. Please, Louise.'

'She's only a child. Charles, how could I let her go through this?' Charles's voice was usually light and faintly mocking when he spoke to her, unless he was angry; now its earnestness intrigued her. 'But why?' she asked again.

'It would be better, Louise.'

'You know nothing whatever about children.'

'I know about Emily,' said Charles ... I like my daughter Emily, said Charles, but he did not say it aloud. If only Louise would not get in the way I should like her very much. Binnie reassures me too, she is the answer to a question that has troubled me for years, but I have a peculiar faith in Emily. There is something vagabond about her, especially the way she moves her elbows and her head, that shows me she is tough and gay and sufficiently hard, while her eyes and her hands and her stomach, poor brat, show that she is duly sensitive. She is capable of taking proper treatment, she deserves it; but Louise will keep a hand across her eyes, and for Emily that means a struggle and fear – a misunderstanding, needless fear. Emily would rather suffer and understand, not at the time perhaps, but afterwards. Presently she would understand; however tragic and deep the suffering, presently she would digest it; digest is the perfect word, Emily could absorb and take what she needs from it, mix it with her own philosophy and discard the rest. It could become an integral part of her. I am acquainted with death, she could say, and death is the other side of life – together they are complete, the two sides of a coin, light and darkness, good and evil, death and life. Necessarily I must know both, or I cannot know either. Emily would presently understand. I, Charles her father, am certain of that; but I am not allowed to help you, Emily. I cannot reach you while you are beyond Louise. How could I help you if I reached you? I would remind you of the little words I could not teach Louise; you know them already but I should continually remind you of them: – *I am* – *It is* – *I see* – *I am*. And those, said Charles, are the best and the only things you can ever learn of life – learn them in a minute – go on learning them always. That is truth … He did not say any of this aloud to Louise, he stared at the bricks on the floor silently, until he said, 'Let me fetch her when Das has been. Let me fetch her and you can tell her yourself what you think it best to do.'

'No,' said Louise.

'Very well,' said Charles, standing up, and she could see that he was passionately angry and moved. 'Very well. Take the power of the angels if you must but, by God, you can do it alone.' He flung over the netting, scattering the Pekingese, and shouted for the groom to bring Delilah.

Louise stayed, smitten into silence with a chill of superstitious shock.

Don lay on the ground at her feet, pressed down on the bricks that were cooler than the air, pressing his throat down on them and then getting up, stretching his head out as if something were in his throat, moving his head, hanging it down so that the shadow of his ears hid his face; when he looked down his face fell into its customary soft peaceful puppy folds, but when he stretched out his neck there was a staring panic look in his eyes and his body seemed wild and strained. He stood up stretching out again, his feet slipped on the floor and he staggered and fell, and choked, his claws scrabbling wildly on the bricks, and Louise stepped quickly out of his way, waiting till he lay still again. The Pekingese stirred and whined.

She picked up the thermometer that Charles had not let her use; in the hot air the mercury had gone up. She shook it down and at once, in her hand, it ran up to 105° ... No wonder in this country we cannot be reasonable; even the weather is unbalanced, a parabola outside normality. The hot sun beats sense and resistance out of us, there is another virus in it that attacks us all, nothing is normal ... There was nothing friendly and nothing normal to her, the country was a hyperbole of heat and terror and disease, she found only perpetual enmity, abnormality, perpetual strain ... But if we have to be inoculated for this, we shall surely have to go away and we must. I must. I can't bear it any longer, cried Louise. I hate it, it hates me. It is destroying me. It hates me ...

The back of the stable had brick holes for ventilators, and a pigeon came through one and looked at her. Its neck was a deep glistening green, its eyes bright and gentle; it bobbed its head two or three times in surprise to find her there and murmured 'Coo.'

Louise had to laugh and immediately began to cry.

At the sight of her tears Narayan stopped aghast.

Tears. Nothing but tears. What was the meaning of so many tears? Anil had been in tears last night, Narayan had left Shila weeping; now, here was Mrs Pool with tears running down her cheeks and they seemed a continuation, a culmination of the tears of Shila and Anil. He stood, not knowing whether he had better go away or stay, and superstitions chased one another through his mind ... Three times tears! Oh, what is going to happen? ... Tears, very very painful tears – what did they mean? A warning? An omen? He was sure that something had happened and from that happening rings of other happenings would spread out and out from it. He was ominously certain of it.

Mrs Pool was graceful in her crying. Her face was not reddened or made ugly by her tears, it remained pale and her hair and her skin in the shadowless light of the stable reminded him of pictures he had seen of the Mother of Christ; perhaps it was the stable that put that into his head, but he found himself thinking it was a pity she was crying over a dog, not a baby. Still she disturbed him; with her eyes drenched in tears she seemed to him too much like Shila, and Shila herself was not unlike Anil; they were each a sad echo of the other. He wished they would not cry; but for him, if not for them, there was, he began to think, good in those tears; they seemed to be washing a throng of previous conceptions, old carelessness, and impossible illusions from his mind; Anil, perhaps, could not be perfect as Narayan would have him, his bright, other, wished-for self; perhaps he was simply Anil, an exasperating, intensely human and delightful friend. And Shila? Perhaps he had never seen Shila properly, she was his wife whom presently he might discover, with all the loves and frailties of a wife. And Mrs Pool was not a species apart from him, with an insurmountable impossible difference; she was Shila's sister crying her eyes out as Shila had cried. His life had a promise as if it would soon be washed clean, and though he was a little uneasy because he had up to then preferred it coated in mystery, he was immensely cheered.

He walked steadily up to the stable door, snapping his fingers at the Pekingese to announce his presence. The Pekingese burst into short affronted barks. 'Mrs Pool?' said Narayan above the din. He stepped over the netting and came in; he saw Don, and came at once to him and bent down. 'Is this the patient?' he asked jauntily.

'Don't touch him!' cried Louise.

'But what is the matter?' said Narayan, ruffled. 'Please. You must have confidence in me. I am a qualified veterinary surgeon and will not hurt your dog.' His dignity was touched. Don had made no movement and he bent down again.

'I shouldn't be so hasty, Maharaj,' said Kokil sarcastically over the stall front. 'Don't be in such a hurry. He is mad.'

'Mad!' Narayan stayed where he was for a moment, his hand out, stiff, where it had been ready to touch Don, his eyes suddenly, intensely fixed on the panting black heap below him; he could not have moved, half for pride and half for fear; the inside of his collar was suddenly wet but his mouth and his throat were horribly dry.

'You needn't be afraid.' He felt scorn in Louise's voice. 'I don't want you to do anything for him. I want you simply to give him an injection and put him to sleep. I will muzzle him and hold him myself. You need not touch him.' She spoke as if she were not sure he understood English and the effect of that was slightly insulting, but in his new-found understanding Narayan did not take umbrage. 'You have only to put him to sleep,' said Louise.

'Without examination? I could not do that.'

She was surprised. 'I have been watching him all morning; so has my – husband. It is quite obvious what is wrong.'

'All the same I prefer to make an examination. I must do so, in fact.'

'I tell you it isn't necessary. There can be no doubt.'

He found the courage to be obdurate, though it was hard. 'Madam, you may be wrong,' and he said without meaning any offence: 'You are not qualified, I think, to know exactly what the matter is.'

She answered curtly, 'Mr Das, if you are rude to me I shall report you to my husband.'

She could. She could also give to her report any complexion she chose; he was helpless to stop her and his confidence in Charles did not go as far as thinking that Charles would believe him, Narayan, against his own wife; but still he held firm. He put his bag down on the shelf and opened it with a click. Don started up, but Narayan compelled himself to stay still though the backs of his knees were damp against his trousers and the finger trembled. 'I do not intend any rudeness,' he said, 'but Madam, you must kindly allow me to examine the dog.'

That succeeded; she swept aside and he went up to Don, pulling on a pair of gloves. Don sprang up to bark but before a sound came he gave a silent choke; he stood on all fours but his tail and hind-quarters were down, his head was strained and his eyes rolled back showing the whites. He seemed to be fighting to swallow something, he panted and saliva frothed on his jaw; he made a dragging movement and collapsed back on the floor. Narayan stood there looking.

'Well?' asked Louise. 'Do you have to see any more?' He did not answer and she asked, 'What else is that but rabies?'

'The symptoms are of rabies, but – I am not sure.'

'What else could it be?'

'He should be kept a day or so for observation,' said Narayan. 'In these cases we can never be sure until death approaches. It may be that it is not rabies—'

'Nonsense.' Don was up again staggering round. 'Isn't that enough?' cried Louise. 'Must you torture him any more? Damn you. Can't you be quick?'

That was as real as a shaft – it quivered through him; it hurt like fire. He turned his back and went to the table setting out his things from his bag. He could see nothing, only a confused silvered shine of instruments and the glass shine of his bottles, and his hands were shaking so that the things chinked against each other as he took them out. In his ears were other sounds, the dry rustling of the banana leaves outside the stable, the whispering rustle of the little dogs behind the netting, the sound of water dripping gently, gently into the trough; and then, across them all, the hooting of the morning mail steamer and answering it, close beside him, a pigeon, and nearer than all of these the sound of the dog panting and the low sound of sobbing. The doctor in him told him that she did not know what she had said, she was hysterical and overwrought; he should treat her firmly and resolutely, but still he smarted and stung. He had only one thought now; he longed to end it and get away ... Anything – anything to be away. *'Damn you. Can't you be quick?'*

The words seemed to creep down through him; through his heart into his blood, into every fibre, and he gave up. He went on quietly working but the whole of him felt cursed, and Louise looked at him surprised by his sudden quietness. 'Please, please – hurry,' she said.

He did not answer. His hands were doing their work; here was cotton-wool, here the phials; this was the metal case of the syringe; with care his fingers opened it, unpacking it, unrolling the barrel from its protecting gauze, fitting in the needle. Presently he turned. 'Stand aside, please,' he said.

'What are you going to do?'

'I have something here which is instantaneous,' he said, and once he had spoken he could not stop. 'It was used in the last war; it cannot last but a second, one prick and it is over. Please do not cry. It shall not be so very terrible. It is not terrible at all, it is most humane, I promise you he shall not suffer at all.'

Louise only bowed her head and said, 'Be quick,' as if her teeth were clenched.

He was instantly silent again, running the drops off the syringe. Then he repeated curtly, 'Please stand aside. I have to bandage his jaws.'

'No!'

'I do not wish to risk a snap.'

'You needn't. I shall hold him.'

'I mean that he may snap at you even, whom he knows so well.'

'I have on gloves.' There was a fanatical determination in her voice.

'When he feels the needle he may reach your arm.'

Louise went down on both her knees on the ground and lifted Don across her and twisted her handkerchief tightly round his muzzle. 'Get on,' she said. Narayan shrugged and then he knelt beside her with the syringe; he took a loose fold of Don's loose skin and ran the needle in and pressed the plunger, a hideous long prick. Don gave a sudden surprised groan and died.

There was a moment to wait. Narayan kept his finger on the plunger looking down past the white of Louise's sleeve to the dog; it was all out of perspective and for a moment the dog looked bigger than them both, and he was seized with terror at what he had done – as if this prick were an unwarrantable presumption; the moment went on and on, blasted by his usurpation, filling him with fear. He put his fingers on Don's side and, pressing, pulled out the needle; and under his fingers he felt the heartbeats lessen – lessen. They died while his own were sounding loudly in his ears. Then the heart under his fingers was still; he had done something he had no right to do; he would have given anything to start that heart again.

He stood up with the syringe dangling in his hand. 'I shall go now,' he said. 'I shall wait for you in the house.'

When he had gone the stable was quiet. The Pekingese, who had decided there was nothing more to wait for, were tumbling on the lawn with their balls; the grass shone under the sun, the sky was perfectly serenely blue; nothing had changed or moved an iota. Nothing had changed; only Don had died. He was gone though he was here in the stable. A calm cloud, glossily white, sailed across the sky and its shadow passed over the lawn and over the Pekingese and left them in the sun again.

Don was heavy on her lap and she knelt up and lifted him on to his bed, where he lay most naturally, his legs still curled from the way she had held him in her arms, his ears fallen forward, his face in heavy sleepy lines; but his eyes were open. She sat back to look at him. He looked perfectly alive, but his eyes were more surprised than she had ever seen them. With a rise of horror she tried to close them and at last he lay peacefully, his eyes shut, laid down on his bed. She knelt beside him, absently stroking him, chiefly because she was too tired to get up and leave him. She was terribly tired, and soon, when Emily came in, there would be so much – so much to wrestle with, and fight … Emily is getting too much for me. How absurd. She is only a child; but I am so tired …

Kokil stole out to look at her and stole away to report; all the servants waited, not daring to interrupt, longing for Charles to come in, and order the dog to be taken away.

After a time he began to stiffen, but he still stayed remarkably warm.

Narayan pedalled furiously all the way home. Dust whizzed from his wheels and hens ran shrieking to the shelter of the house steps; babies rolled over and sat up in surprise and small naked children shouted 'Wah!' and pelted him with little stones and flew away in terror. For all these signs of his power, the feeling persisted. Why? He had done nothing wrong, but he felt that he had done something unforgivable, infinitely in the wrong. The sound of Louise's crying was in his ears and as he came nearer his own house the crying seemed to be Shila's. Why must he listen to this perpetual crying? He had had it all the way there, now he must have it all the way back. Why must this feeling stab him and nag him and threaten to rise from nagging into a pain that filled his soul? He rode faster and faster as if he could outride the crying and the wrong and the pain.

When he reached home he left his bicycle by the gate and no one heard him come in. The house was empty, even the kitchen was empty; on a slab were a row of little rice flour cakes, his favourites, pressed into shapes, a pannikin of chopped vegetables and a little curry powder ground on a stone. They were for his morning meal. He went into the study. The first thing that met his eye was the telephone, scrupulously dusted and silent on his desk; and he looked gloomily at it, for it increased his sense of wrong, and he thought suddenly and inexplicably of Anil's father.

Why should Anil's father come to his mind, of all people? He saw him as clearly as if he were in a little mirror inset into the room, quite quiet and still in the mirror, prisoned into quietness on his wooden bed on the terrace above the fields, sitting in that posture for hours, while only the light changed on the fields and the folds of his shawl lost the gleaming whiteness of midday and took the deeper colours of the sunset. On the wall of Narayan's study was a real mirror with oil flowers painted on the glass and now he saw that someone had stuck a flower that was real too in the corner of the frame; it was a small rosy spray of oleander, the kind that is deep dark rose, and looking at it a tinge of peace crept into his mind.

He had now only a soft reflection of his trouble and he was filled with tenderness for all of them: himself, Louise, Anil, and Shila. He sat down at his desk and wrote a note to Anil on the paper put clean and ready for him, with a blotter from the Asiatic Gas Company, with which he had no connection. He wrote it and finding Tarala in the kitchen told her to send it off.

'Where is your mistress?'

She pointed to the window, and he saw that Shila was in the little court outside; thinking he was away she had gone there where the sun was very hot, to dry her hair. She was sitting on a low stool, not moving, a book in her hands; but she was not reading, she was dreaming, looking at the river, her posture stupid and soft with dreams. Immediately the old irritation rose in him and he put his head out of the window and called energetically, 'Shila! Shila! What are you doing?'

Her voice answered him from far away, 'Nothing.'

It was lazily indifferent and it felt to him almost impolite. She always sprang up at his voice and came to him, or waited, standing silently to hear what he would say; but for the first time he was near her and felt that she was not thinking of him and he was startled and a little shocked.

He immediately went out to her. The sun had baked the walls of the little court to a flaky whiteness and the house tree, a pipal, made leaf patterns on it; sharply they fell over the light muslin that Shila wore, damp and clinging, nothing else but its thinness to hide her body. Her hair lay in wet strands, so black that they had a blue polished gleam. As soon as he touched her she started and the face she turned up to him was damp too, the temples exposed from the weight of her hair dragging back; her eyes were ringed and looked up at him wide and startled, the whole of her face seemed suddenly alive, brittle with life, vulnerable.

'Shila—' he began. She gathered up her things to go.

'Wait. Don't go. Why do you run away?' She did not answer and he looked at her book. 'What is it?'

'*Ramayana.*' Her answer was a whisper.

'And you don't read it. You sit with it and dream.'

She looked down so that he could not see her face and shook her head. He asked gently, 'Do you want our son to grow up a woolly head? Couldn't you read a little every day for him?'

She looked up at him and her eyes glowed with delight.

'Did you put the flowers in the mirror?'

Her lips parted in apprehension. 'I am sorry.'

'Why should you be sorry? They were very nice.' And the little court and the house, the field where his cow was tethered, the garden and the jetty above the water seemed to him very nice as well. He forgot the sense of wrong that had filled him; he had left it with the outside world, away from this intimate and suddenly precious one of kitchen cakes and drying blue-black hair and oleander flowers and whispered confidence. He stood there with Shila, watching the patterns of the leaf-shadows, warmed by the sun, and he was soothed by the gentleness that was the core of the house, that the running of the river seemed to tell, and wondered why he had missed feeling it before ... I was too busy, said Narayan ... How often had he himself violated it? And how often had Shila said nothing and patiently put it together again? ... I must grow more thoughtful ... And he had again, more strongly, that sense of promise for himself ... I shall begin again and differently, said Narayan ... 'Shila!'

He did not know he had spoken until she looked up again questioning. Now he could not remember what it was that he wanted to say. He asked, 'If Anil Banerjee comes tonight, have you something good for us?'

Her eyes fell and the happiness was wiped out of her face.

Anil came. The house was waiting clean and fresh for him; Tarala had swept even the paths and courtyard and, while Narayan was not looking, sprinkled them with cow-dung. About Shila was an air of implicit obedience without a tinge of welcome in it; she had cooked the dinner herself, platters of crisp, light *luchis* that were a kind of puffed biscuit used instead of bread, a lentil curry, and sweets; sugar balls and sweet dumplings and diamond-shaped cream toffee, glittering with gold and silver sugar paper; she had even cut up mutton to make a second curry when Narayan stopped her. 'Don't give him flesh. He will not eat it.' She looked at him, in surprise. 'Yes, yes. I know. It amused me to try to make him eat it, but I don't wish to force him any more.' She dressed herself, putting a fine gauze sari over a petticoat and bodice of red, edged with lace, and pinned a line of jasmine flower heads round the knot of her hair, and went into the study to meet Anil as Narayan liked her to do, quite resolved that she would neither smile nor speak all evening.

As Anil came in she lifted her hands, pressed together palm to palm and finger-tips to finger-tips, in front of her face in salutation, bending her head without a smile but he did not notice that. He said perfunctorily, 'Good evening. I hope you are well. Where is Indro?' He thought it strange of Narayan to try to make a companion of his wife – strange and rather embarrassing and, anyhow, useless; and without waiting for her answer he passed her, filling the room with his young lordliness, and called, 'Indro, are you there? Or are you out?'

'I am out,' called Narayan gaily. 'You are at any rate early. Shila, don't you ask our friend to sit down?' But Anil waited standing, calling out remarks at his ease.

'Where have you been all day, Anil?'

'I have been fishing.'

'*Fishing*? And it is three weeks only to the Examination?'

'Three weeks – three years – what does it matter?'

Anil had always seemed laconic about the Finals, but Narayan knew how he had seethed and fussed and worried with the rest of them; now in his voice there was a genuine lightness as if he truly did not care.

'What made you go fishing?'

'I don't know.'

Like Binnie he had walked and thought he would go fishing, even though his tutor was coming to coach him that day. He thought he would go fishing, not for pearls but for the *rui* that breed in tanks, and taste a little of tank mud when they are caught.

He knew Professor Dutt was waiting in his room, but once he had started to fish the hours were lost to him; he had to borrow a rod and line from the headman of the village that he knew outside of Amorra. The tank was quite deserted. It was in leafy green shade, the water a sleepy sunlit green, and dragonflies hovered still in one place above it. With his rod out he sat in a dream and a kingfisher sat opposite him on a post. It had beautiful feathers, but what he liked better was its knowing head and its eye that it kept all the time on him; it had a cheeky, gypsy knowing look for all its beauty.

They spent the day together. Anil did not catch a fish but the kingfisher caught three and swallowed them immediately and whole.

Anil thought of nothing all day, but as he stood up to go he said to the kingfisher almost mechanically, 'Your feathers are as bright as my dreams,' and as soon as he said it, it flew away. Was that an omen? 'Perhaps I shall not pass after all,' he said, and he said it again now to Narayan as Narayan came out of his room.

'Perhaps you will not if you take your time off to go fishing.' And Narayan put his arm across Anil's shoulders. 'Seriously, you shouldn't do that now. You must not only pass. You must pass with honours.'

'And why?'

'I am ambitious for you.'

'Thank you. But why? Why for me?'

'You are your father's son,' said Narayan. He said that but he did not mean to say it in the least.

'Indro, why do you have this notion of my father?'

Narayan did not answer at once, but the evening was flawed; into the light bantering smile on his face came a remembrance – Anil did not know what else to call it – and a look of worry, almost fear. He said suddenly, 'Anil, your father would not kill – any form of life.'

It was a statement, not a question. Anil was quick. 'Ho! Who have you murdered now? I thought you were a veterinary, not a doctor.'

Narayan did not laugh. He said again, 'No. He would not take life, I think.'

'You know he would not.'

'But why?' cried Narayan. 'Why? What is his reason? There must be a reason.'

Anil did not know the reason but he answered in the oblique way of which he was so fond, 'Perhaps, because each time you kill, you kill yourself.' He said it at random but it struck a look of dread in Narayan.

'Supposing – death would occur in any case.'

'Then why interfere? If it is fate let it be fate. You need not upset it. You should not upset it. There is poetry in fate. I like fate very much. It is cruel but the world would not balance without it. I heartily agree with it.'

'Even when – it is yourself who are caught in its workings?'

'What could I then do?' Anil barely hid a small yawn. 'So very British, my dear Indro, this mania for interference.' Even that did not draw Narayan, and Anil went further. 'If you interfere you are a cog. Yes, a cog in a wheel. Have you been a cog, Indro? I believe you have.'

'I am not a cog.' Narayan's face and voice were fiercer than the words and Anil looked at him in surprise.

'You are not angry? I was only bantering.'

'Formerly—' said Narayan, and his lips trembled. He broke off and then said as if he were justifying himself, 'I work. I only do my work.' He tried to speak more lightly. 'I am – not a cog. I am like oil in the wheels. Anyone who truly works is that.' He could not help a little spite in the last words.

'The oil of life?' Anil countered it.

'Are you not thinking of the salt?' But under his apparent eas-iness Narayan was still troubled. Later he said, 'You do not strictly follow your father, Anil. Is it against your principles to kill? I myself belong to the world today—'

'But all the same you do not like to kill,' said Anil shrewdly. 'What is this, Narayan? Before you had no interest in princi-ples.'

'I had no time,' said Narayan slowly. 'I was not you – I had to work.' And as always when he talked of the difference between them, his voice grew disagreeable. 'Everything I did I had to do. There was no time for anything else. That is the difference between us. You quibble – Shall I pass my Final? Shall I not pass? – it doesn't matter to you, I dare say, but to me it was death, and it was life. There was always too much, too much to be done.'

'There is always too much to be done,' agreed Anil, and another yawn came up to his throat. He did not think he could talk of Narayan and his principles any more. 'Always too much. That is why I am not sure that I have time to pass the Examination.' To his surprise, instead of pouncing on him Narayan said slowly, 'That might perhaps be so.'

'You were cross at me just now for wasting time. I was bene-fited by that waste,' said Anil, and he said prettily, 'I spent the day with a kingfisher, Indro,' but even this did not produce the little shock, or the smile, for which he was waiting.

Narayan only nodded. 'Once – do you remember?' he said – 'we went for a walk. I did not want to walk but you said it would be jolly. We went off the road down into the fields . . .' But Anil was bored. He went to the window and now it was dark and there was the night mail steamer passing upstream, her jewel red light showing, her searchlight stretching out before her, another yellow light in her nose, and below the garden came the sound of her wash breaking in a wave along the bank ...

We went off the road down into the fields ... There had been no path; the little rutted fields were hard as clay, dried with rotting weeds, but among them were patches of mustard. They came near a village where a path of beaten mud sprang up and led through a mustard field and Narayan, walking behind Anil, picked a head of mustard. Naturally, Anil was talking and Narayan listening, and as he listened he began idly to examine the flowers he had picked. He had seen the mustard fields in flower only as a whole, deep spreading yellow, in fact he did not remember ever really looking at a flower in his life. Now he looked at the mustard flowers; they were a dozen on a spray, spread in a shape like a parachute, each flower with five flat yellow petals, and in its centre a green seeded heart; each flower was perfectly mounted on its stem and as he held it nearer his eyes, it blotted out its own whole field, in fact it blotted out the earth; behind the flowers he could see only a glimpse of sky ...

And I had too much to do, said Narayan, ever to look at a flower before. What a shocking thing! And I have been so busy that I have not looked at one since – unless you can count the oleander that Shila brought ... And beginning with the oleander, his thoughts went away on a small trail of peace. He jerked himself back. 'It is shocking. It is disgraceful,' he said aloud.

'What is?'

'Not to have time to live.'

'It's your own fault.'

... Well, who has the wisdom to save his own soul? Hardly anyone. It is not sense. Is it sense to retire as Anil's father had done, to give up business and politics and friends and opportunity and go apart to a lonely country village? No it is not sense, but it is more divinely wise. Since there is nothing divine in me I shall do nothing of the sort. I shall get a better job, as I have said before. I shall buy myself in, and reimburse myself, I shall batten on the others and they on me, I shall go on until I reach the top; and then what shall I have gained? Nothing. Nothing at all. But that will not stop me doing it ... And silently he cried: I do not want to be divine. I want nothing divine in me. And still in front of him came that tiresome picture of Anil's father, sitting in his shawl; and he felt suddenly and extremely tired ... I can't help it, said Narayan wearily, there is God in the flower, and in the folds of the shawl, and in me – in all things, animate – inanimate – whether I like it or not. I cannot help it! ... And aloud he cried: 'I shall give it all up and go away.'

The steamer had passed, the waves were dying down along the bank. 'What did you say?' asked Anil.

'I shall give it all up and go away.' But, said a second time, it merely sounded peevish.

'Now what has upset you?' said Anil, more interested. 'Are you really in trouble? What have you done?'

'Nothing.'

'All this talk of life and killing – you must have done something.' Shila came in carrying a tray with betel leaves she had prepared on it, and Anil spoke to her. 'Indro has committed a crime and will not tell us what it is.'

Narayan flamed. 'Will you be quiet?' he shouted. 'You are driving me mad. Leave me alone!' And he cried, 'I wish never –

never – to be reminded of this again.' And as he said it, there was a reminder knocking in his brain. Something – something in this affair which he ought to remember – something he knew but could not think of. Impatiently he put it out of his mind.

VI

'Don! Don! Don! Don!'

Emily's voice floated in from the garden, shrill and persistent. 'Don. Don. Don!' And Binnie's dutifully echoed behind it, 'Hullo, Don. Hullo!'

Louise went on writing, but her pen bit a little deeper on the paper than before, wavered, jerked, made a blot, and stopped; she threw it down and it rolled with a shower of blots across her letter, spoiling it. Furious, she went out on the verandah to chasten the children, but the quick words did not leave her lips; Emily was coming across the grass with Don's lead in her hand and it swung heavily, at just above the level that a small spaniel's neck might be. It danced up and down as she walked.

'Don't jump up, Don. Bad dog! Down. Down. Down!'

'Hullo! Hullo, Don.'

It was silly, babyish, stupid, clumsy, but it was ghostly. Even in the bright sunlight it was macabre and a little indecent. Louise held the verandah rail and the warmth of it creeping up her arms told her that she was cold. 'How *ridiculous* and absurd!' she cried indignantly . . . But – but – Why did Emily do it? Why did she keep it up? How could she keep it up? It had been going on for three weeks now, persistently, never stopping, never resting. It was not the game or the trick that Emily was playing that upset Louise – that was merely childish, absurd; it was the way she persisted – and that was neither childish, nor absurd; it was beginning to be diabolical ... I mean that, cried Louise, it *is* diabolical, devilish in the way she has thought it all out ... It was much too pat to be accidental.

Last Sunday ...

('Read about Noah's Ark, Mother.')

('... *And they went in unto Noah in the ark, two and two, of all flesh wherein is the breath of life.*')

('Charles says that is God,' Emily had interrupted.)

('What is?')

(The Breath of Life.')

('I suppose it is – in a way.')

('Charles says it is. Charles says, God is in me – see?' She blew on the palm of her hand. 'That's my breath of life. God is in me, in everyone. Professor Dutt says if we kill anything, we kill God. You could kill God in me and in Binnie and in you and in Delilah and—' Her eyes, unblinking, fixed themselves on Louise's face. 'And – in Don.')

Unwillingly Louise had to speak of it to Charles. Charles looked at her and said, 'I know nothing about children.'

'Charles. Please.'

'Nor do you. Nor does anyone. They are unfathomable.' And he added, 'If you are wise you will ignore it.'

That was easy to say. It was impossible to ignore it. It was even beginning to disturb the servants. They were adopting an exceedingly respectful, propitiating way of speaking to Emily baba.

Why did she do it? Why?

Emily herself did not know. At the beginning it had been done too quickly for her to realize it, and for a day or two she had kept it up blindly, covering her hurt; then gradually, as that hurt began to be felt harder and deeper, she had grown angry; and this was not rage or temper, it was angry, adequate, revengeful reason; it was even more than that, it was an inspired campaign. Very clearly and persistently Emily seemed to know what she should do next ... I am not like a child now, thought Emily, I am grown up ... And she remembered the tales she had heard of people whose hair had turned white in a night ... I have turned old, said Emily ... and the drama in that helped to bolster her up; her sense of drama was completely as strong as Louise's.

I have turned old ... It was true, she felt infinitely removed from the Emily who had gone out to breakfast with the Nikolides ... Something left off being in me then. I put on my clean clothes – and she remembered them, her spotted sundress, her sun-hat and sandals – and I went out to breakfast. Mother was clever. She knew how I felt about the Nikolides, she knew I would forget everything for them ... And it seemed to Emily sheer treachery that Louise should have used them against her. One thing – said Emily – I shall never go blind like that again. I shall never be blind ... And even to so young a girl as Emily there was something pitiable in the loss of that heedlessness. Breakfast with the Nikolides was always to be the last hour of her childhood.

In the first few days, in spite of the way she clung to his name, she almost succeeded in shutting Don out of her mind ... I will not believe it, she said, I will not believe it. I will not have trouble here. Don shall not be dead ... Slowly, from that, began the second stage: If Don is dead, and – Oh! he is beginning to be dead – it is somebody's fault. I put my hand out on him in the night and he was there and he was beating, quite alive. What did they do to him? They did something. I know he did not die in this – *untruthful way*. (That is what Louise would say to me: '*Emily, why do you have to answer me in this untruthful way? You are telling me a lie*.') Now that is what I say to you, Louise. You are telling me a lie. He did not die in this untruthful way. Somebody had a hand in it, and I think it was you, Louise.

You had no right to do it!

Don is mine. Mine. Even if he is dead – if he is dead, still he is mine. You cannot take him from me like this. You do it because you think I am a child. I shall keep him alive until I choose to agree he is dead. I asked for him. I wanted him, even if he were dead, to hold in my arms, but you said he had been taken away. Where? You would not tell me. I ought to know, he is mine. He disappeared while we were out . . . You sent me out of the way, you used the Nikolides as a – a – Emily could not think of the word, and then it came – as a *decoy*. You have spoilt them. You have changed them from a private lovely thing to a decoy, and I shall never forgive you for that; and I will not accept it that he has disappeared and I shall not let Binnie accept it either. I shall go on and on and on until I have found out the truth; I shall not give up and I shall not forget. However difficult it is I promise I shall not forget, and Binnie shall help me whether she likes it or not. She says it frightens her; let it frighten her. I shall say to myself in the day and in the night, 'Pay attention, Emily,' and I have taken a book to my private place in the tomato bed where I shall write everything down in truthful writing . . .

Emily sat in the tomato bed with an exercise book and a con-centrated expression on her face; this made her look very ugly, her face was quite tied into knots with thinking, her hair was stuck to her forehead, which shone sticky and white in the heat, her sun-hat was pushed back and its billiard-green lining sent a sickly reflection down to her chin. She knelt, her dress above her knees, and with one hand she wrote and with the other she picked at the earth, picking it up in lumps, crumbling it and letting it run away between her fingers. The tomato plants made a malodorous forest round and above her, with their yellow five-pointed flowers and balls of unripe fruit hanging down; the ripe ones, poppy red, shone between; some had burst and lay rotting on the ground.

Her knees hurt pressed into the lumpy earth, her back ached, but she would not move. She longed to stretch out and lie flat in the sun, making the whole of her warm. For days she had had this curious coldness all over her body, in her legs and arms, even in her breath, a cold uncertain feeling that made her partly sick and partly tired ... The sun makes me feel better. I feel the sun through my clothes and my bare legs and behind my eyes and after a time in the sun I cannot think of anything, I can only feel sleepy; I like the sun but I am going to stay out of it, I am going to stay here until I have written this all down in my book, in truthful writing.

The most difficult part is to pay attention; the sicker I feel the less attention I pay. Well, they always told me I was bad at paying attention, now I am tasting that for myself. The first thing I shall write in my book is: *Pay attention, Emily. Pay attention, Emily* ... It was difficult to write. She was feeling so sick ... Huh, that's nothing. Think what happened to me after the Nikolides! ... But thinking of that she immediately threatened to be sick again.

It was better to think of things from the outside; better really not to think, but only to see, to put the pictures on one after the other, like pictures in magic lantern slides. There was a magic lantern in the College with slides. There was a magic lantern in the College with slides of insect pests and ... Pay attention, Emily. See, here we are coming back from the Nikolides': *Binnie and I came back from the Nikolides' – in time for lunch. It was hot* ... I remember I thought what a pity it was that we had lunch at one o'clock and the Nikolides only finished breakfast at eleven ... That was trying a stomach more than it could bear, and a plate of soup had kept reappearing to Emily all the way home, the soup they had had instead of mulligatawny: a kind of sausage of spiced mince in a soup of dark thick gravy, with strings of macaroni, ham and onion. The feeling of it stayed in her mouth.

'You are not going to be sick, are you?' said Binnie.

Silence.

'If you are, Mother will never let us go again.'

Emily did not answer. The launch went buoyantly along bouncing her gently in her chair; she had thought that delightful on the way out. The sun on the water sent blinding diamond sparks into her eyes and from the engine and the Lascars' galley came whiffs of hot oil and curry smells and garlic.

'You're sure you're not going to be sick?'

'If I am I can manage.'

'You had better,' said Binnie. She was not really severe, but so many things had gone from their lives because of Emily, because of her bilious attacks and her head and stomach aches; as she grew older Emily had become magnificent in concealing them. 'If you can only not look too yellow,' sighed Binnie. 'I thought you would be sick. When I saw that soup, I thought you would be.'

'Don't.'

'I brought one of Charles's handkerchiefs,' said Binnie.

She offered it. It had holes in it, and it had been starched almost stiff, but Binnie had dosed it with eau de cologne and Emily held it to her face. Immediately a wind rose from offshore and blew coolness across her and the launch turned to the jetty so that the deck was in shade. She was better, and they were jubilant as they walked home. Inside the gate the Pekingese came tumbling and barking to meet them, and it was then – then – that ...

The pencil stopped. Emily's thumb dug into a hard lump of earth, pounding it, breaking it, spoiling her nail; she blinked her eyes; the lids were smarting, and she had to press her lips firmly together before she could go on.

'Kokil, where is Don?'

'The Memsahib says I'm not to tell you.'

The answer had been so unexpected that at first they did not take it in. Then Emily's heart and Emily's face went still, but Binnie asked gaily, 'Why? What is the matter with him?' No one answered. Kokil's stillness, like Emily's, penetrated even to Binnie. 'What is the matter?' she asked again, but this time it was a real question. 'Is he ill? Is he hurt?' Kokil was silent, moving the dust with his toe, not looking at them, and Binnie gave a sharp anguished howl. 'He's dead. Emily! Emily. He's dead!'

Kokil looked at them, quite haggard with distress. 'My orders are not to tell you. I'm not to tell you, but – Don dog is dead.'

'No, he is not,' said Emily crisply. She could not have told why she said it, but she said it clearly and loudly. 'Don dog will never die,' and she walked straight upstairs to Louise. Outside Louise's door she jerked Binnie to a stand.

'You always like to do what I tell you, don't you, Bin?'

'Y – es.'

'You always will do what I say?'

Binnie nodded. Her eyes, wet and blue, were fixed steadily on Emily.

'Then, listen,' said Emily austerely. 'Whatever they tell you, whatever they say, Don is not dead. He – is – not – dead.'

Binnie seldom asked questions in words, but she had a singular power of making her whole body ask them for her.

'—?' said Binnie.

'He met us just now when we came in.'

'——?'

'He is here now and he is always with us. Don! Down, Don!' Emily brushed down her dress. 'Do you see? Come out of that corner, Don. He thinks there's a rat. Come out, you naughty dog. You can't dig there. *Come out*, I say.'

'——?'

'He's invisible now, you see,' said Emily.

Light began to break on Binnie's face.

'Say, "Hullo, Don."'

'H – hullo.'

'Louder.'

'*Hullo – Don.*'

'And if you want to be any help to me,' said Emily, 'you will go on saying that whenever you can remember. We have to give him all the encouragement we can while he's invisible, you see.'

Louise was sitting at her dressing-table, picking up the brushes and putting them down again, taking the tops of her jars and bottles off and putting them back unused. She said in her careful voice, 'Is that you, children? Did you have a nice time? Emily, I hope you were careful what you ate.'

There were bright patches on her cheeks and in her voice, and a dead cold weight sank in Emily. Up to that moment she had had a little hope that it was not to be true; up to that time there was even a feeling that it could not be true, there would be – must be – a miracle – It was not to be true. Now that died. It was dead as soon as she saw Louise.

'Emily, come here.'

Her track across the room came to a full stop at the back of a chair. She stood there waiting, her eyes on Louise, and she put her arms up defensively on the chair back.

'Emily – and Binnie, there is something I have to tell you. You must be brave.'

They did not answer. They only stared.

'Emily – Don was killed – this morning.'

'No he was not.'

'We did everything we could. The vet came – but he died.'

'He didn't. He met us just now as we came in.'

'Emily, you have just heard me say he is dead.'

'You say it, but it isn't true.' She and Louise exchanged stares. 'Go on,' said Emily. 'Tell us how he died.'

'He – was very badly bitten – by another dog.'

'In a fight?'

'Yes. In a fight.'

'Don doesn't fight,' said Emily scornfully. 'He never fights, he always runs away. He's one of the greatest cowards that have ever been' – and she asked desperately: 'Where is Charles?'

'He is out.' And there was a hesitating, painful pause.

'Stand up and don't fidget with your mouth,' said Louise sharply. 'Emily—' she controlled her voice – 'I tell you – Don is dead. I am very very sorry about it, more sorry than I can say, but it's no use being angry—'

'Wouldn't you be angry if someone said that about one of your dogs?' demanded Emily, and suddenly her anger choked her; but it was not only anger, it was the soup as well, come back at this most inconvenient hour.

There was no hiding that bout of sickness. She was most mortally sick; she knew that point was reached when everyone gave in to her, when Louise ceased to scold or cajole and became suspiciously reasonable.

Emily did not know then what she was saying, but they told her she had cried all the time, 'I want – Don – by my bed. Tell – them – to bring his bed – and – put it – by mine.'

'Very well, darling. We will. We will.'

'So that – I can touch him.' And, 'Where is Charles? I want him – badly.'

'Yes – yes. But don't talk now.'

And so the day went on until the evening, dragging through the familiar misery of all such days: the bursting pain in her head and eyes, the thick yellow taste of her mouth and the burning unhealthiness of her body; even her skin hurt. There was the smell of eau de cologne, the basin beside her, the towel spread under her . . . But the misery then was not as bad as the misery now. All the time she was so sick she was numb . . . *And*, wrote Emily, *it was days before I could feel again and I am not sure that I can feel properly now, I still have the feeling in my head of being sick and very tired and still not feeling properly. So one day I shall feel it even worse than this, probably.*

At the beginning, in the first shock, she was laid low – and she came very near then to an armistice with Louise.

I woke from a doze . . . And there was Louise sewing by her bed, with her needle glinting in and out of a thread of light that came from a chink in the shutters; Louise looked up and caught her eyes; Louise was pale, hollowed with pity, and her eyes as they met Emily's were anxious, almost timid.

'If you sew in that light,' croaked Emily, 'you will hurt your eyes.'

It was a terrible effort to say that and it was not wise; at once she began miserably to retch again. Louise held her head as she leant over the side of the bed, and Louise's hands were cool and slim and their skin was faintly scented. Luxuriously Emily let them put her back on the pillow and smooth her hair and stroke her forehead. 'Poor – little girl,' said Louise. 'Poor little girl.'

Emily gave a small fluttering sigh and pressed Louise's fingers under her own. ('Why can't you always be like this?' asked Louise's fingers as clearly as if they had spoken. 'Why can't you?' And Emily's answered, 'I can. I can.') And immediately and clearly she said aloud, 'Mother, if you put your hands round Don's chest from behind you can feel his heart beating. It's like a little engine.'

After that she lay alone.

She closed her eyes and presently she was sick again, but this time she had to manage by herself.

While she was retching over the side of the bed, Charles came in and stood there looking at her . . .

Charles came in and looked at me . . .

Again Emily dug and twisted her thumb in the earth. What had she expected of Charles? She did not quite know, but she had waited all day for him to come in, reaching out for that moment, certain of relief, and then ... The tomatoes were hanging absolutely still but they seemed to be swaying and shimmering dangerously.

*

Charles came in to see her after he had changed, not straight up; she heard him ride in and waited for the curtain to lift and for him to appear, but she went on waiting. He came upstairs, she heard his voice, he was talking to Louise and then he went downstairs again. When at last he did come to her he walked up to her bed, and did not speak. He looked ashamed. Emily lay there dumbly, looking at him, and he still looked ashamed, and she, at once, became embarrassed, almost prim. It was a pity – after all that waiting there did not seem anything to say. Why did he look ashamed?

She made an effort. 'Charles—' but she could not go on. Tears of weakness filled her eyes; she closed them trying to prevent the tears escaping under her lids; she succeeded and presently she asked the question she wanted to ask. 'How do – you – say Don died?'

He did not answer at once but she felt him change and he said, as if he were angry, 'Your mother has told you – he was killed in a fight.' Emily knew he was not angry with her.

Charles did not lie – if you asked him a question he answered it; he did not lie. Charles said, 'Your mother has told you – he was killed in a fight.' Charles did not say, 'He was killed in a fight.'

She looked at him. 'Don didn't fight. He ran away.'

Charles did not answer.

'Don isn't dead,' she said.

'Yes he is,' answered Charles promptly, and suddenly he added, 'Emily, if I were you, I should be quiet over this. Don't worry Louise.'

Emily turned over and lay with her back to him. He knew it was a lie? . . . Charles does not tell lies, but he is going to be with Louise against me, in this. Why? I don't know . . . What mysterious power had Louise over Charles to make him join in a lie with her like this – to make him uphold her? . . .

I don't care. I don't care, – wrote Emily, proudly, though her lids were smarting, – *I will be by myself.*

She knew now that was going to be true for her. She was to be alone – not even with Binnie. Binnie and Emily were sisters, children of Charles and Louise, but there was something in Binnie that made her especial to them, something that left Emily out.

Binnie was loyal, but Binnie was no one's ally. Binnie was like a sea-anemone, she took in as much as she could digest and spat out the rest into life; she made no attempt to retain anything more than she comfortably could. *She will help me just as far as she can, and then leave off helping; but she is a help. I met her on the stairs just now with Louise. 'Hullo Don, Don,' said Binnie as I passed and I saw Louise set her lips.* Binnie was useful as a machine gun, she sent in a stream of identical little bullets all on the same spot.

And mark you, Louise, wrote Emily and liked it, *mark you, I shall get what I want in the end* . . . *There is no escape for you. This time I shall win. I am learning to pay attention. I am thinking of this even in my sleep. You think I shall forget, but I shall not forget and I shall not give up even if am alone* . . . And she thought of the Jerusalem song that Charles sang on the steps in the morning. *I have no bows and arrows, I have no sword or a spear, but I shall not cease from mental fight till I have found out everything, Louise.*

The next page was headed: *Inoculations!*

Now this was a very curious part of the affair, and that it was a part of the affair Emily was convinced. The children had been inoculated before, on board ship for typhoid fever; they had been vaccinated; now it seemed that there was a new disease and they were to be inoculated for that.

'What is it?'

'You would not understand.'

They would not understand but they were to have seven ghastly inoculations that were done in the side of the stomach.

Even Charles protested. 'But are they necessary, Louise?'

'Dare *you* take the risk?'

'If we examine them carefully for bites and scratches ...' What could bites and scratches have to do with a disease?

'It doesn't harm you if they are done. Especially,' she said with an edge of resentment in her voice, 'as they can be done here. It isn't worth the risk, just for a few little pricks.'

Little pricks. As Emily thought of them the whole of her seemed to recede leaving only her stomach, and her stomach seemed round and flat like the side of a tambourine with a brittle, stretched, thin skin across it. The Doctor Babu was frightened of the needle himself, he approached it towards them with his hand trembling and once he missed and had to start again; and then there was the long moment to stand with the needle quivering in and out, the plunger going down before he started all over again on the other side.

'O Mother, let me take the risk,' begged Emily.

'Emily, how can you be such a coward? Think of Binnie. It isn't as terrible as all that.'

'It is. It's simply dreadful,' cried Emily, 'and it isn't necessary, either.'

'Would I ask you to have it done if it were not necessary?'

'Yes, you would. Don't you believe anything she says, Binnie!' shouted Emily, and from an overheard tag she cried: 'It's just a form of propaganda.'

Charles walked hastily away. If the disease were so bad, why was Charles not done? Emily counted up the people. Louise, she herself, Binnie, Kokil the sweeper, and the Pekingese. Such a curious and peculiar choice.

'Shah, will you be done?'

'Not I!' said Shah, and laughed.

'Why not?'

Shah was evasive. He shrugged.

'Have you ever been inoculated?'

'Inoculated? Wah! When I was a soldier – for plague, for typhoid – and *langwana* – vaccination.'

'But dogs can't get any of those diseases, can they, Shah?'

That was the most mysterious of all. Why were the Pekingese inoculated? She had discovered that they were done – only by accident. Every morning, very early, they left with Kokil in the car. Where to go? To Dr Das's house and Dr Das was the vet. He was in the telephone book, the only Dr Das. Dr N.C. Das, Vet. Surgeon.

'Charles, why do Picotee and Sun go to the vet?'

'To be inoculated,' said Charles incautiously.

'Like us?' pounced Emily.

'Yes.' And then he added sharply, 'What did you say? Well, yes, as a matter of fact, like you.'

'For the same thing?'

Charles stared at her, but under his scrutiny she kept a bland, inquiring face.

'Yes, for the same thing,' said Charles. 'And I'm too busy to answer any more questions.'

What diseases do people and dogs get? . . . I have to find out that.

Can people get distemper? Can dogs get malaria? What disease do dogs and people get? . . .

All these things Emily wrote down and conned over in the tomato bed, and every day she held a session there and every day she had garnered a little and achieved a little more; the sessions grew longer and longer.

'Emily, what have you been doing to your knees?'

'Kneeling on them.'

'Kneeling on them? They are filthy and stained with something green. Kneeling? Why?'

'To pray,' said Emily pertly.

'For whom?'

'Not for *whom*? – for *what*?' said Emily, and she fixed her eyes on Louise. Their ordinary hazel glowed with a yellow-green light and she looked like a young tiger cat. 'I'm praying for something I mean to have, and I shall get it. I shall get it soon,' said Emily.

War had opened between Emily and Louise.

'Kokil,' said Emily in the evening, 'why haven't you brought Don's food?'

'*Don's food?*'

'Yes. Don's food. He's hungry. Go and get it at once. Bring it.'

Kokil hesitated, looking at her. 'Emily baba, the Memsahib told you. Don dog is dead.'

'She says he is dead but he is not.'

'With my own eyes I saw him dead, Emily baba.'

'With my own eyes I see him alive. Don't talk to me. Go and fetch his food.'

He did not know whether to go or to stay. Emily's nerve broke and she screamed, 'Fetch it! Fetch it at once!'

To placate her he brought it, and Louise, coming down the stairs, saw three empty bowls where only the two Pekingese had fed.

'Why three?'

She could not understand his answer. 'Why three?' she asked again.

'Don dog,' said Kokil simply.

'Don't be so stupid!' cried Louise angrily, but next day they were there again.

('Mother, don't you think Don's *sweet*? Do you know what he did ... ?')

('Hullo, Don. Hullo, Don. Hullo, Don.')

('Good night, Mother. Good night, Binnie. Good night, Don.')

'Emily. Stop it!'

'Stop what?'

'You know very well.'

'I don't. What do you mean?'

'Emily, once and for all, will you stop this clowning?'

'I don't know what you mean.'

'I forbid you – either of you – to mention Don's name again.'

Silence. They were lying on their backs looking at her.

'Why?' said Emily.

'Don is dead, Emily. This – this – play-acting is senseless and – horrid.'

'Not as horrid as being dead,' said Emily.

Louise caught her breath. She was standing between them and in front of her was Don's small empty *charpoy*, its rug folded, a bowl of drinking water beside it, and his lead coiled on the bed.

'You are not to say it. Not to. Understand! You are not to say his name again.'

'We shall have to learn to whistle then,' said Emily.

After Louise had gone and Binnie was asleep she had another

fit of crying; as she lay exhausted after it she looked up at the sky through her net and wondered for the first time where Don had really gone ... Where did he go? I know they put him away somewhere; buried him; but where is he, the breathing part of him? That made a gap of terror in her, and she hastily put a thought over it, an anodyne. 'There has been so much dying lately,' she said, 'that anyhow he won't be lonely.' But the stars all slid together in the blur of tears.

VII

'Charles, I must speak to you.'

Louise was standing by the piano looking out of the window as he came in. He thought she must have been standing there for a long time, she looked so strained and white and her handkerchief was twisted into a string in her hand. There was only one lamp lit in the room, a lamp with a deep shade that made a circle of light on the floor round it and left the rest of the room in dusk; only the flaky shapes of the pigeons in Charles's picture shone on a background that had sunk away into the wall. The sky outside the windows in relief was a clear blue, the blue of blue flowers; the stars were still small and fresh in the sky, and the tops of palms showed indistinct and feathery in their blackness. A chatter of sounds came from the bazaar, not loud but shrill and never ceasing, and with it nearer, in the garden, were a dozen indescribable sounds of an Indian night: lizards, crickets and an owl, a flute from the servants' houses, but more than anything else Louise listened to the tom-toms and the cymbals from the temple in the bazaar and beyond them – somewhere, the sharp yapping of a dog.

'Noise. Always, always noise. Never for one moment is it quiet.' The handkerchief twisted and jerked. 'It never stops. It goes on all day; it is worse at night. It's driving me mad. I have nothing to do but listen to the noise.'

'It isn't a bad one to be listening to as noises go just now,' said Charles quietly. 'Don't forget that, Louise.' But Charles knew himself how the noise came into every corner of the house. He knew how the high vaults of the ceilings gave back every drum-beat as they gave back the piano notes, with an empty mocking echo. Every room had its grey lizard with an incessant *tck tck* in its throat, and just outside the window on the cork tree wood-peckers and cockatoos hammered and squawked all day and at night a cricket scraped in a Chinese whisper. 'That cricket has sent me nearly mad quite often,' said Charles gently. 'Come and sit down and I will get you a drink.'

'That's your cure for everything, not mine,' Louise lashed suddenly at him. 'You know it isn't only the noise ... Charles, let me go away. It isn't any use my staying. I hate it, I loathe it. I can't bear it any longer. You don't know what it is doing to me, I don't know what is happening to me, and I'm afraid. Sometimes I think it is I who am going mad. I'm always alone – always. You don't know ... '

'Why shouldn't I know?' asked Charles. 'I was alone for eight years. Quite alone.' He did not sound in the least sorry or bitter about it. 'There is one thing I can promise, to comfort you: it gets better after about three years. The longer you stay, the better it gets. In the end you may decide to stay for ever.'

'I would die first.'

'You would have to,' said Charles pleasantly. 'It happens quite naturally. When you are alone, you grow – you alter completely. You are changing, Louise.'

That was true. Something of Louise was struggling to live but giving itself up slowly to die. She was angry. She was being killed by them all, by Charles and Emily and the remembrance of Don, by the silence and the noise of the place, by the heaviness of the sky and the stretch of water and the empty dusty plain, by the nearness and the cruelty and noise and stench of the bazaar . . . Who would not die? cried Louise. No one could be herself here. No one could exist here and remain herself. I am dying, dying, dying, cried Louise, and I do not want to die.

Charles watched the struggle in her face, the tense nervousness of the way she stood, with set shoulders and quick fingers, plucking at her handkerchief; and he said, 'Why don't you give in, Louise?'

'To Emily?'

'I was not talking of Emily.'

She turned suddenly and dramatically appealing, her eyes dark with tears. 'Let me go away, Charles—'

Charles waited a moment before he answered, watching her, 'You can go, but – I shall keep the children.'

'Keep the children!' That had not for one moment occurred to her. '*But you can't.* They can't stay here with you.'

'Why not? All these years I have worked honestly for them, faithful to them – and to you; and I think that is more than you can say – isn't it, Louise?'

'I . . . It doesn't matter to you what I do. That is nothing to do with it.'

'Isn't it? It most certainly is. I am very particular and fastidious about my children and – Emily is getting older.'

Slowly Louise's face was stained with a sudden deep painful red.

'That matters, doesn't it?' said Charles.

He wondered why she always wore these soft falling-away colours that he hardly noticed at the time and could not forget afterwards. He wondered why her hair shone so deeply in the light that it had all the shades of gold in it, ending with the brilliance of dark wallflower gold in its knot. He wondered why he still could not keep himself from the thought of touching her hair – and her skin; he could not forget the touch of her skin, he could not be satisfied until he touched it again. But she was talking of Emily.

'Emily!' she cried. 'You are obsessed with Emily.'

'I would be if I had any sense,' said Charles.

'Why are you helping Emily against me?'

'I'm not,' said Charles. 'She doesn't need me. She doesn't need help. She is fighting a large-sized battle, not only against you – and I should like to see her win. I hope she doesn't hurt herself too badly in the course of it, but I can't help her. I think she will win,' said Charles; 'she is remarkably full of power, poor brat.'

'Nonsense.'

'She is a very tenacious person,' he said. His lips twitched; he was thinking of Emily's attack that morning . . .

('Charles, what diseases do people get besides whooping cough and measles, mumps, scarlet fever, dysentery, malaria, and chicken pox and smallpox and plague?')

('Quite a lot more,' said Charles.)

('Tell me some.')

('Here in India – tuberculosis.')

('Do dogs get tuberculosis?')

('I believe they can, but it's not common.')

('Is it terribly dangerous and catching?')

('It can be dangerous and it can be caught, but not all in a minute like that.')

('Oh! Have you heard of people getting distemper? Or worms? They don't get tick-fever, do they?')

(Emily!)

'She is only a child,' said Louise.

'That is no reason why her powers of tenacity should be smaller than mine – or even yours. She is fighting you, Louise—'

'I know. That is what I can't understand. How can she keep this up – for so long against me – as if she hated me?'

'Perhaps she does,' said Charles.

'She couldn't, Charles.'

'It's against all tradition, isn't it?' And he asked, 'What are you going to do about it?'

'What can I do? What can I do? I try to ignore it, but after a time – it's ridiculous to say it – but it's becoming – eerie.'

Charles said nothing and in the pause the cricket's scrape seemed to rise a notch higher. Above the drums the dog still yapped.

'Charles – the servants don't like it.'

'No, they don't.'

'Things are happening. That is the odd part. Things that Emily could not possibly have thought of. Have you heard – about the footmarks at the washing *ghat*, for instance?'

At the northern end of the College tank, the washerman had his *ghat*. The College was walled on all sides, its gates kept shut, the washerman told this story, and it spread quickly through the College servants to the bazaar:

'The only dogs in the place are the small cat-dogs of Pool Memsahib and cat-dogs have paws with little pads that print small shapes when they run. It was not the cat-dogs. Well, we carry the clothes from the boiling and they are dipped and beaten and then spread on the grass for bleaching, but now – if we leave them to turn our heads or go inside – all over them are lines of footprints, a dog's footprints – too small to be confused with anything else, a leopard or a cow – too large to be the cat-dogs' – footprints the exact size of the black dog that used to run on them before, the black dog who is dead, the black dog that the Missy Sahib says is still alive.

'It could not be the black dog. The black dog is dead. Well, who has seen another dog? What other dog is there? How could a dog come into the College grounds? No one has seen it, no one has heard it, but the prints are there.'

Only the washerman's wife, sitting by the clothes at the verge of the tank and eating what her husband left for her in the pot, had heard the English children calling and whispering in the garden next door and felt something go by her like a clap of wind that sent coldness into her stomach so that she retched and the food fell out of her mouth.

After this it was alleged that Kokil had caused the body to be tied to a brick and thrown into the tank and that anyone who chose to come there at night would see the *bhût*, the ghost, rise from the water and drag the brick across to a certain tree. Now nobody swept leaves up under that tree and a little lime was put on the trunk and a few rags tied along the branches; and every-one was very careful not to look at Emily, the familiar of the ghost, if they should chance to meet her.

She noticed a curious falling away from her wherever she went. 'They don't seem to like me any more,' said Emily; 'but you don't mind me, do you, Shah?'

'I don't mind,' said Shah amiably. 'I had an uncle possessed of a devil myself.'

That shook Emily. It was flattering but it was frightening. Frightening ... When she saw the paw marks on the sheets, her eyes went bright with fear.

'Do you know anything about this?' Louise was peremptory.

Silence.

'Answer my question.'

At that moment Emily could not answer the question, her throat and her tongue were dry.

'Emily. Answer me.'

She licked her lips. 'It's Don.'

'Don't be absurd.'

'It's just like Don,' she argued. 'He was always doing it.'

'You did this yourself.'

'I? How could I?'

'That is what I want to know.'

'I couldn't do that. Could I? Could I?' Even Louise caught the appeal, and the perplexity and doubt in her voice.

'She has started something that she can't stop,' said Louise, and suddenly she cried, 'Why doesn't that dog stop its yapping?'

'Now you are being ridiculous.'

'I know I am. Do you think I don't know that? I know I am – and I can't stop it! I can't help it. It's this house and this place – and all of you. All of you!'

'That is a *pai*-dog tied up on the other side of the bazaar,' said Charles; 'and a *pai* must get in and run over the washing too. You know that, Louise.'

She answered slowly, 'I think – I'm beginning to be haunted. Everything is worse since this started. Something dreadful is going to come from it; it will fall on someone, somewhere. I know it will. I'm haunted by it. Why? I *think*, I truly think that Don was mad.'

'And you wanted to get away, didn't you?' said Charles.

'You mean I used Don—'

'I mean Don was convenient.'

'That is an abominable thing to say.' Charles shrugged. 'You will see,' she cried, 'you will see. I shall prove to be right in the end.'

'I expect you will,' said Charles wearily. 'It doesn't matter much. In the end there must be such a small difference between being right and being wrong—'

'And what of the risks?' asked Louise.

'I am not denying the risks.'

'What would you have done then?'

'I should have recognized the risks,' said Charles slowly. 'I should have pointed them out, particularly to Emily. We should have treated them with the dignity they deserved, because they are grave risks. We should have given Don every possible chance; and then we should have carried him to his appointed end. It would have been appointed then, you know,' said Charles.

'You are even beginning to think like an Indian.'

'That is no bad thing in a way,' said Charles, and he asked, 'Why don't you give in? Tell Emily, Louise.'

'That is what she wants me to do. What she is trying to make me say.'

'Well, why not? It is true.'

'No. You must speak to her,' said Louise. 'I shall not give in to her. She must learn she is not her own master. She would listen to you.' She tried to speak lightly but there was anger in her voice. 'She has always been fickle, perhaps because her

feelings are not very deep, and she forms these – these attach-
ments for people – the Nikolides for instance; I remember at
Bellevue she was ridiculously fond of Félix, the cook, for a
little while.'

'And now she has a ridiculous attachment for me,' said
Charles drily. 'Well, as it happens, I rather value that and I won't
do anything to harm it. You can speak to her yourself.'

'I can't—' and she cried, 'I seem to have lost her since I came
here.'

'What makes you think you ever had her?' asked Charles.

Louise was stung. 'If you had seen her in Paris—'

'I did not see her in Paris. Nor did you,' said Charles. 'You
have never seen Emily in your life, not Emily as she is. Come to
that, you have never seen anything as it is in your life. I am
warning you, Louise, you are doing something unforgivable. One
day you will do more than you mean – some serious damage. If
you don't take care. If you don't take care, Louise ...'

VIII

It was easier for Narayan to wish to forget than to forget. To begin with, every morning the Pool car drew up at the gate and Kokil came in with the Pekingese. They delighted and interested Shila very much.

'What kind of dogs are those?' she asked, 'or are they cats?'

'Of course they are not cats. They are poodles,' said Narayan. 'Moreover, they are very valuable.'

Shila knew that already. They were sent in a car. Tarala for instance had never been in a car; they were having injections, costly ones from Calcutta as if they were humans; Tarala had asked Kokil how they were fed – they were fed on mutton and chicken and fish; and they had come in a steamer from England.

'And meanwhile there is starvation and famine and war on every side,' said Narayan.

The injections given these rare and valuable dogs that had never been heard of in Amorra gave him a certain prestige, but at the same time it offended him. Again he felt as if he were interfering ... But if I go on like this, I shall have to give up practice, he said. If I am interfering with fate by giving an anti-rabic injection, I interfere by giving a drench to a horse or a cow. Pool is interfering with fate by teaching the people to fertilize their lands. That is not sense ... And it seemed to him in that depressed moment that it was unspiritual to have any sense at all. He said this aloud to Shila simply because he had to say it aloud.

She offered timidly, 'Perhaps you are fate, you and Mr Pool.'

That salved him for a moment but his conscience was so tender that anything that reminded him of the morning at the Pools made him wince. Yet all the time he was trying to remember ... what? Why should he need to remember when he wished, so much, to forget? What could have happened in this affair that he ought to remember? He could not think of it. He gave the Pekingese injections each morning as soon as the serum arrived from the Pasteur Institute. With it came a yellow paper that he had seen before.

Under no circumstances, said the paper, *should the dog be destroyed – for by doing so one of the most important signs of rabies, viz. the short duration of life, is lost and proof cannot be obtained* ... You see, you see, the thought that was haunting him burst out, there is no proof. I am sure, now I am sure, he was not mad ... And he longed, would have given anything, for a proof – a proof. If one of the Pekingese died of hydrophobia, that would be tantamount to proof, but as he looked at them – even for that relief – he could not wish death on them. So he continued gloomily to give them injections.

'I don't know if it is necessary,' said Charles, 'I don't suppose it is, but my wife wants them to be done.'

'I see.'

'You have no objection to doing them?'

'No, no. I shall be glad.' He did not sound at all glad.

Charles looked at him and paused. 'Das – I know my wife is – nervous. You had no doubt, had you – in your own mind – that the dog was mad?'

That was the question Narayan had been dreading, but while he was still wincing he answered, 'None whatever.'

No bites or scratches were found on Sun and Picotee. He gave them seven injections each.

Sun stood without a sound, his forelegs braced, his head turned thrown back and his face drawn into lines of acute silent suffering, every hair stiff; Picotee's tail dropped between her legs in a hopeless trailing, and she would not stand up. She lay limp and abandoned to her fate on the table and every morning she gave a piercing cry as the needle went in. All the same Narayan would rather have injected her than Sun. Sun's silence was unnerving, but after it was over every day they both went into rhapsodies of relief and joy, leaping and dancing and barking.

'They are nearly human,' cried Shila in delight, but Narayan found this study in character disturbing; character in a Pekingese, character worth respecting, like Sun's? He was glad when the injections came to an end and they need come no more.

'Send me the bill,' said Charles. Narayan did not want to send it, but Charles insisted.

'But – what shall I charge you?'

'I don't know. Charge by the visit.'

He wrote out the bill:

To seven visits from Mrs Pool's poodle dog   Rs 7.
To seven visits from Mrs Pool's poodle slut   Rs 7.

He did not charge for Don.

The money came by return and with it, in Charles's writing,

a postscript *Attending a dog at my house, Rs 4*. It lay on the desk untouched. Narayan kept looking at it all day.

He would have liked to confide in Anil. No, he could not possibly have confided in Anil, and anyway Anil was curiously elusive at the moment . . . I have not seen him for days. He does not come near me, grumbled Narayan. Soon it will be the end of term . . . He recalled himself sharply, he had forgotten the Examination . . . Of course I have not seen Anil. How could I? He is working every moment . . . but his vision of the end of term refused to be of Anil sitting in the Examination Hall, pinned to his papers; it was of Anil going home for the Durga *puja* holidays, where all the ritual of the *puja* fortnight would be prepared.

They will have Durga *puja* in their own house, said Narayan. They will have ornaments for the Goddess, of real gold – all the rapacious and idle and greedy will gather there to be fed. Money will be poured out on a ceremony that has no reality at all. Ceremony is the curse of this land . . . But in spite of his scornful and sensible words his mind was already following the story of the *puja* and it seemed to him simple and beautiful. Nearly all the Hindu festivals have a quality of naïveté, and it is this that keeps them fresh; they come with a piquant shock of promise and surprise each year. It does not matter how many Durga and Lakshmi *pujas* are lived through, the *puja* is perpetually new.

The Goddess Durga is the consort of Siva; she keeps house for him, but once a year she too goes back to her father's house; the festival celebrates her visit and in her wake all the sons and daughters of Hindu Bengal go back to their homes. Durga ends her holiday on the fourth day and her spirit is returned to her husband by the immersion of her image in the river; but the sadness of her leaving is healed in the worship of her daughter

Lakshmi, the Goddess of Good Fortune, on the day and night of the full moon ... Childish nonsense! cried Narayan, but suddenly he called Shila.

'It is getting near the holidays,' he said. She did not answer but he knew by the sudden constraint on her face, the trembling of the edges of her lips and nostrils, what she was waiting for. The festivals start with the autumn new moon, and last, with a short break, through the nights when the moon grows, until the full moon. Last year Narayan had forbidden Shila to keep the sacred days; nothing was allowed into the house, not a gift or an extra cake, or the smallest image. 'It is silly superstition,' said Narayan.

Shila's heart had been hot with shame; in every Hindu house the festival had the significance of Christmas; the chief and most joyful days of the year; the Government observed it, offices were shut, universities and schools closed, everyone went home on holiday, everyone joined in worship – except Narayan; and Shila's shame was sharpened by fear for him; goddesses were easily offended. If arrows of fire shot from an invisible bow had pierced him now as he sat at his desk, she would not have been surprised.

But instead, Narayan was handing her a small pile of notes. 'Take this money,' he said, 'and buy whatever is necessary. You can use it and more. Make a list of the presents we should give, for Tarala and whomever it is suitable.'

She did not move. He had to open her hand and put the money into it.

'But last year ...' She was mystified, trying to find out from his face why he had changed. 'Last year, we did not have – anything ...'

'Is that any reason why this year we should not?'

He saw himself beneficent, a patriarch, as if his family were twenty and not two. Then he was aware that a delicate struggle was filling Shila.

'What is it?' he said. 'What is it you want to ask me?' and with a return of his old irritation he cried, 'Well, ask. Ask. Ask.'

'Indro ...' she asked. 'Shall you ... go to the temple?'

He hesitated. 'I may go to take you' – and he said magnificently: 'It is necessary that I should inform myself of these things from time to time.'

He stood up and went to the doorway, where the steps led to the verandah, and he looked down past them to the river and the bank stretching out of sight. Everything he could see was either green or blue or white; the flat blue-white of the water, repeating the sky, the green of the bank and the foliage in his garden and the floating water weeds, and sharp touches of white, the clouds, a water-lily that had opened under the jetty, and along the banks, the tossing white heads of the pampas bushes.

'Wherever I see pampas I know it is autumn,' said Narayan.

'And when it is autumn the festival time is here,' whispered Shila. 'We shall keep it in our house. We shall make Durga *puja* at the temple – we shall have our tiny *Sree* – we shall have gifts ...' and she began to plan them.

'Tarala shall have new clothes – I shall make cakes for the children. Indro – you need new shoes, and new shirts.'

'Not from that money,' cried Narayan; 'that is the condition. All, all of it is to be spent on the festival only. It is not for gifts. Spend it for worship. Give it for the feeding of the beggars. Take it and make it good. Give nothing of it to me.' And he said, as he had said before, 'Do not remind me of it ever again.'

IX

There was nothing of autumn in the night. It was hot with the heat of September that is deadly and stifling, as if all the months of stifling nights and days had culminated in the end of summer. The moon was old, nearly gone, the stars seemed to shine for themselves without shedding their light, there were clouds, and the heat was manifested in the blackness that was still and black and hot, pressing down upon the town and on the houses; pressing round the beds where some people lay in an exhausted slumber, where some people could not sleep.

The College was silent, without a light; it was possible only to make out the darker buildings against the dark sky; on the tree that wept into the tank, the flowers were dying with a sick heavy smell. The watchman's lantern was on the drive but the watchman had disappeared, he had gone into the shadows and lain down to sleep, with his stomach pressed into the cool verandah stones. Shah had sensibly gone to bed in nothing but a loincloth, and his stiff-cut starched and polished uniform was left by itself in his house, where it could be seen by the light of his oil lamp, looking strangely more like Shah himself than the thin dark sleeper on the bed.

In the bazaar the unknown dog was still yapping, and Louise was awake in her room. It seemed to her now that she had not slept through a night since she came; and the endless void of dark wakeful hours culminated, like the heat, in these tonight. She heard Charles downstairs, she heard him get up and go into the garden; once she thought he came upstairs and she lay, tense, waiting, and held her face down into her pillow so that she would not call out to him in her loneliness: 'I am awake – and bitterly lonely – lonely. Lonely—' But the pillow muffled the words.

Once she heard Emily turn, and move her bed. What did she want? Louise was not alone in the night; Emily was awake too; but Louise shrank from speaking to her; Emily still had Don's bed beside her.

It was dark; she longed for a light but lay perversely in the dark. There was a sound on the stairs that might have been a rat. A lizard slid down the wall near her bed with a *tck* that sounded loudly in her ear, and outside with the babel of night sounds, jackals began to howl; they howled like all the lost souls and banshees and ghosts in the world wailing together. The wind stirred in the sides of her mosquito-net and the blown-in sides touched her bed with a slurring animal sound that made her catch her breath, and she screamed for Charles.

She held her hand across her mouth struggling to hold that scream. She wanted Charles. She wanted his actual physical presence here beside her, she wanted to feel him and to touch him ... How can I? she cried. She must be shocked at herself; she tingled. What are you thinking of, Louise!

It is only the night, she reasoned; it was the night and the heat and her sleeplessness and the worry over Emily. It was only Emily that made her think of Charles . . . Emily, I blame you for everything that has happened . . . I see you, Emily . . . And exasperation swept up in a storm at the way she had to see Emily now. For days Emily had worn a blind and wooden face, blind with obstinacy, wooden with determination, chalk-white; even her hair had a toneless look. Emily was so plain these days that the sight of her gave a pull to Louise's heart; and she was taller, grown long in the legs, even her hair had outgrown its little-girl length; she had begun to look adolescent . . . Nonsense, she is only a child, said Louise; but Emily was exhibiting every sign of developing into a girl, with new glimpses of grace under her gawkiness, and soft swellings round her nipples of which she was secretly conscious and ashamed . . .

It's the country, cried Louise; I hate it. Look what it has done to Emily. I don't want her to grow up. She is still a child. She shall be a child . . . And she had a vision of Emily as she had been when she was a baby, between her and Charles, a baby girl, precious as a nest, bright as a star, with yellow silky fluff standing out from her head, in that sentimental glance, like a Holy Child's halo . . . what has happened to her since? asked Louise. What has happened in between? I don't know. What have we been doing? . . . And the answer came back to her. *What have you been doing?* That question seemed to be asked her again, with a deafening loudness: *What have you been doing?*

It sounded through Louise, loudly, accusingly, and she sat up in bed, shaking, pushing off the darkness. The whole of her body was wet, and she felt as if she were suffocating with blackness and heat and remorse and fear . . .

Emily, stop. Please, please stop it, Emily. I am coming to tell you: This cannot go on any longer. It must be stopped. I will give in to you for ever if only you will stop it; if only you will take that look off your face, try to be more natural and more childish, grow more flesh on your bones, show life in your hair. I did kill Don. You guessed it and you were right. I did lie to you. Yes, I did. I did. I did. I did it all so swiftly that it happened in one impulse. I was caught in it even before it was done and that is why I did it; under the laudable, plausible motives, that is why I did it. Panic comes like blood to my brain – you cannot understand that. Of course not, you are too young . . . Charles was the only one who did understand! Charles! Only Charles – and at the thought of him she began to cry.

She swung her feet down off the bed to the floor, the solid stone floor checked her crying and she groped in the darkness for the switch of the light. The light hurt her eyes, smarting with tiredness and tears, and she sobbed again, calling Emily and Charles confusedly – 'Charles – but I must talk to Emily. I have to tell her what I did to Don . . . ' And she knew, surely and certainly then, that Don had not been mad . . . I killed him . . . She saw the doubtful, unwilling face of the veterinary doctor . . . I made him do it, I made him guilty too . . . And she listened and heard, still, clearly, across the night noises, the yapping of the dog.

'Emily,' she cried. 'Emily! Emily!'

She ran down the verandah to Emily's bed. She stopped and there was a long silence.

Emily's bed was empty.

X

Idleness stayed with Anil. 'What has happened to your work, Banerjee?' Everyone asked him that, angrily, sternly or reproachfully, with curiosity from the other students, without surprise from Professor Dutt. 'Young men are folly. All, all of them,' the Professor would often say, and he gave Anil back his books without a scolding. 'You have not made up your notes. Why do you hand them to me?'

'He will not get his pass, will he, Sir?'

'I expect that he will not,' the Professor said mildly and Anil looked back at him with a smile so sweet and brilliant that the old man stayed, his breath caught, staring until he picked up his ancient umbrella that sheltered him across the quadrangle, and scurried off the dais out of the room.

'What is the matter with you, Anil?' His friends crowded round him, but Anil pushed them away.

'I am engaged on an idyll of idleness.' They thought he was being humorous, but it was true. In Anil's room was a little glazed image of Saraswati, the Goddess of Learning, and now she was wreathed in jasmine flowers though Anil did no work. It was reported that he lay on his bed and looked at her, and sometimes he sauntered alone in the garden, holding her on the palm of his hand. This quixotic behaviour violently confirmed public opinion that he would take all the prizes, and other aspirants grew sulky: it was awkward for them, they dared not copy Anil and leave off their studies abandoning themselves to Saraswati, they needed every hour for study, and they were forced to appear to their admirers as neither so clever nor so pious as Anil. Naturally Anil had more adherents than they.

He did not want them. He spent his days alone. He sat through his lectures in a veritable fortress of thoughts, it was so impregnable; or else he cut them and lay on his bed in his room, not answering when anyone knocked at his door. In the evening he went out walking, so far and so fast that in such weather not even the most devoted cared to follow him. He left Narayan's letters unanswered and did not go to his house.

People began to stare at him. He looked different, there was an elation about him and his eyes were excited though he was usually quiet, but sometimes they would hear him singing loudly and nasally and when they asked him, he did not know he had been singing. A rumour began that Anil Krishna Banerjee was drinking.

His walks were long and solitary. He walked by the river, far beyond the easy trodden paths where the students walked to get the breeze; he left the houses and the path behind, until the only path was a narrow deep-pitted one where the men who towed the boats put their feet; he had seen them, when the breeze fell, drop out from the boat near the land with a rope, and putting the loop of it round their chests, strain on it and draw boat and cargo and family along. Anil would have liked to try it but he was shy of the narrowness of his chest and his lightness; probably the boat would pull him off into the river.

On the low ground, when the river had receded after the rains, it had left great shallow lakes; and there he found water-lilies, and hyacinths and grasses of a bright surprising green, and villages built out of the water on stilts; once a flight of duck lifted out of the water almost over his head with a flash of their white breasts; a feather drifted down, it was the same white as the tufts of pampas grass.

He went into the fields and here the water had dried and the earth had a richness it had only at this season; paddy birds, white and long in leg and bill as little cranes, pecked in it and the farmers were finishing their ploughing; all across the plain they could be seen over and over again – in a repeating pattern of a little man, a yoke of oxen, and the earth turned up in dark lines on the fields. Weeds were stacked in the fields and these made, on the pattern, round purplish dots – some of them were fired in the evening and then the pattern altered: the chequered lines of the field walls were lost in the rising mist, the men and the oxen had gone and in their place the dark bone shape of the plough was left alone, and one after the other the fires burnt red and a spiral of white smoke went up into the evening.

With his power of bribing, Anil stayed out late. When he came home he wrote poems, he sat up writing them most of the night and with unusual reticence he did not show them to everyone. He showed them only to Narayan.

Narayan was always enthusiastic over Anil's work. That meant nothing. 'I want you to show them to Sir Monmatha Ghose,' said Anil, 'I want you to show them even to Mr Pool.'

Narayan showed them to Professor Dutt. 'But these are good!' said Professor Dutt in unflattering surprise. 'I must show these to the Principal,' but before he could do this, Anil asked Narayan to get them back. 'I can't spare them,' he said, 'I want to finish them first.'

'There is no hurry. Let him show one or two for an opinion.'

'I don't want an opinion,' said Anil crossly. 'I know what they are like for myself. I want to finish them first.'

'But Anil, it is to your interest—'

'Let me finish them first.'

That was the only thing that spoiled these days for Anil. He was oppressed by a feeling of hurry; nothing else mattered but the finishing of the poems. He must finish them. He must get them down and he did not know how many there would be nor even what they would be; he knew they would follow one after the other, but to achieve them took a great deal of idling and dreaming and moving about. He had to shut himself away. Often, now, he went out at dawn and slept out under a tree at midday and walked on in the evening.

Often he missed the evening meal at the Hostel and then he would ask the villagers for food. One night, at dusk, when he had been out all day, he asked an old man sitting on his house step, where his and his son's supper was laid out on plantain leaves; he had a little rice and vegetables and sauce and a brass *lota* of pepper-water.

'May I eat with you?'

'How can you eat with us? You are a Brahmin.'

'I can eat with anyone,' said Anil happily and he joined them, but when supper was over and the women had taken away their share, the father began to scold. The supper had been too small to stop his hunger and he wished he had not given any of it away.

'You are a Brahmin. You should not say the things you say, let alone do them,' he scolded Anil.

'It does not matter what I do,' said Anil dreamily.

'You are not yourself. You are your caste!' said the old man. 'What would they say?'

'I shall not be there to hear it,' answered Anil as he drifted away.

It was dark. The moon was over and ready to rise again. As he followed the dark path only the dried jute stick stack, white and brittle, piled in the branches of a tree, showed him when he had come to the edge of the village, and it was difficult to find his way across the fields though some of the weed piles were still smoking. As he came through the back streets of the town where the electric light had not yet been taken, every doorway was filled with the warm soft light of wicks in oil, except where a more wealthy family had the roaring glare of petrol lamps. He passed those quickly and looked in at the door of the huts where the earth walls were turned to gold, for they looked attractive and a little romantic. Sometimes a woman came to the door with a light in her hand, a bowl with a single wick floating in it that lit her neck and chin and left her face in darkness; the effect of that seen over and over again was mysterious and quickening. Outside the men were talking and smoking a hookah or cheap cigarettes, and their voices followed Anil down the road. He knew they all looked after him. The bicycles passed continuously and some, like those of the clerks who went to Charles's house, had bicycle lights and others had none and their riders carried wicks with shields made of paper bags. They passed him and whizzed into the night . . .

Why do they go so fast? Why do they all hurry? . . . One of them seemed to recognize him. A voice cried out of the darkness, 'Good de luck, good de luck,' as it went by. Why should it call 'good luck'? And suddenly he remembered with a jar that tomorrow was Examination Day. For a moment he was startled, but the Examination seemed oddly remote and he discarded the thought of it; but it had given him a small shock ...

How quickly time has gone, he said. What have I been doing? I have so much to do ... and a nervous tension filled him over the finishing of his poems. On a verandah as he passed, women were working, rolling betel leaves for the festival; one had a tray of round cakes made of coconut and sugar, *puja* cakes ... And soon I must go home, cried Anil in dismay. I cannot go till I have finished my poems ...

He walked on and on, out of the town and into it again, thinking, composing, thinking. He sat down on a doorstep under a street light and wrote down his poem with a pencil he had in his pocket and a piece of paper he found in the road, the side of a torn paper bag. It was the best he had done and when it was written, safely caught, fixed on the paper, he was tired, very tired. The tiredness was perfection. He was sure it was the best poem he had written, he felt it was very near the best poems in the world, and it had been as difficult as if he had caught something as wild and terrific as a star and induced it to lie pulsing in his torn piece of paper. Very tired, he stood up to go home.

As he walked a mood of bliss lapped him; he discovered that he was gently drunk with it. The spirit of festival was already in him ... I feel excited, full of undercurrents of excitement ... And the undercurrents threatened to well up and swamp him ... What is the matter with me? I feel – too much ... That was the only way he could describe it and for a moment he felt alarmed, but he answered himself ... It is the poem. The whole of me is full of my poem. At the moment I am my poem. What a good thing I wrote it down quickly. If I had not written it down it might have choked me. I should have been choked by my own poem. I must be quieter. I must distil – yes, distil my poems – as the moon distils itself, surely and certainly. The moon ... And he stumbled in the dark and stubbed his toe.

Slightly chastened, he arrived limping at the gates of the College and gave a gentle double knock and the porter in his sleep let him in and sank on to his bed again.

Anil walked across the grass where the trees made thickets of blackness in the dark. The tank lay dark and opaque with only a faint spread reflection from the stars. Suddenly Anil stopped. At the top of the steps was a figure, sitting with its back towards him. After a moment he went on towards it and now he saw in the uncertain starlight that it was small, very pale in the darkness, with a fall of colourless hair. He had almost believed it was an apparition when it heard him and he saw it jump. It put up its hand and said in a clear imperious English, 'Hush!' He saw it was a child of Charlie Chang's.

If Anil had met Emily or any of her kind in everyday life he would have been nonplussed, but in this mood of exaltation under the darkness, he came up to her and asked, 'Why hush?'

In her ordinary senses Emily would have been paralysed with meeting a stranger, Indian or English, suddenly and alone in the dark; but she would also have been terrified of going out alone even as far as Shah's house at the gate, and she was particularly afraid of jackals. She was exalted like Anil but it was an exaltation of ecstatic bravery, almost hysterical, brought on by fear and misery and amazement at herself. Anil's voice reassured her; she could only see his white clothes blown a little by the night wind that had started in the garden, and the flickering movement of his hand as he held down the tails of his tunic, but she could see he was an Indian.

'How do you do?' she said. 'I suppose you are a student at the College.'

Anil became equally formal. 'Yes, I am a student, and you must be Miss Pool.'

'I am Emily Pool.'

'My name is Anil Krishna Banerjee.' He began to have the slight joviality of a grown-up speaking to a child and Emily became immediately more distant.

'How do you do,' she said, and Anil knew at once that she was displeased, just as he knew at once that he liked her. He could not see more of her than her shape and the fall of her hair but he liked the way her voice came back to him in the darkness like a bell with a clear certain tone. She quieted him; he felt that he was meant to meet her, that she was bound in with his destiny, and he hated to offend her. He wanted to amend what he had said but he did not know how to and there began a stilted social conversation between them.

'Do you like it here in India?'

'Yes, thank you.'

'I expect that you find it hot.'

'Very hot.'

'You came from France in the war, I think.'

'Yes.'

'Was the war then bad?'

'Very bad,' said Emily briefly; it was plain she did not want to talk about it. Anil could think of nothing more to say though he wanted to say more and the silence grew longer and longer between them. Then Emily, feeling it was her turn, asked the only question she could think of, 'Do you like being a student?'

'I have enjoyed it, yes.'

He did not know he had answered in the past until she asked, 'You are not a student any more then?'

He said suddenly, 'Miss Pool, I ceased to be a student about three weeks since.'

'Oh. What are you now?'

He answered at once because he knew exactly, 'I am a poet.'

'Oh,' said Emily again.

'You think that is a pity?'

'Yes.'

'But why? It is very nice to be a poet. Shouldn't you like it? Shouldn't you like to be a poet?'

'No I should not,' said Emily decidedly. 'Poets die young.'

Anil laughed. 'What a funny girl you are.'

'They do. There was Shelley, and Keats and Chatterton. They all died young.'

'You learn that in your books. It is not necessarily true. I am happy as a poet. I will sit no more in class. I will not study in books when I can study in the world. All these years I have been glued to work. I wonder that I let them make a fool of me so long.'

Emily objected. 'When you are young you have to do lessons.'

'Yes, that is so. When I was a boy, for instance, we had a very disagreeable schoolmaster; besides our lessons we had to wait on him, we even had to press his legs and rub them when he was resting and he had very skinny legs.'

For some reason that soothed Emily and pleased her; she laughed. Anil felt success spreading through him and he said, 'Now I am wondering what you do here for lessons.'

'I do lessons with Professor Dutt.'

'Old Granny Dutt? This is a link between us. He is my tutor too, at least formerly I was with him.' He was surprised that so small a girl could be so advanced. 'I thought you would learn with your mother.'

'No.' There was an edge to that and he did not miss it. Anil, who did not really listen to any voice but his own, was curiously alive to Emily's.

'Miss Pool – no, I shall call you Emily – what would your mother say if she knew you were here tonight?'

There was no answer.

'I think you should not have come here by yourself. Would she not be angry if you were to be seen?'

'No one will see me. No one will come here now when it is dark.'

'I am not surprised,' said Anil. 'It is very spooky. When first I saw you I thought you were a ghost.'

'Did you?' asked Emily breathlessly. 'That is – odd.' And she said as if she was surprised at herself for telling him, 'I came – to see a ghost.' And she added quickly, 'Of course I know it isn't here.'

'Then why did you come to see it?'

'Because—' reluctantly she said – 'it is something to do with me.'

'A ghost and you?' But they did not seem such odd companions.

'I heard them talking and I came to see. It's my ghost.' And she said a little defiantly, 'It is the ghost of my dog.'

'Then the dog is dead?' said Anil gently.

'Perhaps he is dead,' said Emily in a still flat voice.

That was the best of talking to Indians. They asked you questions without limit but they would never press you for any particular answer; they understood perfectly how to slide from one thing to another. 'Come – he is, or is not, dead?' Anil might have asked her, but instead he told her, 'My father used to keep dogs when I was a boy. They were Great Danes and they were very costly, but he gave them up; my mother used to make him take them and feed them outside the house.'

'Why?'

'Because we are of Hindu faith; we are Brahmin; and the dogs of course ate meat. That we do not allow and my mother was extremely orthodox. My father also is orthodox now, more so than my mother. Before I left they asked of me a vow that I would not take anything forbidden, not even eggs – but milk of course I take.'

'But don't you like eggs?'

'I don't know. I have not tasted them.'

'But you are grown up,' said Emily with yearning in her voice, 'you can do what you like.'

'No. Still I cannot. I have taken this vow and it would be wicked of me to eat these things.'

'In France,' said Emily thoughtfully, 'it was wicked not to eat,' and she thought of Madame Souviens and how she would kiss her fingers when she spoke of her onion and cheese cake, and the voice in which she said, '*une bonne soupe*,' and she remembered the soup at the Nikolides'. 'Can you eat soup?' she asked.

'There are certain soups ...' but Emily had gone from Madame Souviens to the morning with the Nikolides; through the cracks of the jetty the water looked miraculously clear blue, and she saw first Binnie then herself pass inside the house to breakfast and she smelled the champac flowers as she went ... And all the time – all the time – while I was away ...

'Your ghost does not come,' said Anil.

'I didn't think he would.' He heard the same bright-edged break in the words and he tried again to see her face. What kind of child was this that could have such grief and contain it? Anil was profoundly stirred. 'But you hoped?' he said gently.

He felt a tremor go through her. Though she was sitting only on the step beside him, even her hand not touching him, he felt the tremor clearly. She gave a little cry like a choke and hid her face in her hands. He could only catch one or two words dropped from the confusion of crying. 'No one ... gone ... in the night ... tell them ... no one ... no one ... Mother ... no one ...'

Anil could not bear it. He put his arm round her and drew her close and through the thin muslin of his shirt he could feel the wet heat of her cheeks and eyes, and the movement of her lashes and the shaking of her body; the whole of her was throbbing with sorrow and emotion, trying to escape, beating its way out in a tumult of words and tears. Anil did not know what to do, so he simply held her, and from her an unaccustomed smell rose to his nostrils that made her even more incomprehensible – the mild fresh smell of a well-kept English child – and it disconcerted Anil; he held her and muttered small cajoling words that he did not know he remembered and that he had not heard since he left his nurse; gradually they penetrated to Emily. She could not understand them but she was comforted by them; they were friendly and his shoulder was slight but firm and she too was arrested by the unfamiliar smell of him; she began to cry a little less and sniff a little more.

'Have you no handkerchief?'

Emily shook her head and wiped her nose on the back of her hand; Anil appeared to think that would do as well. He did not like to ask her any more questions in case she began again, but he tightened his arm and said: 'Let us talk of this a little more, perhaps to talk may make it better. Truly I am very much concerned in this—' As he said that, very earnestly, a tremor like Emily's, but not like Emily's, seemed to run through him too – not of grief but of something even more solemn. It surprised him. He went on quickly, 'Suppose you were to see his ghost – now,' and he pointed dramatically, 'there—'

She turned sharply and quailed and looked across the tank as if she expected to see a devil, but there was nothing there but the still black tank, the few stars in it, the few fireflies above it.

'Now, now. You will not see it.' Anil comforted her. 'I think you will never see it. Once I heard of the spirit of a tiger, but not of any other animal. See, we watch for him to come. No. No. He does not come.'

There was no answer, only a grateful small rustle.

'And there is another thing,' said Anil, 'and why should you not do this? We, of Hindu religion, when we wish for the repose of a soul – that it shall rest in peace for instance – we make a small *puja* . . . '

'*Puja*?' asked Emily.

'Worship – celebration,' said Anil. 'In the month there are two periods, *devipaksha* when the moon is growing, and *Krishnapaksha* when the moon is going away; light nights and black nights; and the black nights are the times for ghosts. You will do your *puja* then. You can take, in some place under the tree for instance, a few good things: some fruit or sweets, some good sugar or rice or cakes, even some vegetables; and you will place them on a little table or platform that you have made look pretty, and if possible you will have flowers and a small light – and you will offer these things with prayers to the spirit for whom you wish to make peace, though by offering to one soul you offer to all, and for one year he will gain rest. It would not be irreverent for this especial dog, I think. Why should you not do that, please, Emily?'

Emily considered it. 'Soon – not yet.' But there was a distinct relief in her tone. She gave a sigh that came from the bottom of her heart.

Presently she asked, laying her hand on his knee, 'You are not a medical student, are you?'

'No. There are no medical students here. Why? Is there some question you wanted to know?'

'I wanted,' said Emily, and her voice was alert again, 'I wanted to know what diseases there are that people and dogs can get the same.'

'You should ask Das, my friend.'

'Dr Das, the vet?'

'He is a vet, he is also a very nice fellow.' Anil yawned. It was tiresome of Emily to turn this suddenly into a definite conversation; and then he looked down at her head below his shoulder – in the brightening starlight it looked pale, ruffled and worried; he could see one hand clenched against her cheek, she was thinking, and in front of her the dim spaces of the tank shone empty, and paler now there were more stars.

'Come,' he said, 'you should not be out at this time. Come, you must let me take you back to the house. We will ask for your spirit another night. When the moon is over – though I shall not be there—' and again that brimming of extraordinary excitement rose in him so that he caught his breath. 'Come,' he said when he could speak, and helped her to her feet. They walked across the grass; his stubbed toe hurt him abominably.

'Why do you limp?' asked Emily.

'I hurt my foot.'

'Lean on my shoulder.'

Anil smiled, and very lightly put his arm across her shoulders. They came in at the gate, past Shah sleeping soundly on his bed, and went up the drive between the dark shapes of the poinsettias to the house, where a light showed a width of railings on the top verandah and the shapes of two mosquito-nets. Anil looked curiously around him, he had not been so near a European house before. 'Who sleeps on the verandah?' he asked.

'That is where I sleep. That is my bed.'

They were pinned and held in a circle of light, they were blinded, their eyelids fluttered like moths' wings as they stood there fixed. Emily's shoulders jerked under Anil's arm and she shrank back against him. 'It's Mother,' she said.

Anil's stomach made a surprising movement on its own, totally unrelated to him; it gave a sudden terrified rumble; between shame and his premonition of fright he almost decided to go, but pride ran down his legs and stiffened them. He knew that he ought to go straight to Emily's mother and speak to her, but he could not bring himself to do quite that. Instead, he shook Emily's hand and said, 'Good night. You will be safe now. Someone is coming to find you, I think.'

'Wait! You are not to go.'

Louise's voice startled and shocked them, especially Emily. Anil was a visitor, even though it was the middle of the night. She said in rebuke, 'Mother, Mr – Anil is here.'

Louise brushed her aside and behind her and said to Anil in a suppressed icy voice, 'I cannot speak to you. You must wait for my husband.'

'Certainly.' Anil's own voice was high with dismay and the beginning of serious fright. 'Certainly I will wait, Mrs ——Mrs ——' He could think of nothing at all to call her but Mrs Chang.

'Don't speak to me.'

'Moth – *er*.'

'Emily, go and wait for me in my room. You are not to go near Binnie.'

Emily was really frightened. Louise looked like an apparition of herself, her hair streaming down, her face blenched, and the strong porch light made odd shiny planes and shadows in it; why did her skin look so queer? And then Emily saw with a shock that Louise's face was wet, and immediately Emily broke out into a cold wetness too. It was a relief, it took some of her fright away.

'Mother,' she said boldly, 'don't be so angry. Did you think I was lost? I'm sorry – Mother.'

'Go upstairs. Don't speak to me. I will deal with you later.' Emily put out a hand and Louise screamed, 'Don't touch me! Get away – upstairs.' The scream and recoil were so dreadful that Emily was struck dumb.

Anil at last began to speak. 'I demand explanation,' said Anil. 'I am a student at this College and as such am not under your authority, Madam.' The 'Madam' came trippingly to his tongue but his surprise and hurt swamped it. His voice grew shrill with indignation. 'I was just now returning from an evening's excursion—'

'That is a lie,' said Louise, and her voice was low after his; breathless and rapid. She was beside herself. 'The College is closed at eleven o'clock.' Anil, from sheer fright, smiled, and that drove Louise on to dramatic fury. 'If I were a man I should horsewhip you. That is what they would do to you in England. Flog you so that you should never forget. Don't try to defend yourself. I saw you. I heard you. How long has this been going on? Emily has been queer for days—'

And suddenly Emily could bear no more. She burst into loud

terrified wails like a baby and fled up the steps. Charles was standing in the doorway and he caught her just inside the door.

'Look at me,' said Charles. Trying to hold her sobbing she looked back at him from a tear-sodden face, ugly and swollen with crying, from tired tear-red eyes. He noticed that she was tidy, her hair was still held back from her face by her narrow white night ribbon, and she wore her old checked coat buttoned over blue and white pyjamas; except for her slippers that were wet and stained with grass, and her face that was wet and stained with tears, there was nothing to show for her expedition. Charles's face, very serious, relaxed as he looked at her. 'Go upstairs,' he said gently. 'Dry your feet and wait for me. I shan't be long.'

He went quickly down the steps. Anil and Louise were still there, Louise still fanatically speaking, Anil with his back to the darkness. The light threw their shadows a long way on the grass, Anil's was still but Louise's was exaggerated, mocking her movements, making them into antics and melodrama. Charles came up behind her and put his hands on her elbows holding them against her sides as if he wanted to crush them together. Louise screamed, but the ugly poisonous words finished abruptly; she struggled; he held her rigid in his grip, while his voice came over her head, quite politely: 'I think you had better go in, Louise. Emily is not hurt. She is quite all right,' and to Anil he said, 'Will you wait and talk to me for a few minutes? Don't go.'

Anil was a long way from going – or speaking. He was so absolutely shocked that he could not speak or move or think.

Charles was bruising Louise; the soft flesh of her arms was pinched under the hardness of his and his fingers pressed her down and back against him. 'Charles! Let me go! Let me go!'

but he turned her towards the house and impelled her up the steps.

He loosened his hands and the blood flowing back into the bruises made her cry out again and she fell back against him, faint and sick. He lifted her and carried her upstairs, where Emily had already gone.

But, for Louise, neither Emily nor Anil was there.

She was in another night, in another house; it was another flight of stairs. The pain was the same and she remembered the flash of the enamels on the shelf, the last flash of reality as Charles swept her up past them, crushed and giddy and sick, in his arms. She remembered the night outside the window when he had torn the curtains down ('Damme, we must have gala stars!') and she remembered the sound of her sobs coming in breathless gasps as they were coming now. She remembered how she had escaped over the side of the bed and he had put out a hand and thrown her savagely back. It was always his strength. ('Don't provoke me too far, Louise. You don't know how strong I am.')

Suddenly, at dinner, he had stood up and thrown his whisky in her face and pulled the cloth off the table and thrown the candles down on it. Emily was there too; she remembered how helplessly the baby Emily had woken up and cried, and how the frightened little Anglo-Indian nurse had popped her head in at the door. 'Don't be afraid, Nancy, I am only mad, not drunk,' said Charles, and he bellowed, 'Go into your room and shut the door.' He drove the servants out of the house and locked the doors and windows. 'I wish I could shoot out the lights,' he said, 'but I haven't a gun'; he looked at the Dutch axe over the fire-place: 'But I have an axe and by God you shan't miss anything!' and then he had smashed up the house.

She remembered the nightmare of broken wood and glass, the shrieking of the nurse and Emily – and she remembered the struggle when Charles caught her by the stairs. She remembered the dreadful, mingled taste of whisky and blood in her mouth where her lips had bled, and her clothes torn off her on the floor and her struggles with the softness of her bed muffling her cries, and the naked heat of Charles pressing down on her when at last she gave in and lay still. Now, powerless against his strength, in his arms again, she knew what she knew then and had known ever since – that secret moment would never be lost between them, between Charles and Louise, whatever they did to it, whatever it did to them; the flow from his body to hers, from hers uprising to his, had a fire that could never be put out, that burns them still. That night, stretched on her back, she had lifted her hands to him in ultimate surrender when she forced them down again.

But now she clung to him as he put her down at the head of the stairs. 'Can you stand up?'

'Don't go. Don't go.' She moaned.

He steadied her sharply. 'I must go. That wretched boy is waiting.'

'Let him wait.'

'You have done enough damage already. I must stop it if I can.'

'Charles. Please come back. I want you. I want you, Charles—'

Charles had gone downstairs.

For a long time she stood where he had left her. The colour came back into her face. She looked at her arms where the bruise marks were already turning dark, and she clenched her hands and gave an angry pitiful sob. Then a sound struck her, an exhausted dreary sound, and it had been going on all the time.

It was Emily crying unheeded, as she had cried when she was a baby in the broken house.

Emily . . .

Anil was obediently waiting. In fact he had not moved. He had dimly seen how Charles had taken Louise away, but her voice seemed to go on still – though long before Charles had come he had lost the sense of the words. He was numb, and when Charles touched him he only looked up dully.

'Will you come into my office? We can't talk here.'

'Thank you,' but as he walked up the steps and heard his own shoes on the stone, it grew real and he started back and cried, 'No. I prefer not.'

'We can't talk outside – in the dark,' said Charles reasonably. 'You must come in.' Anil hesitated and walked in after Charles, who was turning over and over in his mind what he possibly could say.

'Sit down.'

'No' – but a nervous whimper shook Anil like a hiccough and he had to sit down, on the edge of a chair, his head bent. He was shivering.

'You are exhausted,' said Charles, and he looked at him puzzled. Could Louise have done all that? And then he saw that Anil's shoes were caked in mud; there were splashes of mud on his legs, and on his *dhoti* that was not white any longer but bedraggled and limp as if it had been soaked and dried and worn a long time. 'Where have you been? What have you been doing?' Another shivering hiccough. 'If I give you a drink,' said Charles, 'will you take it?'

Anil only shook his head. He wiped his hand and his thumb across his forehead and the sweat dropped off on his shirt; his shirt was soaked to his body on his shoulders and chest. He shivered in silence, looking at his shoes – and then he choked, suddenly and painfully.

'You are ill,' said Charles.

Anil shook his head again. 'I have had,' he said, 'a small swelling in the throat, and I am very tired.' As he spoke he lifted his head and Charles recognized him. He could not remember his name, but he remembered him from his lectures, at the debates, at the meetings, and his heart sank. This was a difficult boy to deal with, a turbulent popular student, a ringleader, one of the College bloods, and then he looked at Anil again and was struck by the look of peculiar excitement on his face; it was more than immediate excitement or misery, it was unearthly, and Charles was nonplussed. Now he had Anil here, more than ever he did not know what he could say.

Anil said it first. 'I have done nothing. Nothing,' he repeated. 'Why does she accuse me? I have done nothing.'

Charles tried to cover his confusion and growing dismay by asking business-like questions. Anil was in no state to resist them.

'Why were you out so late?'

'I – had been walking.'

'So late?'

'Yes – I had been out a long time—'

'You know the College rules, you were breaking them—'

'Yes.'

'Have you done this before?'

'Yes.'

'You bribed the porter, I suppose. Anyone else?'

'No.'

'Didn't the Superintendent know?'

'Sometimes – I have given him present—'

'I see. Where did you find my daughter?'

'She was there by the tank. She was afraid. I comforted her and brought her in because I thought you would not like that she was out alone, but I did nothing to her – nothing, nothing, Mr Pool,' and he shouted. 'Why does she accuse me then?' The sound of his own voice, loud in this room, terrified him, and he sank into frightened silence, shivering again and wetting his lips which were suddenly dry.

'My wife should not have accused you,' said Charles; 'I can see that, and she will apologize. She found the little girl missing from her bed and she was naturally upset. I am sure she did not know what she was saying—'

'No—' Anil agreed; and he looked up and cried, 'But she insulted me—'

'She did not know what she was saying. I have told you, she will apologize—'

'She was most cruel and wicked to me, when I had befriended her child.'

'Meanwhile, it appears that you have been breaking College rules for some time,' said Charles thoughtfully, and he picked up a pencil. 'Tomorrow is Examination Day and you, I am told, have a great chance. It would be a pity to spoil it – wouldn't it? Listen to me. We do not want to make a fuss. If you will promise me that you will go straight to bed and say nothing of this to anyone, I shall see Sir Monmatha Ghose in the morning and tell him the whole of the story, and I undertake that he will over-look your breaking the rules this time. You shall see him too, if you wish, and you will get your apology.'

Anil's fingers, working nervously, had found his poem in his pocket, the poem that was a star caught on a dirty piece of paper; he thought of the night with Narayan when he had seen the firefly . . . It was not a shooting star but an insect . . . And a desolation filled him and he nearly threw the poem down in Charles's wastepaper basket, but something even in the feel of the paper it was written on contradicted him, its words seemed to run from his fingers into his soul . . . But there can never be another like it. My freedom is ended. I can stay out no more . . . And it burst from him in despair, 'You must report it? Oh Sir!'

Charles was puzzled again and he was tempted. There was something here that mattered deeply to the boy. More than his chances in the Examination, more than the fear of being found out. Charles was tempted but he sighed and said, 'I am afraid I must.'

'And they will not take action against me? Or against them?'

'Not this time, but probably they will be warned.'

Anil said nothing.

'Otherwise I must send a servant for the Superintendent now. That will be very unpleasant for you.' Anil still said nothing but his tongue came out and wet his lips and his eyes were on Charles, pleading and oddly bright. Charles felt an increasing distaste for the whole of it but he forced himself to insist. 'Do you promise?'

'Yes—' . . . It is all over now. What does it matter?

'You understand. Not a word to anyone.'

'Yes.'

Charles asked, 'What is your name?'

Anil was startled. 'But I know you. Why don't you know me?' his look said, and Charles answered the look. 'There are hundreds of students,' he said, 'you will have to tell me your full name.'

'Hundreds,' said Anil. The word seemed to sink into him in the silence.

'What is your name?'

'My name is Anil Krishna Banerjee.'

'Das's friend?'

'Yes.'

'You will get your apology in the morning,' said Charles, but Anil hardly heard him. 'Remember you have given your promise,' said Charles – but he had the feeling already that he was speaking to an Anil that changed as quickly as the ripples on the river. It was impossible to catch or fix him. Anil had given him a promise; was that Anil here any more?

He hesitated. Almost, he decided to ring up the Principal. After a moment he let the boy go.

Emily waited for Louise. She knew Louise would come before Charles and the waiting was very long. She stood at the foot of the bed and though she was shaking with tiredness she did not attempt to sit down. She could not even approach Louise as far as that and she stood taking in as little of the room as possible. Her mind would not think about Louise, it refused to; it froze itself into terror; now and again it dodged this way and that, then crouched again and was frozenly still.

What had she done this time? What could she have done? It was more than going out of bed. ('You are not to go near Binnie.') . . .

I know your voice, Louise, your coaxing voice, your charming voice, your angry voice, your cutting voice and your frightened voice, but I don't know this one. There is a tone in it I have never heard before and it makes me shake and shrink and freeze, but I don't know what it is. I don't know what I have done, except what I have done, and this is something worse than that. What have I done? What have I done? ...

She looked up at the high vaulted roof where the stucco of the pale walls glimmered up into darkness; outside the windows the sky seemed to swing a little with its panoply of stars, but that may have been because she was swaying on her feet. The sky was luminous with starlight, lit and blue, why had the earth been so dark then? The walls and the windows seemed to fall away, opening Emily to that marauding darkness, darkness where she had escaped from what dreadful thing? Or done what dreadful thing? ... But what, but what, Louise?

Now I am beginning to be afraid. What happened to me out there in the dark? What did I see? A man? A ghost? A dreadful bogy? What? When? Where? When? Where? That was my shriek going up to the stars, bursting my chest, hurting me, hurting the whole of me, but there was no sound; the scream was too high for anyone to hear, tearing through me, cutting its way out of me. Now I am afraid. I am afraid. I am afraid ...

A puff of wind moved a shutter; the slats of it creaked and in the wind she smelled the garden outside, the earth cooling, the smell of dew and nightstrong plants; it blew reasonably and coolly on her hot forehead and it seemed to blow into her head. ('You went out and sat by the tank to see Don,' said the wind, 'nothing else, nothing more. You talked to the student who was kind and brought you home but you told him nothing that was not your own to tell. That is all you have done. Nothing more. Nothing else.') The moment passed. She was calm ... I am glad, said Emily, I am glad Louise did not catch me then ... and, as always when she had those moments by herself and kept them to herself, she felt strong.

Presently Louise came in; she took no notice of Emily but sat down on the bed as if her knees had given way, and hid her eyes with her hand. Emily was not as frightened; Louise looked angry and miserable but she did not look strange any more. 'Come here,' she said, with her eyes still blinded.

Emily advanced an inch.

'Closer.' That was reassuringly like Louise, imperious and impatient.

'I'm sorry I went out, Mother—' At the sound of Emily's voice Louise took her hand away from her eyes and that expression came back into her face. 'What have I done, Mother?' cried Emily in panic. 'What have I done?'

Louise did not answer. Emily and something else seemed to be fighting for importance in her mind. 'Where did you go tonight?'

'I went to the tank. I heard what the servants – the people – are saying about – about Don. I wanted to show it was not true.'

'Of course it's not true. You know that,' cried Louise. 'You are using that as an excuse. You are so sly and deceitful that nothing is beyond you. I don't believe you. Do you hear? I don't believe you,' and Emily had the feeling again that Louise's anger was not only for her, and Louise seemed to sense that too. She stopped and, as if she meant to make herself pay attention to Emily, she took her hand, and Emily knew she forced herself to do it and that she did not want to touch her and again Emily cried despairingly, 'Mother, what have I *done?*'

'Emily, you wouldn't be afraid to tell me the truth, would you?'

Her mind ducked and froze.

'You wouldn't, would you?'

Emily shook her head.

'*Would you?*' A good human exasperation overcame the

falseness in Louise's voice. It gave Emily a breath as if she had come up into the air.

'I wouldn't.'

'Emily, I want you to tell me: what did that man talk to you about there in the garden?'

'Man?' Emily wrinkled her nose trying to think. Anil had passed out of her mind. Then she remembered. 'Mother, you *were* rude to him.'

'You are getting to be a big girl now, a girl not a child.' As she said it Emily seemed to sink into smallness; to Louise who had wanted to keep her child she now seemed aggressively child-like. 'Get bigger. Get bigger,' said Louise's hand and Emily sank faster and faster into little-girl stupidity. 'You are old enough to know that you must never speak to strangers – strange men,' said Louise with that same breathlessness. 'And if they speak to you you must go away from them at once. At once,' repeated Louise sharply. 'You know that, don't you?'

A flicker of curiosity ran through Emily. She wanted to ask why, but she only said, 'Yes, Mother.'

'Do you understand what I mean?'

'Yes,' said Emily hopelessly and she cried out miserably, 'Why can't I go near Binnie?'

'Of course you can go near Binnie.'

'You said I couldn't. Why not? What have I done?'

'Emily, be quiet. You're not trying – to be sensible. Now listen. You went out tonight—'

'I told you I did. Punish me. Punish me if you like.'

'I don't want to punish you. I'm trying to make you under-stand.'

'I *don't* understand. First you are angry with me. Then you are not. What do you want? What do you want me to say?'

'You are deliberately trying to provoke me, Emily.' Louise sprang up from the bed. 'I don't want to lose my temper with you but you make me do it.' She came close to Emily, who shrank back until the edge of the bed was pressing into her legs. Louise seemed to tower over her with the power of a giant, but again she stopped herself. 'Emily—' Her voice altered, it was coaxing and cajoling. 'Try to tell me what happened tonight. What did he say? What did he do? How did he come? Can't you tell me anything he said to you tonight? Anything you talked about at all?'

Emily felt a touch of understanding and pity that was not childlike but completely mature ... How old I am now, she thought, and then she lost it ... Her eyes looked this way and that, searching for inspiration.

'Emily?'

She shut her eyes. Her mind went backwards and forwards trying to remember. She felt a wave of sickness coming over her.

'What did you talk about?'

(You are not going to be sick, are you? Emily asked herself. The words rang in her head and they brought back the breakfast with the Nikolides and joined it to this trouble tonight; it began then – with the Nikolides; it has been getting bigger ever since ... 'What did you talk about?')

'Soup,' said Emily suddenly.

Louise gave a sharp breath like a hiss and slapped her cheek.

Emily jumped and all the colour went away from her face except from that one mark. She did not cry. She looked at Louise quite silently, her eyes brimming with dignity and hurt.

'You are impossible. Impossible!' cried Louise. 'I try. I do try, but you are impossible. What am I to do? What am I to do?' She walked up and down, as if the pain were too bad to keep still, and she said, as if a repellent little snake had crept into her room, 'Get away. Go away to bed.'

Still with those baleful eyes on Louise, Emily crept out and away along the verandah. She was cold. Cold. Charles did not come. The coldness numbed her. Her pyjamas were wet, but she was burning, and in spite of the burning she was cold and she lay shivering, sick and dry with a brittle cold dryness. How can you be wet and dry, burning and cold? There was no warmth or live feeling left in her, only her head felt hot and her eyes burnt with shock, and her cheek where Louise had hit her.

She heard Charles come up. She waited, trying not to cry. She waited. Charles went into Louise's room and after a while he closed the door.

She put out her hand and rubbed the edges of Don's bed; the wooden edge was still rough with his biting, the rug was there that he had scraped up into a nest before he lay down on it, and the lead that he had broken. The lead dangled limply in her fingers, nothing at the end of it. Before, there was a pull, warmth, sturdiness. Now only limpness, emptiness. There was no one. No one. In a rush of despair she thought, This is what it feels like to be dead.

Charles came upstairs to go to Emily but Louise's door was open and he saw Louise. She was walking up and down the room, up and down, until she turned and faced him; her hair was on her shoulders and with heat and anger she had a flush of colour in her cheeks and the heavy white folds of her dressing-gown swung in round her feet as she turned, showing the shape of her hips and thighs and legs in folded slender lines. 'You are always right,' she cried. 'Always! You are hateful. Hateful.'

'And you, even when you have been as poisonous as you were

tonight, still remain so beautiful,' said Charles, and he leaned against the door surveying her. 'Why is it? More than beautiful. You have an angelic face, Louise, the face of an angel; you ought to be so kind. I wonder why you are not. By the way,' he asked, 'what have you done to Emily?'

'Can't you hear her? She is crying in her bed,' and she said defiantly, 'I slapped her face.'

'Charming,' said Charles, but he made no move to go to Emily.

'Well – what are you going to do now?'

'What can I do – except what I have always done? Take the consequences. I expect there will be consequences,' said Charles. 'I don't think that boy will hold his tongue. I told him you would apologize.'

'I won't apologize.'

'You will have to. God knows what you have smashed this time—' and he said softly, his eyes on her, 'Last time it was a house—'

'You smashed that . . .'

'No, you,' he corrected. 'You had made a mistake. You see, you married a man, when all you wanted was a money-box.'

'That isn't fair.'

'Of course it isn't. I find it hard to be fair to you, Louise. You call me hateful. For years you have made me feel hateful, and I shall never forgive you for that.'

'You were hateful,' said Louise hotly, 'you didn't trust me.'

'Were you to be trusted?' asked Charles. Louise did not answer. 'That was it,' said Charles, 'you were not reasonable. You did not want something – you wanted everything. You wanted to spend all your money and be rich, you wanted to have a child and have no worry and pain, you wanted to marry and not be married; and when it naturally didn't fall out like that you made an outcry and a moan. You wanted to be trusted and have the fun of being untrustworthy – you did have fun, didn't you, Louise? And you wanted me to be jealous – without being inconvenient.'

'You forced yourself on me.'

'What a villain. Go on.'

'You behaved abominably.'

'I behaved like a fool. Look at the statistics,' said Charles. 'You stayed with me for nearly three years – say a thousand nights, Louise; on one night out of a thousand I lost my temper with you. Why was it only one?'

'It isn't a joke,' said Louise icily.

'No. Nor was it then,' said Charles, and his eyes grew hard. 'Can a man assault his own wife? Apparently he can – if she chooses to make a scandal of it ... and, incidentally, make it impossible for herself to see him again – for eight years, Louise?'

'I had no wish to see you again. You were bestial.'

'And the result of that was Binnie,' said Charles thoughtfully; 'and Binnie, the child of violence, is very nearly perfect. That doesn't make sense, does it?' His voice was not steady, he had forgotten his bantering. 'I tortured myself over Binnie. You knew that, didn't you, Louise? That is why you never wrote and were so careful not to let them tell me anything. *Dear Sir*,' he mocked bitterly: '*Mrs Pool has instructed us to inform you that a daughter was born on the 4th April.* I thought she might be abnormal. I thought I might have made her blind or ill. I believed all the old wives' stories. When I walked up on that steamer I was shaking – and then she came across the deck and put out her hand and made me look ...' He did not go on.

'Why didn't you ask?' said Louise.

'Because you wouldn't have told me. You were very angry, Louise. You did everything you could. You separated me from Emily – finally. I shall never have Emily again. You refused to see me.'

'I couldn't bear to see you.'

'You didn't dare. There was one thing you could not forgive me about that night, Louise,' said Charles, 'and that was that you liked it.'

'That isn't true.'

'Isn't it? Why didn't you ask me for a divorce? Why wouldn't you take it when I offered it to you? Why didn't I divorce you?' – He came closer – 'Why, when you were frightened to death, did you come back, Louise—'

'You didn't want me. You don't want me now.'

'Who in their senses could want you?' shouted Charles. 'You make nothing but trouble wherever you go. I can't escape it, and neither can you.' He looked at the bruises on her arms. 'I hurt you tonight, the first time I have touched you for eight years. It seems I'm beginning where I left off – because I touched you tonight I can't go away,' and he said, 'You are eight years older, Louise. This time are you going to run away?'

Anil was so tired that he walked out of Charles's room, across the garden and across the grounds, up to the stairs of the Hostel and into his room without feeling anything at all. He did not wait to take off his clothes, he simply dropped his shoes on the floor and fell over on his bed asleep. He must have slept only a little while when he woke up choking . . . I have caught cold, he thought again, and it seemed to his tired, over-tired brain that his nuisance of catching cold was something terrible, an accident that might finish by exterminating Anil . . . I hope it doesn't hurt me too much, he said, and jerked himself back to sense ... I must be sensible ... But to wake with a dry choking throat is a peculiar kind of terror, worse when the arms and legs are so deadened with sleep that they cannot rise off the bed and fetch a drink of water.

He fell asleep again and dreamed that Mrs Pool was suffocating him.

This time he woke by sitting violently up on his bed, literally tearing himself out of the dream. Sitting up, presently he began to breathe properly ... I cannot lie down, my throat is too uneasy ... and he leaned against the wall and went to sleep in that position; but every few minutes he woke.

XI

Charles called early at the Principal's house. It was outside the town and remarkable because it was three storeys high and looked all the higher for the flat land round it. He left Delilah by the steps and was asked to come up, past the first floor, past the second and on to the roof, where he saw a small marquee built into the sky with a top that was lined inside with a quilting of patchwork flowers. Sir Monmatha Ghose sat under it, his legs folded neatly into each other, on a bed with a mattress tied down with a cotton sheet and two of the enormous bolsters called 'Dutch wives'. Sitting as he was, on a cloud, between two clouds, with the real clouds rolling slowly past him, he was like a god being carried in his palanquin of flowers through the air; he could see his domain, all the College, Charles's house, the Farm, the new houses, the road to the river, and the river; and in the very distance, the Nikolides' chimney smoking against the sky.

'Welcome to my seat in heaven,' he said. 'Now you see how I spy on my students. It is truly heavenly. From up here I can see just how big they are – so small that they are not important at all. Down there they are sometimes so important that they blot out everything else. Then I come up here to readjust my eyes.'

'And I have come to drag you down again,' said Charles. 'Monmatha, something very unpleasant has happened—'

'Not on Examination Day,' pleaded Sir Monmatha as he sat up and unfolded his legs. 'What is it?'

Charles told him.

'Anil Krishna Banerjee?' said Sir Monmatha Ghose. 'Yes, I know him. Yes, he might do it and he might just as easily not. It is impossible to predict. You are quite satisfied, of course, that he did not; but I do not think he can keep it to himself. He will make a fuss, undoubtedly, and they are ripe for trouble today. They will probably go on strike. Well, it has happened before.' He sighed. 'Troubles in College are not usually sexual ones, though the authorities make arrangements for all foods of mind and body except that.' He looked at Charles and it struck him that Charles had singularly the look of a man who has been fed; he had lost a haggardness that he used to have, most noticeably for instance on that night when he had come to listen to the news. 'You have heard the news?' said Sir Monmatha. 'I think Greece will be next. The Nikolides were going home to Athens for the winter. Now they are not going.' He sighed again. 'Yes, I am afraid it will make a stir. I am sorry, Charles.'

'I am sorry too.' Charles did not go on.

'Does the little girl know?'

'Not so far. I shall tell my wife to keep her in. I left them asleep.'

'Das may be able to help. He can influence the boy. I shall be going down to the College, could you have a word with him?'

'I will go now. If we can stop it at the beginning . . .'

187

'The beginning.' Sir Monmatha pointed down. 'My dear Charles, it has begun.'

When Anil woke for the last time he was sitting in his chair with his arms on the table and his head on his arms. This time he woke completely; he had a dry electric wakefulness and his throat refused to swallow. He took off his shirt and took his drinking cup and went outside; after a drink it was better and he washed out his throat and cleared it with noisy spittings.

'Who is it who makes such filthy noise?' He did not answer. The water had eased him and he splashed his face and chest and arms. It was beginning to be light; the darkness was raftered by light, but in between were mammoth wedges of blackness, and Anil had a sense of heaviness as if the darkness would never lift; but the birds knew that it was morning, they were beginning their earliest sounds in the trees and then, far over their heads, dropped from the minaret into the College grounds, came the first call of the muezzin from the mosque in the bazaar. The lights were on in the Moslem Students' Hostel.

Anil splashed himself as if he would never finish in the cool water; he could feel his body burning through his soaked waist-cloth ... I think I have some fever, he said.

As he went back along the verandah the daylight was grow-ing; voices spoke to him, on the beds a white mosquito-net was lifted, a bolster thrown out, arms stretched; there were yawns, hawkings, spits over the verandah rail, laughter, the opening noises of the day. Anil was revived by the cold water, and as he passed among his friends, he began to smart with remembrance.

There was the tank, turning green in the growing light, the cool glimmer of water, the shadows, still liquid, of the trees. That was where he had sat with Emily and there was the slumbering outline of the house, and one after the other, smarting bitterly, came those moments, there in the porch, when Mrs Pool had lacerated him. *Mrs Pool. Mrs Pool. Mrs Pool.* Her name was repeated, hammering in his brain, throbbing with bitterness and injustice and wounded pride. *Mrs Pool* – and soon it was running in a whisper down the colonnaded verandah of the Hostel.

The students gathered. They leaped from their beds, they came up from the privy, they left their washing. The whisper passed from tongue to tongue – *Mrs Pool. Mrs Pool . . . Mrs Pool . . . Mrs Pool.*

They all knew Emily and none of them admired her; they all admired Louise; that did not prevent them conveniently overlaying both with their own inventions: Louise was a hag, a siren, a malefactor; Anil could not see anything but Mrs Pool, Charles was blotted quite out of his mind and Emily was a figment who altered as he wished.

She grew and waned also according to the rumours that were now rushing about the College and changing in the same surprising manner . . . Anil Krishna Banerjee had rescued the child Pool and Mrs Pool had accused him . . . Anil had accused Mrs Pool of cruelty and Mrs Pool said she would flog him . . . Mrs Pool had flogged him . . . Anil, who had rescued a little child from assault, was to be flogged and sent to prison and forbidden to sit for his Examination . . . Mrs Pool had hit Anil with a horsewhip . . . Mrs Pool had made improper advances to Anil . . . Anil had made improper advances to Mrs Pool . . . Anil had made improper advances to Mrs Pool and Charlie Chang had flogged them both with a horsewhip . . . Anil (but no one really believed this) had flogged Charlie Chang . . . That monster, the girl Pool, had assaulted Anil. . . Anil was to be expelled . . .

They flew from mouth to mouth, and the quadrangles filled with students; groups of them gathered and surged round corners of the buildings, where on ledges or pediments other students harangued them; where one came down, another sprang up; Moslems joined with Hindus. The Superintendent of Anil's Hostel, attempting to telephone the Principal's house, had been bodily placed on his bed and advised to stay there; and one young Hindu, with cheers, climbed out along the first-floor balcony and cut the wires; only he cut the wires of the electric extension instead, and all the fans went off and it was necessary to cut the telephone cable on the inside, which might more prudently have been done in the first place.

The morning meal at the Hostel was carried round the square, and a procession started with it to the Principal's house. *We shall not eat injustice* – a banner was scrawled; there were other banners – banners of the League, the Onward Movement – and someone had made a straw figure and dressed it in a frock and given it long dangling legs and a head of straight jute hair. It was really not at all unlike Emily. They had garlanded Anil and put a white cap on his head and painted his forehead and he was in the middle of them, but before the procession could start a car was reported to be coming from the Principal's house.

The procession shrieked and swayed 'They are coming to arrest him!' And the shriek passed down its length: 'Hide him. Hide him. Hide him.'

Anil was passed from one set of hands to another, he was hustled and bundled and pushed, his cap was knocked off and the garlands pulled off his neck, until at last he reached the fringes of the crowd, where nobody knew who he was or why they were passing him along or what they were to do with him and they left him to pass himself; they were all pressing in the other direction, watching a party of students who were daringly preparing to surround and halt the car.

Anil found himself in Charles's mango grove at the back of the College; through it a path led to the river road. Anil stood there panting, leaning against a tree, his face against the bank. He felt very ill ... I have much fever. What is it? Perhaps it is tonsillitis. Perhaps it is diphtheria ... But he had no pain in his throat, only the sensation of blockage, of swelling; it made him swallow nervously and continually, but he was frightened by a strange feeling in his head. He had had it all morning; for moments together he had no head at all, he had only a gap ... I suppose where my neck is left ... in which was a noise and a hot light ... as if the sun had sat down in my eyes; but how could the sun sit in my eyes if my head is not there? ... I am quite sensible, you see.

It was very quiet in among the young trees. The hubbub seemed to be moving away from him, there was no one now near the grove but one old woman picking dung off the road and putting it in her basket. The bark of the tree scratched Anil's forehead and he had one thing that seemed to him to need most urgent attention; his toe where he had knocked it on the stone last night was sore and swollen ... It is most dangerous, a swollen toe, thought Anil; I must have it seen to ... And then he remembered that this path led out towards the river ... Indro's house is by the river. Indro will put it right for me. I shall go and see Indro ...

He started limping down the path and presently he began to run, but every few moments he would stop and say, 'Excuse me. I am not to be interrupted. I am going to see Indro.'

*

When Professor Dutt came down to assist at the Examination Hall he could not get in. The students were lying down in the road outside and on the steps.

He did not attempt to insist. He turned round and went home and put his umbrella away.

Narayan's house was preparing for the *puja*. Each side of the door were fresh plantain trees standing in pitchers of Ganges water with green coconut; mango leaves were strung across the lintel. Tarala was busy with rituals of her own in the courtyard, but most of the work had to be done by Shila; there were many things that Tarala as a widow must not touch. Shila loved to do them; she had made the platter of ball-cakes, molasses rolled with coconut, that stood cooking near the window; she had folded innumerable betel leaves, and now she had chosen her best Benares sari to wind below the dais of the *Sree*. Now she went into the garden room where the materials were ready, and loosening the folds of her sari a little because she found it hard to kneel now, she went down upon her knees to make the *Sree*.

It was modelled of rice-flour and Ganges water and it needed clever fingers; she took a lump of the paste to knead in her hand and rolled it on her palm, round and round with the other, her thumbs held back; the movement grew into a rhythm, and the rhythm grew into a song and presently she began to sing.

The tuneless happy sound carried to Narayan in the study, and he began to draw it in shapes on his blotting paper. He was writing an account of what he had spent on *puja* presents and it was far too much, but as his pen went round and round his gloom left him and he tore the sheet out of his account book and threw it on the floor. Shila heard him and, taking it for impatience, stopped singing at once.

Narayan was sorry. Now he liked to hear Shila in the house; he liked the feeling of festivity. Here, on the river, the morning had signs of the cold weather, there had been mist on the river, and mist in the dew. Already, before the *pujas* had come, the wind said, 'After the *pujas* are over – after the *pujas* are over we shall start again ... After the *pujas* my son will be born—' and he was intensely and superstitiously glad, in spite of his extra expenses, that he had given that money to Shila to spend.

Attending a dog at my house ... (Destroying a dog at my house.)

Until that day I worked to save life, never to destroy. My cases have died, but that was in spite of me – not because of me ... what a fuss! What a fuss to make about a dog when men were dying, men and women and children, crushed from existence, hundreds at a time ... But it is the same – even if it is one dog and a hundred men. It is *against* not for; it is *counter* – an offence against life. By my guilt I have laid more guilt upon mankind overlaid with guilt already; and this, when each one of us should be a rock against evil. Each of us – soldier, sailor, tinker, thief, black man, white man, nigger-boy, Chink ... I have done violence, and the stain is deepened because of me ... And he passed to the thought of himself (and he cried, 'Don't let it bring bad luck!' and he shut his eyes and prayed from the bottom of his heart).

He opened his eyes; and as if he had been dropped from the ceiling, there was Anil in his room.

'Anil ... You!'

'Indro – give me some water. Some water, Indro, please.'

He was terribly out of breath, gasping painfully, with sweat running down his neck from his hair, in which were caught a few dishevelled jasmine flowers; his shirt was torn across the shoulder, but it was his face that most startled Narayan; under its dust and sweat, and the vermilion that had run from the mark on his forehead, was a look of the wildest excitement that Narayan had ever seen, his nostrils and his eyes were dilated and his eyeballs were red, bloodshot.

'Anil – are you very ill?' Anil shook his head, too out of breath to speak. 'Where have you been? What has happened?' A suspicion crossed his mind. 'Are you drunk?'

'Water. Water, please.'

On the desk was the tray that Shila always put ready with water and a dish of nuts; he poured out water and Anil drank in gulps, but Narayan was looking at the clock. 'Anil, look at the time. What in the world has happened? Look at the time.'

Anil wiped his face in his sleeve and spat, clearing his throat. He did not go outside but spat untidily on the floor, and sat looking dully at the stain.

'What – time? Why?'

'The Examination. Have you forgotten the Examination?'

Anil lifted his head and the excitement came back into his eyes. 'That is exactly what I came here to tell you. I remember now. There will be no Examination held today.'

'Why? For God – why?'

'We are on strike,' said Anil, and he said it with a kind of primness that had such pride and wanton mischief behind it that Narayan cried out: 'You are behind this – you!'

'Yes. It is all because of me.'

'You fool. You worse than fool. What has possessed you? You have everything and then you throw it away. Why have you done this, you fool boy?'

'Wait till you hear the reason.'

'I don't care for the reason.'

'Listen. Listen.' His voice was uneven, high with excitement,

194

then husky. 'Indro – last night I was out – I came in late – and—'

'And? And? Go on then.'

'I met – one of Charlie Chang's daughters.'

'—?' said Narayan.

'No. I tell you it is not what you think,' cried Anil violently.

'Then why is the trouble ... ?'

'Wait. Listen.' He became rhetorical. 'She was a child. She wept. I comforted her.'

'How comforted her?'

That put Anil off his flow. He said uncertainly, 'I – don't remember.'

'Did you touch her?'

'And what if I did? I am not poison, am I?'

'How old was she?' Anil was picking at the nuts, shelling them and throwing them on the floor. 'Big? Little? Perhaps thirteen?'

'Perhaps, but listen, Indro—'

'Why was she out?' Narayan demanded angrily. 'What were they doing to let her out alone?'

'She was searching for her dog.' Narayan flinched, but Anil said, puzzled, 'And yet I think she said her dog was dead; then why was she searching for it? It hurts in my head if I have to think of these things. Don't ask me questions. Listen, Indro—'

'Tell me what is true. Tell me what really has happened.'

'But listen, but listen.' Anil could not remember in the least what had happened. He could only repeat what they had shouted in the College, what now they said he said had happened. 'I comforted this frightened child, so small and so afraid. I took her in and then – the woman, Mrs Pool, abused me – in a most beastly fashion. She insulted me. She is my worst enemy.

I brought the child to her. She would not listen. I was not per-mitted to explain – her husband came – he threatened me—'

'Is all this true?' Narayan was dazed.

'True? They came to arrest me. I am to be flogged. Incarcerated.'

'This is disgraceful.' Narayan was catching fire.

'Think of my father and my name. I am ruined—'

'But who – who has done this to you? The Principal? The Police? Mr Pool? He has not the power, I think. Has he lodged information about you? Whose orders are these? Who gave them?'

Anil's excitement snapped, his voice dropped to an odd dull languor as if he could hardly speak. 'No one.'

'No one? No *one*! Then why, for God, have you done all this?'

'I don't know.'

Narayan stared at him in amazed silence. Anil's eyes were shut, his hands were round his throat, his lips fixed open, and between them a bright round bubble of saliva winked in the light like a third eye come from the inside of Anil to look at him while his eyes were shut; it trembled and exploded, leaving a smear of spittle on his chin. 'Why are you in this state?' cried Narayan.

Then the gate closed with a wooden thud and someone came down the path to the door. Anil sat up with open eyes. Facing them at the bottom of the steps was Emily.

Her sudden apparition seemed to surprise her as much as themselves. She had come to see this Dr Das; she was forbidden to go out alone but she did not think it mattered now what she did. She had been waiting outside trying to make up her mind to go in and at last she had precipitated herself in at the gate. Now her entry disconcerted her as much as it disconcerted them and they stared at one another in surprised silence. Then – 'This is the girl,' said Narayan in vernacular. He said it as a fact, not as a question, and Anil nodded, staring at Emily.

It was obvious that she did not recognize him. Anil's heart gave a pang ... I thought she was pretty – how ugly she is! At least he wanted her to be pretty and he could see from Narayan's face that to him she looked ugly too: tall and lanky, all knees and elbows, and her hair was no colour and her white face glistened with sweat. Where was his graceful little ghost? She had been small, light-boned in his arms. Now he barked at this gawky stranger: 'Why do you come here? What do you want?'

She opened her lips. They were dry and for a moment nothing came through them. Then she said, 'I want to see Dr Das.' Her voice was the same, with the same clear, slightly imperious bell-like tone, a way in which no Indian girl would ever speak; the voice that had told him at once she was English in the darkness by the tank. In spite of himself he softened. 'Mr Das? There he is.'

'Oh no! Oh no! No!' said Narayan unexpectedly; he had retreated behind his desk.

'Come in,' said Anil to Emily.

'In – my shoes?' asked Emily. She had never been in an Indian house before.

'Certainly,' said Anil rudely. 'Mr Das is Westernized. He does not mind what dirt you bring into his house.'

Neither Narayan nor Emily heard his rudeness. Emily came in gingerly as if she were treading on unfamiliar ground and Narayan watched her helplessly. She came straight up to his desk and said seriously to him, 'I want to ask you a question, Dr Das.'

'Not just now. Not just now,' said Narayan. 'You must excuse me. I have no time to answer now, Miss Pool.'

'It won't take you a minute.'

Her eyes examined him with a child's particular searching-out gaze, quite unabashed; her eyes were some years younger than her voice and he looked back into their foreign green-flecked clearness and the feeling of wrong and shame came up in him so that he said as if she had spoken, 'I am sorry.'

'Dr Das, my mother's Pekingese have been coming to you here for injections?'

The question moved his attention from her eyes to her.

'What disease did you inject them for?'

'Hydrophobia.' She looked puzzled and he said, jocose in his nervousness, 'You don't know what that is, I bet you.'

'No.'

'Hydrophobia. That is rabies. That is madness.'

The eyes flinched, then they came back to him more searching than ever. 'Were they mad?'

'No, no. It was prevention – against the bite of a mad dog.'

'Had they been bitten by a mad dog?'

'No. I do not think so.'

'Then why did you inject them?'

'Your mother asked for it.'

'My mother.' Again Anil heard the edge to that; even now he was sensitive to her.

'Dr Das, you came to our house the day – that my dog died.'

Narayan answered carefully, 'Yes, I did.'

'Did you – bandage up his wounds?'

'He had no wounds.'

'No wounds!' In her surprise the word hung on her lips.

'It did not hurt him,' said Narayan. 'It was all over in a matter of seconds.'

'As quick as that?' Her voice was incredulous.

'Yes. I tell you, he did not feel anything at all.'

'Then – why did he die?'

Narayan stopped and looked at her. 'Don't you know?'

'They told me he died in a fight.'

'And what did you think?'

'After you said hydrophobia, I thought he died in a fight with a mad dog.'

'Perhaps, in a way, he did.'

'What do you mean?'

'Well you see,' said Narayan slowly, and he picked up a pencil and tapped it so that he need not look at her eyes, 'we had to put him down, put him to sleep, because we were afraid that he had been so bitten.'

'Had he?'

'He showed certain signs. Your mother thought—'

'Did you think so?'

'I don't know. Still, I do not know. She would not wait for proof ... proof,' said Narayan, and once more something was ringing in his mind, pressing to be remembered. He grew angry. 'No one can tell what the outcome of this will be, but there has been nothing but trouble and loss. Your mother gave no time for reason or sense ...' He grew angrier. 'Your mother is very difficult and headstrong. You should ask her to answer you for this—'

Emily was still and into her face came an expression of shock and with it of triumph. 'Mother!' she said in a long whisper. 'Mother!' she remembered her manners. 'Thank you,' she said to Narayan, 'I think I will go home now,' but Narayan was looking over her head at someone behind her.

'May I come in?' said Charles.

The whole of Anil's body gave a quick nervous start. He

glared at Charles; he stood on the edge of the verandah, clench-
ing and unclenching his hands.

'Good morning, Das ... Good morning,' said Charles to
Anil.

'Really, really,' said Anil offensively, 'it seems, Indro, that
your house is to be turned into a rendezvous of Pools.'

Charles's hand came inside Emily's arm – 'I came to see you,
Das. I did not know that Emily was here.'

'So you take no better care of her than formerly,' said Anil.

Charles propelled Emily away. 'Wait for me in the garden.'
And he said. 'You are not to go home without me.' Emily had
not even heard him. He ignored Anil and said, 'Das, I have
come from Sir Monmatha Ghose – to speak to you.'

Narayan was trembling, but he stood up with his hands on
the desk; it was easier to stand up to Charles if he had his hands
steady. 'I also would like to speak to you. Most shocking things
are reported to me, Mr Pool. A most shocking thing has been
said to this boy.' His voice, now that he had achieved it, was
over-blustering.

'And you have believed everything he told you?'

'Unfortunately it is only too likely,' said Narayan bitterly. 'I
too have had experience of Mrs Pool. Because he was Indian the
worst suspicion came into her mind. Without waiting, he is convicted—'

'He is not convicted.' Charles was sharp.

'This may very well go to law,' said Narayan, taking refuge in
a side issue. 'There is libel. There is defamation—'

'Don't be absurd. You let this boy run away with you, Das. I
have come to you—'

'You thought that I should help against my friend? You
thought that I should hush him up?' Narayan was now truly run

away. 'Or did you track up your own daughter who came following him here?'

'You are not to speak to me like that—'

Narayan buried his face in his hands. It was not in this way that he had meant Charles to come. Everything was loud, noisy, rude and untidy; the room was a litter of nutshells and stains where Anil had spat. He cried, 'It is horrible. Horrible.'

'It has been made so,' said Charles. 'The College is in an uproar. Four students are under arrest – I had hoped—' He asked wearily, wonderingly, 'How did it have to grow into this?' And he asked Anil, 'Why couldn't you keep your promise?'

But all this while Anil had been struggling, searching, struggling to find his head. It was necessary for him to find it because he could not breathe without it; the noise of the pain in the gap took all breath; there was hurt in the noise now, agony that blinded him. He screamed.

'My God! What is the matter with him?'

They caught him and held him between them. He felt their hands, gripping him in every place and doing nothing to help his head. He tore away from them, beating at his throat with his hands, screaming without a sound coming from his lips. How could there be a sound? He had no lips – because he had no head ... They were there. With a rush of air into his throat, his head was back again. He lay sucking in air, and his lips were wet – and curiously stiff.

'*Anil.*' Narayan was bending over him and he said to someone behind him, 'Water.' A hand passed a glass of water and with those odd, stiff-feeling lips Anil drank. 'That is better.' Narayan's face was anxiously looking into his. 'Anil, can you speak to me? Have you pain? Where is trouble? Tell.'

Anil wanted to tell. He wanted to complain of his head that

had come back to him with those strange lips, of his mouth that felt so stiff, and of his throat, and the noise, and the pain in the noise, but all he could do with his mouth that would not move properly was to croak, 'My toe. My toe is swollen.'

'Your *toe*?' But Narayan went down on one knee to examine it; though he tweaked it and pulled it Anil did not feel it and he cried again querulously, 'My toe.'

'Nothing is the matter here except the toe is bruised.' Narayan examined the foot and the ankle and then he saw at the side of the shin a small pale scar. He saw it; he looked at it; at Anil; back to it. His face changed, into a dreadful silent stare. He had remembered.

XII

Emily, sent away by Charles, went round the corner of the house. The sun striking off the river blinded her; she stood still, holding on to the plaster, and the red hurting glare of her eyes exactly suited her. She was angry; angry with a good right anger; it was in her legs and in her face and stomach and hot in her heart, but it would not overflow until she meant it to overflow. She was compact with rage, dangerous, ready . . . I am coming, Mother. I have found out everything I wanted to know. This time you are going down to me, not I to you. I am up. I am right. There is no mystery left. All of it has been cleared away from you. I see you, Louise. I see you exactly as you are. You are larger than I am and powerful, but you cannot crush me now . . .

This garden was beginning to be adjusted to her eyes. She saw it as a small sunbaked spot, bright with green and a few brilliant heads of marigold against the white sandy soil; and in front of it was the river, a shimmering width of brightness. She liked it. She liked the way the garden was shut in on three sides and open to the river on the fourth, she liked to stand there hidden, not tall enough to see over the walls, and see the sweep of the river and the plain and the huge domed shape of sky ... It matches me; the hot sun matches me, and the water running past. I am hot and I am strong and I can see a great way. I see what I could not see before. I shall call you names, Mother, I shall call you a cheat because you cheated me and a liar because you lied and a coward because you were afraid to tell me the truth, and I shall call you a murderess because you murdered Don. You killed him. You, not Dr Das. I know how you made him do it. I know only too well. I hate Dr Das but I do not blame him, Mother, I blame you. I don't care who takes your part. I shall never have anything to do with you again. You can take Charles and you can take Binnie. I prefer to be by myself ... And all at once there was a crack in her anger and desolation seeped through. Hastily she closed it again ... Don't let my anger go. Emily, stay as angry as this till you get home. Stay as angry as this.

Don was once alive. He felt the sun on his back; his legs, if he sat down for a moment, were up at once to run again. He liked gardens and sun and grass and sticks and leaves; he used to play with them; now all these things are still because he is not here. He loved other things too – cool floors to lie on, his own bed; best of all, food; second best, toys. I don't know which were his balls because the Pekingese have taken them; I let them take them, a ball is a silly thing alone. I shall not cry; I only feel like crying because I have been tired. Now I am not tired any longer. It is nearly over and I am coming, Mother. I am coming now. I shall come straight to you and I shall say, 'Mother, I know all about it now. Liar. Cheat. Coward. *Murderer*.' That is what I shall say, 'Liar. Cheat. Coward. Murderer.' Now, whenever I need to say Mother I shall say one of these ...

She was turning to go when she looked in at a door near her.

She had been standing near the doorway of a room built into the house, and in spite of her hurry, once she had looked in Emily stayed there. There was nothing in the room but a young Indian woman making a little image on a stand. It was like the clay images Emily saw nowadays at the bazaar, of a goddess with a crown and ten arms, but this particular goddess had four.

Emily had seen this phenomenon too often to be very astounded. From her own bed at night she could hear the sound of four religions, the bell from the Mission Church, the muezzin called from the mosque, the gongs that were rung by the nomad Buddhist priests, and the tom-tom and cymbals and bell from the temple. Charles said, from the *Gita*, '*Howsoever men approach me, so do I accept them; for on all sides the path they choose leads them to me.*' Emily liked that. It made God sound big.

Shila had finished the figure; it was both delicate and firm and she was pleased; now she had made the rest of her rice-flour more liquid and was decorating the stand with patterns. With nothing to guide it the pattern came quickly and Emily watched her fascinated; neither of them heard Anil's scream. Emily's eyes followed Shila's hand and, as if there were something soothing in those even loops and circles, she grew quieter. She was more comfortably angry. She leaned against the door post and asked, 'How does your hand know where to go?'

Shila did nothing so jerky as to start; she pressed her fingers together so that the flow of liquid stopped and looked up with surprise in her eyes. To look from the dark room to the garden was a little dazzling and she could see only the black outline of Emily, but like Anil she knew from her voice that she was English and she answered in English though Emily had attempted the vernacular, 'What did you say?'

Now Emily was surprised. Shila's English was not clipped like

Anil's or Narayan's, she gave her words a musical lilt. 'What did you say?'

'How do you know the pattern?'

'I know it. My mother knew it and her mother. Even my mother's mother's mother,' and she knelt up a little. Emily saw at once that she was going to have a baby.

'If you have a daughter she will know them too,' said Emily.

'One day I shall have a daughter. First I shall have a son,' said Shila quite positively and she ended her pattern. Then her eyes came back to Emily. 'How did you come here?'

'I am sorry. Do you mind?'

'Not at all, but how did it happen?'

Emily evaded that. 'My father is talking to Dr Das.'

'My husband?'

'Is he your husband?' Emily saw Narayan in his European coat and trousers, with his desk, his bookcases and his charts, and then this empty room and Shila on the floor, in her single cotton sari that left her arms and part of her back bare. At her face, Shila laughed. 'You have come to the back of the house, you see. Here we are domestic in the Indian way. Won't you come in?'

Emily asked again, 'Oughtn't I to take off my shoes? Your husband said he did not mind, but—'

'You are nice,' Shila said softly, 'but you need not. Often my husband comes in, even into the kitchen, with his shoes.'

'But you would like him to take them off,' said the shrewd Emily.

'In this part of the house, yes.'

'I will stay here,' said Emily, and then she remembered. 'At least, I have to go.' Still she stayed. 'What are you making her for?'

'It is our *Sree*. It means grace, and as that is an attribute of our Goddess Lakshmi, we make an emblem of her. We will offer her flowers, and fruit and rice, all through our holy days.' She smiled at Emily. 'She is the Goddess of Good Fortune.'

'I am glad I have seen her,' said Emily gravely, 'I am glad I have seen how you do it,' and she hesitated and asked, 'Do you think – an English girl could make a *puja*?'

'Anyone can – if they believe in it.'

'I should believe,' said Emily, 'but there is something I have to do first.' And she said goodbye and turned to go home.

The procession had been round the town. It went to the Principal's house to make a demonstration, but when it arrived there was no one to see it; the Principal had left for the College in his car and Lady Ghose was in Darjeeling. Someone suggested they should throw stones, but it was no part of their programme to be undignified and the procession returned through the bazaar. Here among the lanes and side-roads it was forced to split up and many little processions went wandering off by themselves and remained lost for the rest of the day.

The staff and Sir Monmatha Ghose were in conference in the College Hall, where all was prepared for the examination of the B. Ag. candidates. There was something reproachful in the rows of small tables, each with its pile of foolscap, a piece of pink blotting paper, a clean pen and inkwell and an empty chair; along the aisles between them, where the monitor should have paced with a watchful eye, messengers scurried up and down; outside the windows the students were singing.

They had been singing for a long time; the conference had been in session for a long time. No one knew what to do next. There was a hitch.

'We will return to work if you reinstate Anil Krishna Banerjee.'

'But he has never been dispossessed.'

'Has he not? Has he not? He is imprisoned at this moment.'

'You have hidden him yourselves.'

'That is a lie – a lie to cover your actions.'

'Listen to me—'

'Until you release him we shall listen to no one – to nothing.'

'I tell you, we have not got him.'

'And neither have we – where then is he? Is he thin air?'

It was quite a long way from the Das house to the College and Emily wanted to get in before Charles, and Charles was riding; she had seen Delilah held by a boy in the road. It was very hot, even though the road was planted all the way with trees, and the people she passed turned round to look at her curiously. She began rather to wish she had not come out alone.

Charles was a long time talking to Dr Das; Emily was certain she had made slow progress though she hurried; every moment she expected to hear Delilah on the road behind her; but there was no sign of Charles as she came within sight of the College.

Then she gave a little hiss of dismay and annoyance. She had come up with the tail end of a procession that was filing in through the College gates, completely blocking the road. She could see a press of people – students, she thought from their white-clad shoulders – and she could hear a hubbub and shouts and the beating of a tom-tom, and far ahead she could see a figure, a stuffed doll on a pole swinging above the heads of the crowd ... What are they doing now? groaned Emily. She tried to edge her way through. It was impossible. The people were passing against the gate, trying to push their way through.

Here in the vanguard, Emily was among the beggars who had clustered round the College gates; they hopped on sticks or were dragged in wooden boxes on wooden wheels, or pulled themselves along on one another's shoulders; there were armless ones, and legless ones, one with no nose, one with his teeth growing through his cheek; they ran with sores, and from their rags came a putrid old dead smell; and Emily, shuddering and sick, hurled herself away from them into the crowd.

Now she was forced to go with it: step by step, she found herself walking in her own procession though she had no idea whose effigy it was that swung from the pole ahead. The crowd were shouting on all sides of her but she had no idea what they said. She walked, trying to move sideways as she advanced, to reach the farther edges of the crowd by her own gate; she was banged and pushed, flung sideways, in the press of taller people; they could not see her face, hidden by her sun-hat, or realize her difference. The crowd smelled almost as badly as the beggars; a stale smell of sweat, another almost lavatory smell, and mixed with it a sweetness that was like flowers and scented oil; she was astonished that she did not mind it more though the heat was unbearable. She pushed and pushed until the people thinned and she reached the farther side.

She knocked against a woman who carried a water-jar on her hip and the water spilled over and the woman turned to look. She looked at Emily's face, and for a moment she did not take it in, then she shrieked a stream of vernacular and caught Emily by the arm. She was immediately ringed with people, but before they could touch her Shah was there.

He had no more authority than his uniform and a pair of boots could give him, but the ring broke. Shah seized Emily and dragged her to the gate. The moment his back was turned his temporary prestige was over and he had just time to pull Emily inside and shut the gate, on which excited hands began to batter and pound.

Emily did not in the least understand what had happened. She smoothed herself down. 'Why did you touch me? What made you do a thing like that?' she said severely. 'It was only a procession. I shall report you to the Sahib.' Deeply affronted, she walked up the drive to find Louise.

The crowd began to pelt the gate with stones. Someone threw a brick. Then a police sergeant swept round the corner on a motor bicycle and there was immediately a miraculously cleared space along the road. Shah opened the gate.

'Have you a *lathi*?' the sergeant asked. 'You can use it if necessary.'

Shah smiled and spat on his hands.

Louise was not in her room; she was in the drawing-room, sitting at the piano, but she was not playing. She was pressing the notes thoughtfully down with one finger and letting them spring up again. Binnie was looking from the window at the massed students in the College grounds.

Louise did not appear to hear them, or Binnie who was reporting everything they did; she just touched the notes softly and let them spring up again, and there was a small new smile at the corners of her lips.

It was extraordinary how loud those quiet notes sounded after the hubbub and the heat that Emily had been through; they came winging across the room to her and each one was like a very clear, round full-stop.

Emily stood outside and looked into the room; Louise looked up and saw her and she stayed, her finger holding down a note, and while the sound of the note went on nobody moved. Emily stood outside; she saw the room, she saw Louise, and it was a clear completed picture. Everything was in it; the sky was in it, reflected on the walls of the room, held in light between the windows; the shadows of trees fell across them in clear green patches, moving and fretting; there was noise in it, sustained with the vibration of the note – distant shouts and cries and singing; there was dust rising in the light of a sunbeam; simplicity in the exposed backs of Binnie's thighs as she stood on tiptoe to see; there was sleep in the sleeping shapes of the Pekingese, curled head to tail on the rug, and business in the wings of a bee searching with her honey-bags in the flowers; the honey was food and drink; and there were colours wherever Emily's eyes rested. All the colours, and thoughts and shapes and sizes – everything was in the room; and what had happened to Louise?

Louise was suddenly quite small.

Even when she let the note go and stood up, she did not seem so large to Emily, and as Emily went across the room to her Louise said, 'Emily, how tall you are! How tall you are getting.' She stepped back from Emily against the piano.

'Did you go out with Charles?' sang Binnie without turning her head. 'When we woke up both of you were gone. What *is* happening, Emily? Is it what they call a riot?'

Louise did not ask any questions. She seemed to accept the fact that she and Emily were now and henceforth different. She said, 'Emily, I shouldn't have hit you last night.' She said it in an unaccustomed way, stiffly and politely, but with a quietude that Emily had not heard before. Louise was new. 'I am sorry,' said Louise.

'It doesn't matter,' said Emily. It did not matter. She had

touched extremity in the night. Charles had shut the door and she was left alone. Now she was Emily – Emily alone – Emily walking by herself. No, decidedly it did not matter now. She said quite softly, 'I know – what you did to Don.'

For a long time Louise did not answer. Then, 'He is dead,' said Louise. 'It's no good wishing.'

'He is dead,' agreed Emily.

'Will you kiss me, Emily?'

... Kiss you or not kiss you, it does not matter now. I am Emily who walks by herself ... For a moment she had a sense of being cheated; it was her victory and it had flagged, it had brought her nothing – only Emily who was to be alone. As she said that, she was conscious of a new feeling – like stretching, as if she had the power to stretch herself out and touch, with her finger-tips, the sides of a new world. There was no limit to this power – what was it? It was freedom; and though it was a little giddy, headlong in its possibilities of loneliness, there was strength and satisfaction in it ... I was right to have fought, said Emily, I was right ... A sigh that she could not escape from rose to her lips, but even as she sighed she was saying *I am free*, and she kissed Louise.

'It isn't finished yet,' cried Binnie from the window. 'They are all shouting. Listen. They are starting again.'

It was past noon when a rumour began to circulate that Anil was not in jail, not captive in the Principal's house, not hidden in the Police Quarters or in the Hostel: he was in hospital. Before this had time to grow or change it was confirmed.

Sir Monmatha Ghose came out on the balcony of the hall and asked the students to disperse as Anil Krishna Banerjee was ill. There was a momentary effect, they were stilled, hundreds of dark faces and heads turned up on a sea of white towards the balcony; but before he could go on, one cried, 'How – ill?' – another, more boldly, 'He was not ill!' – and a babel broke out, 'What have you done to him? What have you done?'

Sir Monmatha held up his hand, he shouted, and his words were tossed back to him on whistles and cat-calls. He went inside. 'Sir, why not send for the Police?'

'I shall not have the Police in my College,' he said. 'Presently they will hear reason.'

They showed no sign of it. The insane ugly noise went on. Then there was an ebb. Another rumour was filtering through the crowd, more than agitating it; a pall of perplexity and doubt hung over it ... Anil was not ill. Not ill? No. He had been stricken dumb.

It came from an orderly in the Hospital itself, who had seen Anil. Small inside hairs of superstition lifted in every student's head. Dumb! It spread through the bazaar, gaining heat as it ran; but another came to meet it, and this came from Tarala, who also had seen Anil; Tarala said that he was visited, speaking in every extraordinary tongue with demons' voices. The two rumours became tangled and for ever, in Amorra, there persisted a tale of a dumb boy who in trances spoke with the voice of God.

The students poured out of the College to the Hospital. The little hospital at Amorra stood in waste ground, railed off with net railings on a knoll and shaded with trees. It looked innocent and unprotected as they marched down on it, and there at the railings was Charles Pool.

There was a minute of intense stillness and then a shout of anger went up from everyone; some could not remember now what exactly Charlie Chang had to do with this, but they shouted with the rest. Their cries rolled forward as they surged towards the Hospital. 'We – want – Banerjee. We – want – Anil – Banerjee – Where – is – Banerjee? We – want – Anil.'

Charles stood perfectly still behind the railings, two small spick-and-span white ones that reached to his waist; and because of the knoll and his height, he seemed very high to the oncoming students; the sun struck flashes of light from his monocle into their eyes as if, now that Anil was smitten dumb, he would smite them blind. They were moving, he was still; they were shouting, he was quiet; but the power had changed from them to him. He took out his monocle and the students in front stopped as if their feet had gone into the ground.

It was the first time any of them had seen him without it; they had always looked at the glass in his eye, never at his face. Now, suddenly, he emerged before them, a Charles they had never seen. He looked at them with tired naked eyes, and they felt his look pitiful and stern as if he had something to tell them that was grim and sad.

The front ranks had stopped and stood waiting perfectly silent, but those at the back, who were not near enough to see him, booed and called and whistled. 'Pits! Pits! Pits!' they cried. 'Where is your beastly daughter, Charlie?' And rising into a clamour, 'We want – Anil Banerjee. We – want – Anil.'

They pushed themselves against that immovable front line until it could hold no longer and broke and was swept forward against Charles. Legs and thighs and stomachs were bruised and crushed against the railings; some were trodden upon, some thrown over; there were screams and shrieks of pain; and tumult broke, those in front trying to push back and those at the back pushing insanely on, still with their shout, 'We – want – Anil – Banerjee. Anil – Banerjee!'

Charles's head and shoulders were still above the crowd; he could still be seen, the figurehead of the turmoil, with a space behind him; the railings had not given – yet; and suddenly, he filled his lungs and with all the measure of his enormous voice he bellowed 'Hush!'

They were quiet from sheer surprise. It was an extraordinary word to use to a mob, an extraordinary word to bellow in that shattering voice – a child's word in a tumult – but it was right. There was an instant stillness as if even the wind had been put out; they waited and into that hush climbed not Charles, not authority, but the young veterinary surgeon, Dr Narayan Das.

He was Anil's friend, and the sight of him brought more silence and surprise. He climbed up on the railings, hiding Charlie Chang who was supporting him, and there was a look on his face of such woe that a murmur broke out again. 'Speak to them. Speak to them quickly – Indro,' said Charles.

Narayan's lips trembled; the whole of his body, his feet balanced on the thin rail, his hands on Charles's shoulder, trembled; he quivered from head to foot. He saw the crowd as Sir Monmatha Ghose had seen it: the young black heads, the faces, hundreds it seemed to him, on white shoulders, turned to him; only he was not much above them, he was close to them; close; and his lips suddenly opened, and his heart, with all his grief, and his reproach, and his anger and his love; and what did he say?

His voice sounded very large to him; the whole of him was in it, it seemed to break the sky and come back to him, but it sounded very little to the students after Charles's – little but very clear. It reached even to their outskirts. They all heard it. 'You – must – be – quiet,' said the little voice, 'Anil – is – dead.'

XIII

The holidays were over, the queer exotic *puja* fortnight was gone, with the things of which it held so many in its span. It was like Emily's room, everything was in it, but now it was gone; only, washed up by the river on the banks and round the *ghats*, were small fragmentary remains, the straw inside body of the Goddess when the clay had washed away, pieces of coloured paper, flowers like a farewell garland on the water.

The strange light nights were over, when villagers, who went to bed soon after the sun, stayed up and visited from village to village, when their songs could be heard going home across the fields in the dawn; the bazaar had sunk back into its customary clamour: there were no more processions of students or of *pujas* in its streets.

The College was shut and Sir Monmatha Ghose spent his mornings and his evenings on his roof. In the College life a seal had been quite firmly and immediately pressed on the break in it where Anil had been; 'There can be no break in the continuity of our lives,' said Sir Monmatha Ghose, 'we must not make it so.' The students had gone into the Examination Hall next day. There had been no demonstrations.

Anil's brother and the family priest had come on the train. They had taken his body to the river for burning, bound on a narrow litter that was decorated with cloth and green leaves and flowers. He lay with a white cloth up to his chin, his face turned sideways into this necklace of flowers, the red mark of sandalwood, which he had worn so often in life, on his forehead; and presently his friends came and carried him away.

Narayan was not asked to be present at the funeral rites, neither the brother nor the priest would have allowed his presence there, but after they had gone Narayan asked permission to go to Anil's room and it was opened for him.

'I think I can do that for you,' said the Superintendent. 'Besides,' he added, 'there is nothing of value there.'

Narayan found the poems in an old exercise book among the papers on the table. He took them and hid them under his coat. He was ready to go when he turned and looked round the small room. It was just as Anil had left it, no servant had been in to clean and tidy it; the bed was still creased where Anil had lain and tossed, his *lota* was still half full of water, on the floor lay a dirty crumpled shirt. With suddenly blinded eyes Narayan bent down to pick it up.

Something rustled in the pocket as he turned it right side out; he pulled out a piece of paper, dirty but carefully smoothed and covered with a few distinct lines. It was another poem.

It was more than another poem. As Narayan read it, Anil was not on his pyre by the river; it did not matter where he was, he had not died. After a while Narayan folded it and carried it away with the others.

'The brother would not have known what they were,' he said

to Charles. He copied them carefully and sent them to Sir Monmatha Ghose ... He had come, this evening, to hear his opinion. Like Charles, he was shown up on the roof.

There was one more feast that had not come into the large *pujas* – the Kali *puja*, Diwali, the Feast of Lights. Already, as Narayan bicycled through the streets, there were signs of it in the town; now, as he waited anxiously for the Principal's verdict, first one light, then another, came out like pinpricks, and a fire-work sizzled into the blue.

'You are as high as the rockets here. It is barely dusk and they are out already.'

'They are a little previous – like these poems,' said Sir Monmatha.

'You mean they are no good?' Narayan was stung with bitter disappointment.

'On the contrary, they are very good indeed. What a pity he could not have waited longer! But there is one—'

'I found that in his pocket, after he was dead,' said Narayan. 'It seemed very much alive.'

'It is,' said Sir Monmatha, and he promised to see that they were published, in a book after Anil's heart, printed and pub-lished in India on Indian paper, bound in *khuddar*, with a hand-made Indian design. 'Naturally, if his father permits,' said Sir Monmatha.

Narayan had written to Anil's father already but he had had no answer. At first he had been offended, then grieved, then glad; Anil's death belonged to that period of violence in which he had been caught, that he perhaps had caused. He and Charles had not left Anil, and the horror and the helplessness of those struggles would be on him all his life; but it was over. Anil's father had receded into a little figure away over countless fields and peasant huts and to sunset skies. Now something much more interesting was to happen; something that would not stop for grief; that would, in its mysterious fashion, balance grief. He could not at present think too much about Anil. At the moment he was thinking of a row of houses, far too tall and close together, in a street of noise and garbage smells; and he looked down from Sir Monmatha Ghose's roof, and far away, over the lights, he could see his little house set down beside the river; and as he looked he saw a line of lights, tiny as beads, break out there too, along his wall.

'I must go home,' he said.

'How is your wife? She keeps well, I hope.'

'Very well.'

'Are you so modern that you will be disappointed if it is a son?'

Narayan had nowadays a quick friendly smile. 'I shall not be disappointed,' said Narayan.

On the way home, in the Farm road, he met the Pools; winter work had started on the Farm, ploughing and planting for sugar-cane and wheat, the pulses and mustard were planted already, and the rice was growing high. Charles was out early and late, and here he was, walking down the road with Mrs Pool. Narayan heard their voices before he saw them in the dusk and he stiffened; he still could not forgive Mrs Pool. His guilt went beyond him into her and he could not wipe this last trace of vio-lence from his mind ... That is the meaning of religion now to me – non-violence – to be completely without violence to any ... Still he could not accomplish it with Mrs Pool. He passed them without stopping, with a bow of his head that was too quick and clumsy and came only from his neck.

Charles smiled at him and Mrs Pool opened her lips; they just parted and closed again, it was not even a smile, and she tilted her chin . . . She is not altogether changed either, said Narayan, and that cheered him and gave him an affinity with Louise that he had not dreamed of. He looked back at her; yes, she had the same ridiculous elegance, for walking on the deserted Farm road: a light full-skirted dress, a parasol; she was leaning on Charles's arm and before them Binnie danced backwards, speaking to them and walking at the same time. Charles lifted his hand in salutation. They and Narayan passed on down the road.

Where was Emily? Emily was in the deserted College garden by the tank, and she had a small decorated table on which was laid a saucer-light burning in butter, some rice, a collar of flowers, and a paper ball.

She had made it of paper because she did not want anything of her *puja* to be discovered. This was her last secret; and her table was the lid of a cardboard box and she had decided to put it on the water where presently the cardboard would soften and sink and carry everything away; if the flowers floated they would not be noticed. There was *puja* in the air.

Now, in the last light, she placed her table on the water and pushed it out from the steps. With its little flame reflected in the dark water, it eddied round and round, gently blowing across to the shades beyond; but however hard Emily looked there was nothing there.

The student boy had said that. *And if you offer for one you offer for all* . . . I wonder what has happened to him, said Emily; but of course all the students have gone home.

A rocket leapt into the sky close beside the wall and curved over her head into blue and red stars. There would be nearly as many lights on earth tonight as there were in the sky.

Emily's burned steadily as it floated away.

KINGFISHERS CATCH FIRE

Rumer Godden

'Rumer Godden's novels pulse with life . . .
A collision of England and India familiar to
readers of Forster's *A Passage to India*'
Daily Telegraph

Sophie, an English ingénue with two children, arrives
in Himalayan Kashmir to set up home in a tumbledown
cottage surrounded by fields of flowers and herbs. Settling
down to live quietly, frugally and peacefully with her new
neighbours, she is unaware of the turmoil her arrival provokes
as the villagers compete fiercely for her patronage. Sophie's
cook makes a drastic bid to secure his position, and
the unwanted consequences are catastrophic . . .

BLACK NARCISSUS

Rumer Godden

High in the Himalayas near Darjeeling, the old mountaintop
palace shines like a jewel. When it was the General's 'harem',
richly dressed ladies wandered the windswept terraces; at
night, music floated out over the gorge. Now, the General's son
has bestowed it on an order of nuns, the Sisters of Mary.

Well-intentioned yet misguided, the nuns set about taming
the gardens and opening a school and dispensary for the
villagers. They are dependent on the local English agent of
Empire, Mr Dean; but his charm and insolent candour
are disconcerting. And the implacable emptiness of the
mountain, the ceaseless winds, exact a toll on the
Sisters. When Mr Dean says bluntly, 'This is no place
for a nunnery,' it is as if he foresees their destiny . . .

'A very remarkable novel indeed. One in a thousand' *Observer*

THE RIVER

Rumer Godden

Harriet's older sister is no longer a playmate, her brother is still a little boy. And the comforting rhythm of her Indian childhood – the sounds of the jute factory, the colourful festivals and the eternal ebb and flow of the river on its journey to the Bay of Bengal – is about to be shattered by a tragic event. Intense, vivid and with a dark undertow, *The River* is an arresting portrait of three siblings on the cusp of adulthood.

'*The River* will make you laugh, make you cry and, in its way, change you for ever'
Julie Myerson

Available in a Virago Modern Classics
limited hardback edition.